CAE//URA

Dan, Thanks for your support.

Frank

CAE//SURA

FRANK HYLE

Tate Publishing & Enterprises

Published by Tate Publishing & Enterprises, LLC
127 E. Trade Center Terrace | Mustang, Oklahoma 73064 USA
1.888.361.9473 | www.tatepublishing.com

Tate Publishing is committed to excellence in the publishing industry. The company reflects the philosophy established by the founders, based on Psalm 68:11,
"The Lord gave the word and great was the company of those who published it."

Published in the United States of America
ISBN: 978-1-61739-591-8
1. Fiction, Family Life
2. Fiction, General
10.12.16

CAESURA

(si zoore)

In music or verse, and sometimes life,
a brief, silent pause in which time is not counted.

CHAPTER 1

The bookmark proved to be more interesting than the book itself. Pausing in his reading, Michael picked it up and tucked it in place. It was almost time to leave for the airport, but he had a few more minutes to linger. His eyes fell again to the bookmark, which was a postcard-size collage of photos of his mother, Helen Telford.

Photography had long been one of Michael's hobbies. For the past three years, however, it had become almost an obsession with him, as he labored not only to continue to take current photos, but also to catalogue snapshots that had accumulated in his mother's home for the past fifty years. He had been sharing the old photos on a regular basis with his mother in an attempt to slow down the steady decline he had observed in her since the onset of dementia five years earlier.

Michael lifted his gaze from the bookmark and the photos with which he was so familiar and looked around the living room of his home. He was a forty-six-year-old single man who had grown accustomed to living alone. He had purchased the home almost a dozen years ago, just after he had been awarded his Ph.D. in English. It was conveniently located adjacent to the campus of the University of Cincinnati, where he served on the faculty in the English Department.

It was a modest, two-bedroom home, with the unique feature of having an open floor plan. Shortly after he moved in, Michael and his brother, Tom, removed the walls surrounding the kitchen, dining area, and first-floor bedroom. The result was an extremely large open area, suitable for Michael's piano in one corner, his desk in another, and a sitting area surrounding the fireplace on the other side of the room.

Photos of Michael and his parents and siblings were either in frames or in loose piles around most of the room. It was good no one else was around to be bothered by the clutter, he thought. The collection of photographs had been spread out around his home for the last year. During that time he had rummaged almost daily through the collection in an effort to find two or three different photos to show his mother each time he went to see her at Village Green Retirement Center, where she had resided for almost a year until her death two weeks ago.

On the desk was a photo of Michael and Lainie taken twenty years earlier on their memorable vacation. Lainie had been the one true love of his life—or so he thought until recently—but she died shortly after the photograph was taken.

Atop the piano was a small frame with a photo of Michael with Tom and their sister, Mary. It had been taken forty years ago, at a time when the three of them never dreamed of a life without their mother and dad.

Michael put his book down to take stock of his living room. He was leaving in a half hour for a few days in Florida, where he was seeking to regroup after the events of the past year. Walking across the room to his desk to gather some papers for his trip, he paused again to examine a photograph of his mother that was hanging on the wall near his bookcase. It was part of the next group of photographs he had planned on showing his mother, but her last illness had not permitted it. There she was smiling from the kitchen of their home in New York. To her left were a young Michael and his older sister, Mary. He laughed as he thought *Mother looked old even then.* She had always looked old to him. The photo was taken during the time they lived in an old, country home in upstate New York. He was eight years old when they had moved. The family had settled there when his father, Thomas Telford, was offered a position running a shoe factory in the nearest town. The home was located on a large farm. The owner of the factory leased the home to the family while a relative farmed the adjoining land.

The home seemed like a mansion to his parents and his brother and sister. Besides the four bedrooms upstairs, it had a large living room, dining room, kitchen, guest room—and, best of all—a place they dubbed the pink room. The pink room was in the east wing of the home and was the size of the living room, dining room, and kitchen combined. It became the biggest playroom any child could ever have wanted. Even the ping-pong table seemed miniature in there.

Michael loved the adventure of moving to a new town and exploring the vast acreage of the farm. The home was surrounded by beautiful farmland and orchards. Along the driveway, running the length of the three acres they occupied, was an apple orchard. To the rear of the barn, which served as their garage, lay fields for the dairy cows. Beyond those fields were the 1,500 acres of land where corn and peas were raised each year. A dirt road served the dairy fields and surrounded the crops, and was a wonderful route for kids to ride their bikes and explore. Although warned that some of the barbed wire fencing along the orchard perimeter, designed to keep the cows out, was electrified, Michael and Mary couldn't resist sneaking a touch. One time was enough for them to vow never to do that again.

On their first day there, as the movers were carrying in the furniture, Michael, Mary, and Tom explored the outbuildings around the home, while their parents supervised the move inside the house. The barn was the biggest thing the city slickers had ever seen. It could easily hold a dozen cars, although the family had just one. Next to the barn was a small building with old doors secured by a rusty coat hanger wrapped around the two handles serving as a primitive lock. The three of them undid the hanger, opened the creaky doors, and discovered an old, red tractor. With no one else around, they climbed aboard and pretended they were farming the land.

In the middle of the dairy field was a creek that would freeze over in the winter, and had served as their own private ice skating rink. Before moving to New York, neither he nor Mary had ever tried on ice skates. The creek offered them the opportunity to experience a new outdoor world in winter time.

Shortly after taking over the farmhouse the family purchased a second vehicle so that Helen could help ferry the kids to and from school and occasionally substitute at Michael and Mary's school when a teacher was ill. Beneath the photo of his mother in the kitchen of their home was another one of her taken in the schoolyard at recess that same year. Helen had been a teacher before the children were born, and she loved the opportunity to occasionally return to the classroom. She didn't get the call to substitute often, but when she did it was especially nice for Michael. On those days Helen would help supervise the lunchroom during her break. The school had an unusual policy that required all students to purchase the hot lunch rather than bring peanut butter and jelly sandwiches from home. Before students could leave the lunchroom for recess, they would have to eat all the food on their plates. That policy resulted in many unhappy children who just couldn't manage to eat all of the potatoes or vegetables they had been served.

On days when Helen worked the lunchroom, Michael was a hero to many of his new friends, as his mother would come along and help the finicky eaters clean their plates. At their evening dinner after those days, she would laugh at how many potatoes and peas she had eaten to help kids get out to recess, including some off Michael's plate. Though they only stayed two years in New York before the factory was sold and another move was required, the farmhouse for Michael would forever be the home of his youth.

Both of the photographs reminded Michael of the day he first learned his father's age. For some reason his dad had preserved that information to the point where none of the children ever asked anymore, even as birthdays were celebrated. The photos called to mind a time when an encyclopedia salesman was making a sales call at the home. Since Tom was nearing college age, his father thought it was time to equip the home with a set of encyclopedias. The sale was agreed upon in the living room, while the entire family sat and listened. As the salesman was completing the order form, he casually asked Mr. Telford his age. Suddenly, the room was quiet. All eyes turned toward their father. Could this be it, each wondered? Are we going to find out? Or will Dad take the salesman into the other room to answer the question? He paused, and looked around at each of his children. Then, slowly, a smile spread across his face as he saw the anticipation in each of their eyes. "I'm forty-five-years-old," he announced.

It was all Michael could do to remain in the room for the balance of the sales call. He was shocked. *Forty-five years old*, he thought. *My dad is forty-five years old! He could die tonight, he's so old.* Once the sale was completed, Michael crept off to his room where he quietly sobbed, certain in his young mind that his father would not be around much longer.

Looking at the photos again now, Michael smiled. The old man lived a long time after that birthday, and Michael himself was now forty-six, one year past the dreaded old-age number of forty-five. *Forty-five doesn't look too bad now.*

Michael turned his attention back to his desk. He located his flight confirmation sheet and placed it in his pocket. Next he wanted to find a few writings that he would review while he was away. Sorting through the materials on his desk, he came upon another photo of the farm in New York. His mother was not an outdoor person, but there she was standing along a six-foot bank of snow at the walkway that led from the front door to Bluefield Road. She was smiling for the camera, and he was reminded of how his mother taught him his first lesson on the meaning of love on a cold, cold evening nearly forty winters ago. It was on that night that he first realized how his mother was a quiet but determined teacher whose goal was to show her children the meaning of family and inspire love among its members. She showed him with a snow shovel and a determination to keep a walkway open for her husband's return on a snow-filled night.

It was the time of a raging blizzard that created six-foot drifts around the home. Their father was away on business, and the rest of the family was snowed under. The roads were closed, and the closest dad could travel by vehicle was to another house two miles away. No one expected him to attempt to get home that night, but that had not swayed his mother's determination to keep the path open from the road to the front door.

To get home, their dad would battle snow drifts all the way. But once he would reach the walkway from the road she insisted the path be cleared. Never mind that the path consisted of thirty feet, after he would have marched two miles. He was part of the family, so the path to the door, and to his family, would remain open.

Michael recalled that with the winds howling, they would no more finish shoveling than the path would start to fill again. Every hour or two his mother would gaze out the window and suggest that they ought to shovel again, because she just didn't know when dad might get home. The three kids would gripe about going out again, but she was insistent that night. She would peer out the window at the falling snow, then bundle everyone up for shoveling, and finally warm them with hot chocolate when they came in from the winter night. That short path would never have kept their father away, snowbound or not. But that wasn't the idea of the exercise.

It turned out that it wasn't until the next afternoon that their dad was able to walk home through the drifts to the shoveled path. Michael remembered that once dad arrived, he and Mary bragged about the clean walk, and complained about shoveling all evening. And he remembered as well that his mother let them talk, and let them complain, choosing to say nothing at all about the shoveled path.

A year after that picture was taken, the factory in New York was sold and the family moved again. His father found another factory to run, this time in Cincinnati. They left the farm and returned to suburbia where they moved into a three-bedroom home with a small yard.

Michael bent over to pick up another pile of photographs that had fallen off the desk. On top was a photo of his mother sitting under a patio umbrella in the backyard of their home in Cincinnati. It was a great contrast from their New York home, but with time it became the family home where his mother would reside for almost forty years.

Placing the pile back onto his desk, his eyes settled on a shot taken just a year ago, on the day his mother moved to the assisted-living wing at Village Green. He picked it up to examine it more closely. She was smiling, but he could see the anxiety behind her smile, the slight confusion in her eyes. It had been a very uncertain day. In hindsight, he guessed that she had decided that day that she was leaving her home and her known life behind with the move, and she would never have what she would consider to be a home again. She was reluctant, he realized now, because to her the move was the first step in the process of leaving this world. Darkness had begun to settle around her a few years before the move, as she struggled to overcome the confusion in her mind. Her decline was slow at first, but a year ago the pace had quickened. It seemed like only yesterday to Michael, and as he set the photograph back down amidst the clutter of the desk and gazed out the window that sunny afternoon, it all came back to him again.

CHAPTER 2

It was a beautiful August morning. The summer heat had drifted away, and with temperatures in the seventies, Michael felt a sense of early autumn in the air. A nice day to be out. He was on his way to Village Green, driving the short route from his office. His mother had been there four days, and he had taken the time to visit her each morning and evening. As he drove, he wondered whether daily visits would become routine. For now, though, he knew they were just as important to him as they were to her.

His mother had reached the point where the time had finally come for her to leave her home of the past forty years for an apartment in an assisted-living facility. She had agreed in July to leave her home, but only because she relied on Michael's judgment so heavily that whatever he would suggest seemed to her to be the best thing. He had pledged to himself seemingly forever that it would never come to this, that she would stay in her home until her final day. He had made a promise to his late father to always look after his mother, and he had been determined over the years not to forsake that pledge.

But time has its way with all of us, he thought. Time had certainly not spared his father. A few years before he retired from the shoe factory, he was diagnosed with emphysema. The relentless disease would gradually wear out his lungs. And as his lungs were diminished, so, too, was his dominance over his family.

As Michael pulled into the parking lot of Village Green, he thought back to that summer day, six years before, when his dad's health was deteriorating. Michael was having lunch with him in the kitchen of his parents' home. That summer he had no courses scheduled, which afforded him plenty of free time. Helen was off playing cards, and Michael agreed to have lunch with his dad and help him settle in for his afternoon nap. At that time, his father was entering the final stage of his lung disease. Ten years of combating emphysema had taken its toll.

As the years had gone by, his dad began to take Michael more into his confidence, asking him his opinion on investments, and having Michael prepare his income tax return. These were things unheard of in the past. His father even displayed some fear of mortality, which touched Michael dearly. His father had been retired for almost ten years, but by that time he was afraid to be alone, fearful of some complication from his disease. He knew death was calling, and told Michael of his concern for his mother's financial welfare after he was gone. As successful as he had been in running shoe factories all his life, he was never paid an inflated salary or earned a major pension like today's executives. And what with paying college tuition for three children, his big earning years had been depleted. He was not poor, however. He and Helen always lived comfortably, yet well within their means. Michael had no idea of their finances through early adulthood, but as his father began to count on Michael's advice, he became aware of their savings.

At lunch his father rocked on his hands, one of the usual measures he employed to try to get a satisfying breath. "I'm worried about what will happen to your mother after I'm gone," he volunteered.

Although it had been many years since the time Michael had first learned his father's age and had feared his father would not live out the night, he was still troubled about his parents slipping away. His dad would die less than a year later, and the premonition hung heavily over the two of them as they each sipped on a bowl of soup.

"Don't worry about Mother," Michael offered. "We'll always make sure she's well cared for."

Tears slipped down his father's cheeks, something Michael had never seen before. "Promise me you'll take care of your mother, Michael," his father asked.

Michael was unsure of what exactly to say. His father had always been the strong one. Michael had always been the recipient of the promises and the encouragement. His father's display of emotion both moved and unsettled him. He reached his hand across the table and gently placed it on his father's shoulder.

"Dad, you should be proud of what you've accomplished and how well you've provided for mother," Michael said.

His father's eyes still held tears, but there was a gleam of pride, almost as if he were the son and Michael the father now. But the emotion prevented him from responding with words. He placed his hands again under his legs and resumed rocking forward and back before lifting his head to look directly into Michael's eyes. Wrinkling his face into a smile, he nodded his head a few times then broke his eyes away.

Michael withdrew his hand from his father's shoulder.

"Dad," he said, "I promise you I'll be there for mother. You'll always be able to count on me."

His father stopped rocking momentarily, and looked up again into Michael's eyes. It appeared to Michael as if his father was summoning all the strength he could find in his frail and emotional body just to speak.

"I'm depending on you, Michael," he said, then nodded his head one more time and finished his soup.

Michael was struck by the concern his father was showing in the face of his own deepening illness. *How could he not promise his dad that he'd stand by Mother?* The promise he made that afternoon remained fixed in his memory.

After the meal, Michael resumed the conversation on a positive note. Not long before, his brother Tom had been at a dinner party where the host asked each of his guests to list five people each guest most desired to engage in conversation. The names announced prompted some lively dinner conversation.

Michael asked his father to guess some of the names Tom had selected.

"Jesus Christ," his father guessed correctly. He thought a while longer, then added, "Mahatma Gandhi, Muhammad Ali, Babe Ruth." He was sharp in analyzing whom Tom might wish to speak with, and he concurred with all the choices.

"There's another name on the list," Michael said. "Someone whom you'll probably never guess, but a choice you'd be happy with."

His father sat pensively, again rocking on his seat, hands beneath his legs, trying to master his breathing. But no further name came to mind, so he surrendered.

"Who is it?" he finally asked.

Michael smiled. "He included you on the list, Dad. You are one of the top five for Tom."

His father bent his head down, looking at the table, not wanting to make eye contact, and let the silence settle upon them. Eventually he looked up at Michael, tears gathering in his eyes for the second time that day.

"That's awful nice of Tom to include me in that company."

"Yes, it is, Dad. I admire his choice."

The silence returned, and it felt good. Michael cleaned up the dishes, then helped his father move to the chair lift, up the stairs to his bedroom, and over to his bed for a nap. *He is a proud man, even as he grows weaker each day.*

Walking across the parking lot toward the Village Green lobby, Michael noticed a hearse slowly pulling into the lot. It was a grim reminder to him of his father's death. He recalled that it was only six months after that lunch when his mother called Michael at the office and asked him to come over to the house. Helen had just spoken with their family doctor, who directed her to take her husband to the hospital right away. She had called Michael to tell him that she needed his help getting his father to the car. He had been in the hospital many times before, always returning home stabilized after having his many medications adjusted. Michael arrived that afternoon, however, to find his father weak and afraid. His mother was worried, too. His father did not want an ambulance, even though he did not possess enough strength to walk from his bedroom to the chairlift connecting the second floor hallway to the living room downstairs.

When Michael went to the bedroom, he told his father he was there to help take him to the hospital.

"I don't want to go, Michael," his father said, choking back his tears.

His father knew his hourglass was nearly empty, but Michael did not.

"I know, Dad," Michael replied, "but it's time to go. The doctors will take good care of you. Now let me help you."

"I can't make it alone," his father said.

Michael helped him to his feet. They faced each other and Michael wrapped his arms around his father's waist, trying to shuffle him across the room. But his father's strength ebbed after two steps, and he could advance his legs no further.

"Put your feet on mine, and hug me closer, Dad. I'll slide us both along."

His father lifted each of his feet atop Michael's shoes. *He weighs no more than a child*, Michael thought, as he began to slowly shuffle his feet backward across the bedroom and hall to the chair lift, all the while hugging his father to his chest. As they neared the lift his father told him again he did not want to go.

"Dad, you're going to get better in the hospital," Michael replied. But his father knew that would not be the case.

Once they had descended down the chairlift to the living room, Michael helped his father to his feet and had him again place his feet upon Michael's own. They hugged again as they slid across the living room to the kitchen and, finally, to the garage door. As they hugged and shuffled, Michael had a memory of the time his father had hugged him on the day Michael graduated from high school. Now Michael wanted to squeeze him tighter, but dared not. More than anything he wanted just to say, "I love you," but he refrained, thinking that might push his father, and maybe even Michael, over the edge.

Years later, Michael's reluctance to say "I love you" to his father in his closing hours remained one of his greatest regrets. The opportunity during the last, long trek presented itself and he let it pass by.

It was only three days later when Michael found himself with his brother, Tom, and his mother, meeting with Dr. Canton at Christ Hospital. It was eight o'clock on a Friday morning, the day before his father's birthday. The doctor was explaining to the three of them that he did not believe the head of their family would live to see that birthday. Michael and Tom were stunned to hear the doctor's report. This was their father's seventh visit to the hospital in the last four years. Each time before, the doctor had adjusted his medicines and sent him home better than before he had arrived. *Why can't the doctor make him better,* they each wondered silently. *What's different this time?* The doctor saw the confusion in their eyes and answered their questions before they had to be asked.

"Your father's lungs are exhausted. The effort it takes him to breathe has weakened all his other organs, and they are now all in the process of shutting down," the doctor explained. Turning to their mother, he asked, "Are your sons aware of the failures that were happening before you came to the hospital, Mrs. Telford?"

She shook her head no, clutching her white cloth handkerchief, trying to rein in her emotions.

"May I speak of this to your sons?" the doctor asked.

Again she merely nodded.

The doctor then turned to Michael and Tom and said, "Your father's heart is failing now, as are his kidneys. In the last two weeks he's lost control of his bodily functions. Your mother has been looking after your father at home, cleaning him when he could no longer make it to the bathroom in time because he was so weak from the emphysema."

Michael and Tom looked to their mother. "Why didn't you tell us?" Tom asked. "We would have helped, or gotten him here sooner."

"You boys know your father is a proud man," she said in a soft voice. "He wanted no one to know. It was all he could do to accept my help." Tears began running down her face.

Silence fell over the room, broken finally by the doctor's words. His voice was calm. It contained no suggestion that the sons should have known what was going on. In measured tones, he said, "Your mother has been a rock for your father these last few years. And even though his illness could not be stopped, she did her finest to help your father preserve his dignity. Now his time is near. You need to prepare yourselves and say good-bye. I believe he'll be gone sometime today."

After Dr. Canton left, the family returned to the hospital room to wait in vigil. An hour later, Mary arrived. When she entered the room, Michael leaned over to his father and said softly, "Dad, look who's come to see you. Mary's here."

His eyes remained closed as Mary took her father's hand in greeting. After her hello he asked her quietly, "Am I going to die, Mary?"

Stunned at the question, Mary reflected briefly, then bravely replied, "Yes, Dad, you're going to die. But we're all here with you now."

Michael wondered whether he would have had the courage to answer his father's question so honestly. He squeezed her shoulder as she stood next to her father and her first tears began to flow.

Two hours passed with no more words from him. His breathing was labored and his eyes remained closed. Then suddenly, at noon, as if he just remembered something important, he spoke up.

"What time is it?" he asked.

"It's twelve o'clock, dear," their mother replied from her chair across the room.

A minute passed, then he asked again, "What time is it?"

"It's noon, Tom, and we're all with you," she again replied as she stood and walked over to the side of the bed.

Another few minutes elapsed, and then for the third time he asked, "What time is it?"

Now their mother took his hand and gently patted it, and said, "It's Friday, June fifth, honey, twelve o'clock noon."

Although it didn't appear that his mother's words were registering with their father, suddenly, with a voice racked from the battle to breathe, a struggle endured for so many years, but yet a voice still powerful enough to command them all and show them the way, their father said, "The Angel of the Lord declared unto Mary."

Silence descended, as they all stood in amazement at the thought that even through this final ordeal their Dad would remember to pray the Angelus at high noon, a prayer he shared with his wife every day during his retirement. A prayer taught to them all in grade school so many years ago, and one that now only their father and mother remembered.

Finally, his mother broke the silence, responding as she had so many times, "And she was conceived of the Holy Spirit."

Their practice had always been for Dad to lead Mother in the Prayer of Hail Mary that followed. But his strength had ebbed, so their mother took the lead in prayer for the first time any of the children had witnessed.

"Behold the handmaiden of the Lord," she continued, with their father struggling to join in, and together, for the final time, they recited each verse of the aged prayer.

At its conclusion, he would speak no more in full sentences. Some grunts and groans, and a few single words passed his lips over the next twelve hours. Respiratory therapists came in every two hours to offer some help with his breathing. The parish priest, with whom they had shared cocktails in their home once a month for the past nine years, visited late in the afternoon. He offered a few prayers and words of consolation for their mother, but their father was too far down the road to offer any response. Finally, just before midnight, as he neared his birthday, his lungs gave out and his breathing simply slowed to a halt. After a full day of struggling to breathe, his heart could carry the load no further. He was gone.

Though they had been waiting for this to happen throughout the day, it was still hard to believe that it had actually arrived. Their mother continued to hold her husband's hand with her right hand, while stroking the top of his head with her left. After a few minutes Tom looked at the clock. It was three minutes till midnight.

"He didn't make it," Tom said, shaking his head solemnly. Until that point, no one had been rooting for their father to hang on until his birthday arrived. But he had labored so hard that suddenly it occurred to them that maybe they should look at the day's struggle as if their father was hanging on throughout the day just to reach that midnight mark. *Who knows why these kinds of thoughts race through grieving hearts and minds at an hour like this,* Michael thought.

Helen was the next to speak. "What do we do now?" she asked looking up finally at her children. "Shouldn't we tell the nurse what's happened?"

Mary pointed to the clock. It was still two minutes before midnight. "Let's wait until Dad's birthday," she said softly.

They all nodded. Mother turned back to her husband. Tom, Mary, and Michael each exchanged brief glances, silently agreeing with Mary's suggestion.

At two minutes past midnight, Tom pushed the call button and announced to the nurse's station that his father had stopped breathing. Moments later a nurse quietly entered the room. She went to their father, felt for a pulse, then listened to his chest. She then turned to the family.

"I'll call the doctor now. He'll be right in," she said and left the room.

The physician entered the room without greeting anyone. He approached their father and checked his heart with a stethoscope. After a minute he looked up and said, "I'm sorry. Mr. Telford has died."

The doctor looked at the clock. "How long ago did he stop breathing?"

"It was just a few minutes after midnight," Mary responded. "We called the nurse right away."

"Very well," the doctor said. "The time of death was 12:02 a.m., June 6th."

Looking at Helen, the doctor said, "My deepest sympathies, Mrs. Telford," before leaving the room. The nurse told the family to take as much time as they wanted, and she then left the room as well.

When the family was alone again, Helen asked, "Did we just tell the doctor that Dad died on his birthday?"

Even at a time of grief and despair, smiles spread across the faces of everyone in the room.

"We decided that Dad would have wanted to make it to his birthday," Mary said, as she wrapped her arm around her mother's shoulder.

"Well, I'm glad you did," Helen said, as her smile quickly slipped away, replaced by a solemn sadness. "Let's say a prayer," she suggested.

Tom took the lead and started the Our Father. Together they prayed for their departed father and their grieving mother.

Tom stood with one arm around his wife, Janice, and the other upon Michael's shoulder, and said tearfully, "We've lost a good man, Michael."

"Yes, we have, Tom," he replied, as he turned to hug his big brother.

Another half hour passed. Helen signed some paperwork for the nurses and collected her husband's belongings before they all began to file out of the hospital room. Michael was the last to reach the doorway. He looked back at his father, now all alone in his bed, then turned back to the door where his sister Mary stood.

"I can't leave him here alone yet," he said, and Mary urged him back into the room.

"We'll go when you're ready," she said.

Michael returned to his father's side. Remembering the walk from the bedroom to the car just two days before, he wanted so much to tell his father that he loved him while he could hear him still. He leaned over the bed and took his father in his arms.

"Oh, Dad," he cried, "I love you, and I always have, and I always will." The tears came now to Michael for the first time. He held his father's lifeless body close to him for another minute, then gently laid him back on his pillow.

Only Mary had remained in the room. Michael stood then and looked over to his sister and said, "Now we can go."

She smiled and reached out to hug her brother as he reached the door. As they walked out of the room Michael looked back over his shoulder one last time before joining his mother in the hall.

Once they were all together outside the room, Helen asked Michael to coordinate funeral arrangements with Tom and Mary.

"Is there anything special that you want?" Michael asked.

"Yes, there is," she replied. "It's just one thing. At the end of the service I want the choir to sing 'In the Garden'."

"What is that?" Michael asked.

"It's a song that was played at my mother's funeral and my father's as well. Your father loved the music and he insisted it be played when his mother died. It means a lot to me."

"Okay, Mother," Michael said, wrapping his arm around her as they walked to the elevator. "We'll see to it that you hear that song."

CHAPTER 3

Michael's morning at Village Green was to begin with a meeting with Carl Fowler, the administrator of the facility, and Amy Nelson, the head nurse in the assisted-living department. Carl Fowler looked surprisingly young to Michael, who wondered whether this was Carl's first opportunity to head up such a large facility. He had been named administrator less than a year ago. One of Carl's goals was to personally meet with the families of all new residents to try to learn more about the resident and to reassure the family that their loved one would receive good care. He was particularly interested in hearing from the families of the assisted-living residents in order that he could help foster a more supportive environment of care.

Carl ushered Michael into his office promptly at ten o'clock. The attractive dark-haired woman already seated at the conference table was Amy Nelson. Michael had not anticipated someone so warm and endearing would be the head nurse. After being treated to a dazzling smile and noticing her hazel-colored eyes, Michael guessed she must be in her late thirties.

After the initial introductions, Carl thanked Michael for taking the time to meet with them and explained the goal of the meeting was to learn more about Helen in order to help her adjust.

"Why don't you tell us about your mother?" Carl began. "How long has she been a widow?"

"Just over six years," Michael answered.

"Was it a difficult adjustment for her after your father died?"

"Yes, it was. We all thought that after a period of time, Mother might venture out into the world more often. She was in good health, and showing no signs of any mental fatigue. She was able to live independently with few problems for a number of years, but she always missed him terribly."

"What kinds of things did your Mother do to occupy herself?"

"For a long time she enjoyed playing bridge with her friends. She played once a week, and every Monday she helped count the collection money at her church. She went to the library often and read novels regularly. She loved to go out to dinner, and even to travel. For a few years she took trips with her card-playing friends to a hotel where they would stay a couple of nights and play cards all day."

"That must have been good for her," Carl said. "How about close friends? Was there anyone that your mother socialized with much after your father died?"

"Frances Miles was a very good friend for many years. The two of them played cards together for a long time. I suppose Frances was Mother's closest friend."

"What happened to Frances?" Carl asked.

"She died about three months ago."

"Was that hard for your mother?"

"Well, yes, the death was difficult. But they had been out of touch for a number of years."

"Why was that?" Carl asked.

Michael sat back in his chair and reflected on Frances Miles. "That's a long story. Mother watched Frances go through the early stages of dementia. It was very troubling to her."

"Can you tell us about that?" Carl prompted.

"Mother and Frances Miles had been partners for a number of years in various bridge clubs. They each thought they were pretty sharp card players, because they won a few bridge tournaments over the years. Each win netted them about five dollars a piece, but you would have thought it was a thousand the way they talked about it."

"We've seen that kind of happiness around here, haven't we, Amy?"

Amy smiled in agreement with the administrator. "The ladies feel pretty good about themselves when the cards fall right," she said.

"I can imagine, since I witnessed it first hand with Mother," Michael said. "For a few years after Dad died, neither of them had shown signs of serious forgetfulness or mental fatigue. But around that time, Mother began to notice that Frances was getting confused during their games. She watched her friend decline over a year or so to a point where Frances couldn't play cards anymore and wound up in a nursing home. Frances was the first one of my mother's friends who moved into a nursing home."

"So I imagine that scared her," Carl said.

"I remember going over to see Mother on the day she learned that Frances was moving to a nursing home. When I walked in, Mother was kneading the handkerchief that was on her lap and just staring out the living room window. She had tears in her eyes.

"She told me that she was afraid that was going to happen to her some day. I tried to reassure her that she was doing well, but she just sat there in tears, worried that she would be next. When she spoke again she just said, 'I don't want to leave my home.' That became a common refrain over the years."

"What kind of condition was your mother in mentally when Frances entered the nursing home?" Carl asked.

"She was in good health. We could count on her to take her medicine faithfully and without prompting. At that point, she seemed to have all her wits about her. But a few years after Frances left the group, a cloud appeared, almost out of the blue, and her worst fears began to be realized."

"So how did it all begin with your mother?" Carl asked.

"My brother and sister and I noticed it first with her stories. She began to tell the same ones over and over when we were with her. Then she began to fret about money. Her house was paid for, as was her car. Her Social Security check was more than enough to pay her monthly expenses, so her savings actually increased each month. But she began to worry that she was going to run out of money. Then we began to notice that she would occasionally forget to take her medicine in the morning. It was little things at first, but they all began to add up.

"Once the confusion began to settle in, Mother turned more and more to the three of us for contact. She began to find excuses to miss her card games, and decided one day that she would no longer be a money-counter at her church. She told me that she was afraid the pastor would find her making a mistake and the thought was just too much for her to bear. Better to quit before she makes a mistake than be embarrassed, even if that meant shutting herself off from the other money counters who had been her friends for many years. We knew that our role in her life was going to have to increase.

"She began to see many of her friends move into assisted-living facilities, or 'old lady homes' as she likes to call them."

That drew a chuckle from Carl and Amy. Michael joined them in laughter.

"Believe me," Michael said, "We've worked hard to get Mother not to call this place by the same name."

"Oh, we've heard that plenty of times," Amy said.

"Anyway," Michael continued, "many of her card friends were in their eighties or nineties, so she saw more of them entering nursing homes, and some of them pass away.

"Mother began worrying about her future. She occasionally would visit Frances Miles at the nursing home, and she always would report that the facility was dreadful, and she never wanted to have to leave her home.

"We kept trying to reassure her that she was doing well and no one was thinking about asking her to give up her home. But as the days went by, we began to spend more time with her, and we could see that the decline was steady, and it became less of a laughing matter to see that her mind was playing tricks on her.

"Our increased care started with more regular contact. My sister, Mary, began to phone Mother every morning and evening just to say hello and insure she was okay. I began taking her to her doctor's visits to be sure the family kept up with her ailments. I also took charge of her medicines, putting them in compartment trays for morning and evening.

"But after two years of additional care and what we termed some mild eccentricity, preferring not to use the word 'dementia,' Mother began to grow afraid and, sometimes, terribly confused.

"She had been born and raised in Columbus, Ohio, where her younger sister, Louise, still lives. It was in Columbus that she met and married my father, Tom, and had given birth to the three of us. As the years went by, Mother began to visit Columbus more and more in her mind, to the point where she would occasionally wonder aloud when her mother and father were coming home. It had been over fifty years since their deaths, but she could easily forget that fact.

"When Mary would call her each morning, Mother began to ask whether all the kids would be home that night so she would know how many to plan for at dinner. Mary would gently bring her back to reality, telling her that her children were all grown now, but that one of us would be over to have dinner with her that night.

"The number of drugs she was prescribed increased. She began to take blood pressure medication, a medication to help her relax in the evening and sleep through the night, and another drug to try to slow the progress of her dementia.

"For a long time after I began sorting her medicines, she followed instructions well. She remembered most mornings and evenings to take her medicine. But, eventually, Mother became confused over the day of the week. When she began to forget to take her medicines, I placed notes in large print in the kitchen and in her bedroom, reminding her to take her medicine. That worked for a short while, but eventually her memory weakened to a point where she neglected to even read the notes.

"So the three of us decided that even more care was needed, and we began to take turns spending the night."

"How long did the three of you continue to share that duty?"

"We did it for a little over a year, until we moved Mother here."

"And how did that work?" Carl asked.

"It worked well for a good while. One of us would arrive at the house at six o'clock to make sure Mother had dinner and her nightly medicines. By nine o'clock she was usually ready for bed. We would help her change and tuck her in, then spend the rest of the evening reading or watching television before retiring to the bedroom next to hers. But she was still confused, even with all the time we spent with her."

"Can you give us an example?" Carl asked.

"Sure. One evening I had taken her upstairs at 8:30. I helped her change into her night clothes, and within fifteen minutes she was in bed for the night.

"A few minutes after 9:00, just as I had settled in to watch some television, I heard someone coming down the stairs. I jumped up from my chair and went to the staircase. Mother was halfway down, fully dressed. When she saw me, she smiled and said, 'Good morning. I didn't know you were here.'

"I asked her what time it was. She told me it was nine o'clock, and that she had slept late.

"I told her she had only been in bed fifteen minutes, but she continued her descent down the staircase. Once she reached the landing, she looked at me and said, 'you can't kid a kidder.'"

Michael paused to recall the evening's events before Carl prompted him to continue.

"What did you say then?" he asked.

"The first thing I did was take her to the front door to show her that the moon was rising and the street lights were on. She was definitely surprised that it was still evening, but found it hard to believe. She was certain that she had just slept for ten hours. Once she realized that she was mistaken, she was embarrassed, but she was able to laugh about it. "I told her that getting up after fifteen minutes in bed was definitely a new wrinkle. Then I suggested that she must be tired, and that even if she didn't think so now, she was going to be in the morning if she didn't get some rest. When I began to usher her back upstairs to try to sleep again, she just said, 'Okay, boss. Whatever you say'.

"When I went back downstairs after helping her get to bed for the second time, I wanted to laugh at what happened. But at the same time, I knew she had just taken another step down a road that was going to be more and more troubling."

"And did that prove to be the case?" Carl asked.

"Yes, it did. As time wore on, even the mornings became difficult for her. The overnight stays would end at 7:30 after we would get her breakfast ready. She had her morning newspaper and was usually happy to see whoever stayed the previous night off for work. But after about a year, her anxiety was present in the mornings, too. It became more difficult to leave at 7:30, because she would cry and ask what she should do after we had gone. So we hired someone to sit with her for part of the day. Elaine was a very kind middle-aged woman. She would sit three mornings a week with Mother. Elaine encouraged Mother to talk about her family and the old days, and Mother enjoyed the visits. After a few hours, Elaine would prepare Mother's lunch, and then leave. The arrangement helped with Mother's uncertainty for a few more months, but eventually even that was not enough to hold off the fear that was circling around her."

"Did your mother continue to play cards with her friends during all this?" Carl asked.

"She did find a new partner to join the bridge club once Frances dropped out, and she continued for a few years to enjoy her cards. But two months before the move here another event involving the regular card game occurred that reinforced our belief that Mother was slipping beyond us, and needed more attention than the three of us could offer."

"What happened?" Carl prompted.

Michael looked out the window, reflecting on his mother's final card game. It had been an emotional day for both of them.

After a minute of silence, Carl asked if Michael was okay. Michael turned back to Carl and Amy and smiled.

"Yes, I'm fine. I was just thinking back. That's all. That was quite a day."

Then, returning his gaze to the window, Michael began to recount the day as if it was all happening again.

It had been another card game with her old cronies. She hadn't gone to a game since Frances Miles death two months earlier. Every week since then she had come up with one excuse after another to avoid going to the game. He and his sister had been sympathizing with her when she sought out substitutes each week, but they thought it was time she get back with her friends, so this time they refused to let her beg off. She didn't want to go, but Michael had called her partner, Ruth Keller, and told her that Mother was coming. Mrs. Keller had been thrilled to hear that Helen would be back, and she arranged for one of the ladies to pick her up.

That morning Helen called Michael to tell him she wasn't feeling up to going, but he had insisted that she needed to get out. She finally agreed when he had promised her that if she wasn't feeling well after she got to the game he would drive over to pick her up and take her home. So she went, but only an hour into the game Ruth Keller had called to say that his mother wasn't necessarily sick, but she wasn't her old self and they were worried about her. When Michael paused to recall the rest of the day's events, Amy poured a glass of water from the carafe on the conference table and slid it across to him.

"Why don't you have a drink of water before you continue?" she suggested.

Michael studied Amy's face for a moment. He appreciated her simple courtesy, and was struck for the second time that morning by her lovely smile. After thanking her for the water, Michael took a few sips before continuing to recount the memory.

On his arrival at Ruth Keller's condominium, he found his mother sitting in an overstuffed chair, away from the two bridge tables. She was glad he had arrived and told him she wasn't feeling well and that she wanted to go home. She looked so lonely and frightened that Michael was almost ready to cry myself. He helped her to her feet and thanked Ruth for giving him a call.

Then the tables grew silent as the ladies all put their cards down and rose. Where there had been chatter when he entered, now there was none, and he could feel that a sense of sadness had fallen over the room. Some of the ladies had tears in their eyes, struggling to come to grips with the fact that their friend might not return to their tables again. They offered brave smiles, but Michael could see that his mother's fear of being away from her home was having just as great an impact on them as it was having on him. As he looked at the collection of seventy, eighty, and even ninety year old women, he wondered how many times they had witnessed one of their long-time friends fall by the wayside as the darkness settled in.

He knew then that there would be no more card games for his mother with these old friends. And he could see that these sweet old ladies, some of whom were fighting their own brief visits with confusion, knew that this was the last time Helen would be in their midst. It had only been two months since Frances Miles had died, and now another one was going to leave their group.

Usually the farewells at the end of each game were simple. But that day each of the ladies stepped over to give their friend a hug. A few who had played cards with Helen for forty years were struggling not to cry, but it was hard for them not to wonder whom the darkness would overcome next. The darkness that they had seen before with their husbands and their friends, the darkness they each feared someday might claim them.

Michael was standing next to Phyllis Schrand, one of the youngsters of the group, while the ladies were saying their farewells to Helen. He learned from Phyllis that Helen had only played two hands when she asked to sit out. They could see that she was having trouble remembering how to play. When Michael whispered that he thought his mother's card playing days were over, Phyllis nodded that she understood, as a single tear rolled down her face.

"As we were walking toward the car I told her I was sorry she wasn't feeling up to the game today. She looked up at me and said that she knew she couldn't play anymore, and that sometimes when she would look at her cards she didn't have a clue about what was happening around her. It had all just slipped away. I thought that was a striking admission from her, and it seemed pretty feeble to try to suggest that happens to all of us from time to time. I didn't think that would be helpful at that moment. So I just suggested we have some lunch before we go home, and maybe a piece of cherry pie for dessert. She replied with a line she loves to use when she wants someone to encourage her to do something that may not be good for her, like a second glass of wine or dessert at lunch time. 'Get behind me Satan, and push', she said. That made me laugh, so I told her, 'All right, I'm pushing. Let's go'. And that was the last time she went to a card game."

Carl let the story sink in before asking, "And at that point did your family decide to come here?"

"Actually, two weeks after the card game, one more event occurred that convinced us that Mother needed more care than we could provide. It seemed like a simple slip on her part. She mistook me for her husband."

"Had that happened before?" Carl asked.

"She had called me by my father's name a few times over the past two years, as she had drifted back to some memory from long ago. Each time before it was easy to correct her. That Saturday morning in June, however, was different.

"I had spent the night in my old bedroom at the family home. On this particular morning Mother got up around seven o'clock and went into the bathroom. After she left the bathroom she paused at my doorway when she saw me sitting up in bed.

"I put my book down and said good morning to her. She stared at me first before saying that it seemed wrong for me to be in this room and her to be in the other room when we were going to get married. Then she walked in and sat down on the edge of the bed.

"It took a few seconds for me to realize that she thought I was Dad. I smiled at her, and then she patted my arm and said, 'Well, are we going to tie the knot?'

"I felt so badly for her. I thought about how wonderful it would be if Dad could have been there to help her out. But I knew I couldn't act as if I was my father. That would really be a mistake. So I tried to bring her around gently, without causing her much embarrassment."

"What did you say to her?" Carl asked.

"I told her I was Michael. She continued to look at me with a quizzical look. When she didn't respond, I tried again. 'I'm your son, Michael. You married Dad sixty years ago. He's gone now. Do you remember'?

"Then slowly her look changed to one of surprise, as she realized her error. Once she saw who I really was she acted as if nothing had happened at all. 'Oh, it's you, Michael,' she said, and then she asked if I had slept well.

"I told her that I had slept fine, and then suggested that I help her get dressed so we could have breakfast. She said okay and returned to her room, and just like that the confusion ended."

"So was it that event that led you to conclude that a change was necessary?" Carl asked.

"Yes, that's right. After that last bout of confusion, I told Tom and Mary that I didn't think the three of us could really look after her as much as she now needed. Mary had heard of Village Green so we came here first to look for help. We wanted a newer facility that featured a variety of living styles, not one that just was designed for assisted living and skilled care. We felt like this place offered a good support base for Mother. We liked the fact that she could live in a one-bedroom apartment that we could furnish with all her personal belongings. And we liked the fact that her meals would be served in an attractive dining room, and that her medicine would be administered by professionals.

"So, late in July we met with Mother to discuss the idea of moving to Village Green and a new apartment in assisted-living. Not surprisingly, she was cool to the idea. After listening to each of us, she said simply, 'This is my home. I don't want to leave'.

"I asked her if she agreed that a home is a place where some-one feels safe and warm. She agreed, and said that was why she wanted to stay put."

That drew a laugh from Carl and Amy.

"I can see that sometimes she's still one step ahead of you, isn't she, Michael?" Carl said.

"You're right. She can still be a clever one. But we pressed on. We told her that the old home just didn't feel safe anymore. When we reminded her that we had been taking turns spend-ing the night there for over a year she was very surprised. She thought it had only been a few weeks. Then we talked to her about how she was not feeling safe in her home when one of us was not around. Mary pointed out to Mother that she had been crying that very morning because she was afraid of being alone for a few hours. Mother couldn't even recall that.

"I tried to remind her that her mind had been playing some tricks on her. I knew that this decision wasn't going to be easy for her, but that it was necessary, and that it would require us to be gentle, but firm. She finally acknowledged that she does get confused a little sometimes. We told her then that we've been around to help her, and that we're not going away, but that it breaks our hearts to see her so afraid each morning when we leave for work. She asked if we could get her some medicine and make her feel better. We told her that we wished we could, but that there wasn't any medicine that would keep her from feeling afraid. Then she asked me how an old ladies' home would help."

That drew more laughter from Carl and Amy before Michael continued.

"I told her first that we should try not calling it an 'old ladies' home', and that we ought to be a bit more positive. Then I pointed out that there were people of all ages living here, and not just ladies, either. We showed her pictures of the apartment layout, and reassured her that she would have her own place with all her own furniture, but there would be people around to help with the meals and with her medicine and to help fill her day with some fun things, instead of scary things.

"She told me she was scared, and asked if we would still come to see her. We all promised her that one of us would be out to see her every day. Finally, she said that she still didn't want to leave her home, and she asked me if she had to. At that point I thought back to the afternoon where my dad was rocking on his hands, trying to insure we would look after Mother. So I took her hand. I knew this was the point where we had to be firm. 'It's time we find another home that will make you feel safer', I told her. 'We promised Dad we would all help to take care of you, and we always will. So now it's time to find a safer home'. Once I said that, she nodded her head in resignation and the decision was made."

Carl smiled at Michael, and said, "That's quite a remarkable series of stories you've related. I really appreciate your candor. What you've described is common to a lot of the residents who are in assisted-living."

"They're all very personal to me," Michael replied.

"We understand," Carl said.

The three of them stood to end the meeting.

"What you've told us will be helpful to Amy and her staff in understanding where your mother is coming from," Carl said.

"It sure will," Amy said, as she shook Michael's hand. "Thanks for coming in today."

The meeting then broke up and Michael headed down the hallway for a quick visit with his mother.

CHAPTER 4

Fall courses at the university would not begin for another month, so Michael continued to visit Helen every day to try to help her settle in. She'd been in her new apartment for three weeks. As he drove the long, shaded lane on the Village Green site, he passed a landscaping crew planting fall flowers. The grounds were beautiful, and Michael hoped Helen would feel up to a long walk today. He felt good about the move to Village Green. He knew she was still worried and often afraid, but more and more he believed that this was the best place to try to stem off the worries that her age and mental state were bringing on.

When he arrived at the apartment, he let himself in but discovered that she was not there. She lived on the third floor of the senior facility, in a large one-bedroom apartment. They had furnished the apartment comfortably with many of Helen's belongings from home, and had purchased a small table for two that sat in front of the bay window, that looked down over the trees and flowers in the landscaped courtyard.

The grounds were beautiful, meticulously maintained, and lined with an abundance of trees and shrubs. The large courtyard featured walkways, benches, and flowers. Directly beneath her window was a beautifully shaped maple tree. Across the courtyard were two dogwoods and magnolias that would flower beautifully in the spring. The walkways throughout the courtyard were lined with flower beds that contained roses and an assortment of summer plants, now being replaced with mums by the landscaping crew.

Michael lingered at the window, enjoying the view and feeling a sense of tranquility descend over him. After a few minutes, he set off to look for Helen, hopeful that she had gone off to meet some of her fellow residents or participate in a morning activity. As he walked down the wide hallway of her wing, he paused to admire the decorations outside the residents' rooms. Most of the apartments had end tables with a family photograph just outside the front door. Some had a chair and a painting affixed to the wall. One apartment actually had a small piano next to the front door. The hallways were so wide that the decorations didn't overwhelm the building. Michael thought it was a nice touch to permit the residents to decorate this way. Outside his mother's apartment was an old piece of furniture that had served as a telephone stand in her home for the last forty years. Atop it was a marble lamp featuring a ballerina. He and his siblings called it the dancing lady lamp. They all thought that the familiar table and lamp would serve as a kind of beacon for Helen in finding her apartment.

The hallway in Helen's wing connected with a main one that led to the elevator. Michael found her at the intersection of those two halls. She was sitting in an overstuffed chair outside another resident's apartment, talking with an elderly gentleman.

As Michael approached them, he sensed that Helen was lost and uncertain as to what to do, even though she was only six doors down from her apartment.

"Oh, Michael!" she exclaimed as she laid eyes on him. In a voice that sounded as if it had been years since she had last seen him, she said, "I'm so glad to see you. How did you find me?"

"I just walked the halls, Mother. What are you up to?"

"I'm so glad you came," she said again. "I'm lost. I've just been sitting here waiting for someone to come along and tell me where I'm supposed to go. This is Henry. He lives here, too, but he doesn't know where my room is."

"It's okay. I'm here now. Hello, Henry," he said, offering his hand to the tall but stoop-shouldered white-haired man. "It's nice to meet you. I'm Michael Telford, Helen's son."

Henry took Michael's hand in a strong grip. "It's nice to meet you, Michael. I was just showing your mother how I keep track of my room. I have my key here on my wrist band, like your mother does, but I also have a little tag here that tells me where my room is. Once in a while I get lost in these halls too, so the tag helps me."

"That's a great idea. We'll fix one of those up for Mother. Where do you live, Henry?"

"Oh, I'm down this hall and off another one. My room number is," he paused and looked at the tag on his wrist, "Number 314."

Henry looked sheepish as he spoke, embarrassed that he needed to look at his tag.

"I see that tag is a good idea," Michael volunteered. "Thanks for telling us about it."

"You're welcome," Henry smiled. "Well, I'll be on my way now. It was nice meeting you, Helen. I hope we see each other again soon."

"Thanks, Henry," she replied, then looked back to Michael. "Show me where the apartment is, will you?"

"Great idea," Michael responded. "Let's go."

She took his arm and together they walked back down the hallway to her apartment.

Once back in her room, Helen asked Michael to sit down on the couch next to her to talk. Michael wondered what topic she would choose today. He guessed it would be money, and he was correct.

"How am I going to pay for this place?" she asked, in a voice that held a touch of alarm.

Finances had been a major source of doubt for her. She hadn't balanced her own checkbook since Dad had passed away, relying on Michael to take care of that chore. She was not a wealthy woman, just comfortable enough with her Social Security, a few small investments, and a home that was fully paid for. Michael had taken over the bill payments for her once she began to have trouble with her bookkeeping. Many times he had reassured her that she had plenty of money and she would never have to worry about any bills. But her memory continued to fail her, so his financial reassurance speech was becoming almost a daily ritual.

Her monthly income covered only half of the monthly fees at Village Green. The balance would have to come from her savings. He knew that the house would need to be sold in the coming year to keep up with the cost, and, of course, if she went into skilled care they would be out of money in less than two years. But he could never tell her that. If she thought she was going to run out of money she might just give up. Michael had chosen to tell his mother what he thought she needed to hear, rather than the actual facts.

Balancing the need for being honest with his mother and telling her what he thought needed to be said was something Michael had wrestled with over the past two years. In this instance, he chose to calm her with a rosy exaggeration of her financial situation rather than tell her that if she lived long enough, she would run out of money some day.

"You're fine with money, Mother," he said. "You've got Social Security and money in the bank and you're never going to run out. I'm taking care of that for you."

"Oh, that's good to hear. I worry about it when you're not here."

"Try not to worry about this. You're in great shape. You should think about all the wonderful activities they have here, and let me handle the money matters for you."

"Oh, Michael, I can't think about that. I can't even find where the activities are. I just keep thinking about how I'm going to pay for all this. I'm afraid I'll wind up in the poorhouse, and I don't even know where it is."

He laughed. "If you'd like, maybe we could find an atlas and figure out just exactly where the poorhouse is located."

"Okay, stinker," she replied.

"First, though," he suggested, "why don't we look at a few pictures and see what we remember?"

On the coffee table in front of them was a photograph of Michael's father seated in his favorite chair. Mother was behind him to the left. To the right was an end table on which sat an open book.

"Do you remember when this was taken?" Michael asked.

"This is in the living room here," Helen responded.

"Well, that's pretty close. It's the living room at your old home here in Cincinnati."

"Oh, that's right. I moved, didn't I?"

"Yes, you did. You're in a new apartment now. Do you remember anything more about this picture?"

"No," Helen replied. "Just that it was a long time ago."

"That it was," Michael agreed. "It reminds me of one of my greatest achievements ever."

Helen looked again at the photo then turned to Michael. "Okay, I give. What was that?"

"Do you remember when the shoe factory in New York was sold, and Dad was away from home for a while searching for a new plant to run?"

It was coming back to Helen. "I remember. That's when we moved to Cincinnati."

"That's right. This picture reminds me of the day when Dad made it very clear that your title was 'Mother', and not 'Mom'."

Helen smiled. "He always called his mother by that name. He insisted that's how he wanted our children to address me as well."

"I remember," Michael smiled, as he began to relate his memory of the big achievement from many years ago.

"You know that calling you 'Mother' was the only name we ever thought was right for you. But it wasn't until the time this picture was taken that I was actually told there would be no 'mom' or 'mommy' names permitted in the Telford home. And until that time, Dad was still to be addressed as Daddy."

"You called him Daddy for a long time. When did that change?"

"It was almost time for me to begin high school, when Mary and I decided the time had come to approach Dad to discuss his name."

Helen smiled as she recalled her young children. "So what happened?" she asked.

"Mary and I went into the dining room where Dad was reading, and I took the lead. 'Daddy,' I began, because I wasn't bold enough yet to shorten the title, 'I'd like to ask you something.' I remember Dad sat up a bit, and put his book on his lap and folded his hands."

"'Is that a fact?' he said to me. Remember how often he would use that line?"

Helen smiled and nodded, recalling the expression.

"Anyway, Dad said, 'All right, what do you want to talk about?'

"So I summoned up all my courage, and said, 'Well, Mary and I are getting older now, and we were wondering if it would be all right with you if we called you Dad instead of Daddy'."

Michael found as he was reflecting on events from so long ago, he could still recall the anxiety he felt at what was such a simple request.

"And what did your father say?" Helen asked, now very interested in the story.

"He looked at me for a second, and then said, 'I see,' in that strong voice he carried. 'So the two of you think you're getting too big to call me Daddy.'"

"We both nodded our heads, afraid of what he was going to say."

Michael paused to recall the day and how his father showed his warm heart. Then he turned back to his mother and continued. "So Dad said, 'I suppose you are old enough. I think it's probably a good idea that you call me Dad from now on.'

"Mary and I were bubbling with pride at the thought that we had just persuaded him. I remember that we each said, 'Thanks, Dad,' for the first time together. It felt good, like we were adults. I suppose I thought that now I was a more serious force to be reckoned with in the world. Anyway, Mary and I turned to run off, eager to congratulate each other. But we only took about two steps in our getaway before Dad's booming voice stopped us in our tracks."

"What did he say?" Helen asked.

"'Come back here', he commanded. 'There's one more thing to be said.' So Mary and I stopped, and we each looked back over our shoulders. Neither of us wanted to turn around completely to face Dad, because we were still anxious to be off before he changed his mind.

"'Come here', he said a second time, and then we knew that an over-the-shoulder look was not good enough for the message he intended to deliver. He wanted our complete attention. So we turned and stood back before him.

"'You can call me Dad from now on,' he said, 'but don't you ever think of calling your mother by any other name'."

Helen laughed. "That sounds just like your father. And what did you and Mary say?"

"I remember thinking to myself, my God, I would never have dreamed of asking to call you Mom. 'Oh, no, Daddy,' we both said. Already we had failed to take advantage of our new power. 'We'll never ask you that.'

"Dad looked at us both again, then smiled and said, 'I'm glad we're clear on that. Okay, you two can go now.'

"We watched him sit back in his chair with a grin on his face and resume reading his book, then we hightailed it out of the room, anxious to find a place where we could catch our breath and try to regain that sense of confidence we held so briefly just moments before."

Michael smiled at his mother, and continued, "You know, when Mary and Tom's kids were little, they would sometimes tell their friends that their parents never called their mom anything but mother, as if we were some type of dinosaurs.

Helen patted Michael's hand. "Your father was a good man. I miss him every day."

"That he was," Michael agreed. The two of them grew silent again, recalling the old days. Finally, Michael suggested they take a walk around the building again and try to get used to the place.

"I'll help you learn how to get back to your apartment from the dining room. Maybe, while we're downstairs, we'll find a tag for your key bracelet and write your room number down like Henry told us. Then we'll have some lunch together. What do you say, Mom?"

"It's a good thing your father didn't hear that, young man," Helen joked in return. "As for lunch, don't ask if you don't mean it."

"Okay, let's go," Michael said, and together they began the trek back down the hall again.

When Michael returned for another visit two days later, he came upon Henry, as he was walking past the nurse's desk on his way to his mother's apartment. Henry was standing next to Amy Nelson and the two of them were looking over the list of the day's scheduled activities, which was posted each morning in the main hallway near the dining room.

"Good morning, Henry," he offered.

Henry looked over at Michael, pausing to size him up and search his memory. "Good morning, young man," he said. "I believe we met before, but perhaps you'd do an elderly gentleman a favor and tell me where that was."

"Certainly," Michael replied. "I met you a few days ago in the hallway upstairs. You were talking with my mother who was lost and couldn't find her apartment."

"Oh, yes," Henry replied with a smile, nodding his head. "I remember now."

Michael turned to Amy and extended his hand, "Nice to see you again."

"Same here, Michael."

Michael turned back to Henry and said, "So tell me now, do you like the activities they offer here?"

Henry offered a snort and flicked his head toward the list for the day. "I guess it's a fair offering," he said with a trace of mockery.

"What do you mean?" Michael asked. "You don't sound too pleased."

"Well, this is a big place," Henry began. "And there are a lot of people here, most of them with pretty good minds still. I'm having a few memory issues now, I must concede, so I live in this area where people who need a little more help are closer to the nurses. I guess your mother is living near here, too."

"Yes, she is."

Henry grew silent as his eyes wandered off, not just across the room, but to another place entirely. Michael sat quietly until Henry blinked, and focusing in again on Michael, asked, "Now what were we discussing, young man?"

"We were talking about the activities here."

"Oh, yes," Henry recalled. "The activities. Well, you see, it's got to be hard on them to try to schedule things that everyone can do, so the good things, like lunches at restaurants or trips to the art museum are generally restricted to the folks living outside of this assisted-living building, the ones who probably won't get lost on the trip. The nurses don't like it if I try to sign up for a bus trip to the museum, because they're afraid I'll wander off and no one will be able to keep track of me. They may be right about that. I'm quite certain I would want to wander off from the crowd. That's been my style for over eighty years. So I don't go on those trips anymore. For me there's the discussion of what's in the newspaper most mornings at nine, and some silly game at two after lunch. A lot of evenings there's a concert in the main hall, where everyone is invited. That's the activity I look for every day. Otherwise, I just try to do a lot of walking, and avoid getting lost at the same time."

Amy placed her arm through Henry's and looked up at Michael. "We love seeing Henry every day. He's the finest gentleman in the house."

"I believe that," Michael said. "But is it true about the activities planned for the residents?"

Amy nodded. "It's true that most of the activities here are terrific for the independent-living residents who don't suffer from so many memory problems, but there is a concert or a movie scheduled almost every evening that Henry and a lot of others in assisted-living really enjoy."

"Well, I'm sorry that the activities seem limited. The concerts sound good though. Is there one tonight?" Michael asked.

Henry rejoined the conversation. "Yes, it looks like a duet will be singing some of the golden oldies tonight, young man. You should bring your mother along."

"I'll try to do that. Thanks for telling me."

"My pleasure," Henry replied, as he returned to study the daily list. Michael walked away, headed for his mother's apartment. Amy joined him.

"Your mother is a very sweet person," Amy said, as they reached the elevator. "I was just on my way to see how she was doing this morning."

"Well that sounds good to me," Michael said with a smile. "Let's head up."

"How do you feel your mother is adjusting to Village Green?" Amy asked as they walked toward the elevator.

"I think it will be slow going for a while," Michael said. "It's easy for her to get lost, as I'm sure it is for a lot of other residents here."

"Yes, there are a lot of patients that we find wandering the halls. Your mother doesn't seem to venture out much by herself, though."

"You know, that's how we first met Henry," Michael said. "It was just a few days after Mother moved here. I came out to visit her and found her down the hall sitting in a chair talking to him. She was lost and didn't know how to get back to her room.

He didn't know how to find her room either, but he stayed with her and reassured her that everything would be okay. It was really a nice way to meet the man."

"He really is a sweetheart. I just love being around him. And I think I'm going to enjoy being around your mother as well," Amy said.

As they reached the door of Helen's apartment Amy knocked and then opened it and stuck her head in the door. "Helen," she called, "it's your nurse, Amy. I've got someone special with me. Can we come in?"

Helen was seated on the couch watching a television show. "Come on in," she said.

When Helen saw Michael she smiled and said, "Oh, Michael, I'm so glad to see you. Where have you been?"

Michael smiled. "Well it's only been about twelve hours since I last saw you, Mother. Amy found me wandering the halls and brought me down to see you."

"Well, that's not quite true, Helen. But I enjoyed walking with your son to see you," Amy said, smiling at the two of them. "So how are you feeling this morning?" Amy asked.

"Oh, I feel good today. Thanks for asking. I like it when Michael and my other children come around to visit me. That always makes it a good day," Helen said.

"I can see where that would be the case," Amy said. "Let me just check your blood pressure real quick and then I'll let you have your visit."

Amy drew the blood pressure cuff from her pocket and took a reading.

"Good pressure today," Amy said as she pulled the cuff off Helen's arm. "You know, Helen, I just love all these photographs you have here in your apartment. It really makes the place feel warm."

"Thank you. The kids insisted that we hang them all up. Michael likes to quiz me on them once in a while."

"Is that right? That sounds like fun. It looks like there's a story there," Amy said, as she pointed to a photograph of Helen holding a juice glass in one hand and a pretzel in the other, smiling for the camera. "What was going on when that was taken?"

Helen considered the photograph for a minute, then asked Michael, "Was that the night Dad retired?"

"Good memory, Mother. Yes it was."

Michael turned to Amy and added, "They posed that one. It was taken the evening of Dad's retirement, and we all insisted on a re-enactment of the evening ritual Mother had performed for years and years. Each evening when Dad would return home from work, he would open a bottle of beer and pour a few ounces in a juice glass for Mother and pour the rest in a glass for himself. Mother would place some pretzels or other snacks into a bowl and they would carry their drinks and snack into the living room. The bowl of snacks was always on the table next to Dad. Very little conversation was held when they would first sit down. Dad would begin to read the evening news. Mother would patiently sit, waiting for him to sip his drink and scan the paper, knowing that he needed his quiet time. Generally, after perusing the front page and the editorials, Dad would fold the paper and then begin to tell a story about the factory, raising his voice and sometimes even pacing the floor. Meanwhile, Mother listened closely and concurred with the stories. She was always very calm, waiting for him to unwind and return to the fold. And always he would return, thanks to her quiet way."

Michael smiled.

"What a lovely story," Amy said, smiling at Michael and Helen in turn.

Then Helen spoke up. "You know, I never did like the taste of beer. I preferred it when Dad would fix a cocktail for each of us. As the days in the factory grew harder on him, he changed from an evening beer to an evening Manhattan. That suited me just fine."

Michael joined Amy in laughing at Helen's declaration.

"Do you have time for one more story?" he asked Amy.

"Sure I do," she replied.

Michael turned to his mother. "Tell Amy about your M&M bowl."

Helen smiled. "Every Monday in our house was grandchildren day. Tom and Mary's children would spend the day when they were young. If they were still there when Dad returned from the factory, sometimes one of them would try to sneak over to touch grandpa's snack bowl while he was reading the newspaper. I wish you kids would have warned them," Helen laughed. "Dad's snacks were not to be trifled with, and his bark could scare the little ones away. So I always kept this dish on the coffee table filled with M&M's, and the children were always allowed to fill their little candy dishes. This is the bowl I always kept them in. Would you like an M&M?"

"Well, thank you, Helen," Amy said as she scooped a few out of the bowl. "That was a nice story. I've seen a few of your grandchildren here. They look like they've all grown up."

"Yes, they have. But they'll never be too old to eat M&M's."

"You're right," Amy said. "I better tend to the other residents now, so I'll leave you with Michael. One of the nurses will be back in a while to check in on you, all right?"

"I'll be here," Helen said.

As Amy headed for the door she stopped to examine a framed photograph. It showed a younger Michael and a young girl seated together on a piano bench with their hands poised to play.

"Do you still play piano?" she asked.

"A little," he admitted.

"I've always wanted to learn. It was nice talking with you again, Michael. I hope to see you again soon."

"Thanks, Amy. Let's make a point of it," he said.

Amy smiled as she left the apartment.

"She's a nice young lady," Helen said after Amy left. "Maybe you should get to know her better. Say, you could give her piano lessons."

Michael laughed. "Don't tell me you're being a matchmaker, Mother. You just met her."

"Well, you never know where you're going to meet a nice young lady," Helen said.

"You're right. Someone will come along again someday, don't you worry about it."

"I just hope you don't wait forever. It's been a long time since Lainie. You've been so good to me since your father died. I know you've sacrificed a lot of your personal life to take care of me."

Michael smiled, recalling the face of the woman he was certain he was going to marry years ago, before illness struck and she was taken from him.

"I wouldn't have it any other way. I'm not complaining about my personal life. You're not going to get rid of me that easy," he joked. "Now let's get you some exercise." He recognized that Lainie's memory lingered steadily with him, and the need to provide care for his parents had helped to mask the loneliness he felt since her death. Maybe his personal life had suffered since they had each become ill, but what was he to do? There never seemed to be time for another relationship.

On the way outside they looked in the auditorium and spied a grand piano on wheels in the far corner.

"Shall we?" Michael asked.

"Oh, let's be bad," Helen replied, a wicked smile spreading across her face.

Michael closed the door behind them, leading Helen over to the piano bench. They both squeezed onto the bench and Michael began to play. He kept his right foot on the soft pedal, but the classic Baldwin had a clear tone that softly carried through the doorway to the hallway beyond. Amy was just passing by the door on her way to the nurse's station when she heard music drifting from the auditorium. She looked at her watch. No program was scheduled at this hour, so she stuck her head in to see what was going on. She recognized Michael and Helen. Michael would play a few bars of an old song and she could see that Helen was guessing the name. They were both laughing and having a good time. It touched Amy to see a mother and son enjoying their company together like that. Michael began to play another piece, but this time he didn't stop after a few measures. Amy recognized the melody and quietly took a seat to enjoy the performance.

A minute later, Joanne Holly, the director of activities at Village Green, was walking by the auditorium and heard the music. She stepped in to see who was playing her grand piano. When she saw one of the new residents and some man sitting at the instrument her budget had paid so much for she felt like she had to put a stop to it. The piano was reserved for professionals.

Amy saw Joanne begin to walk toward the piano and stood to speak with her.

"What is going on in here, Amy?"

"It looks like an impromptu concert to me. I think it's wonderful."

"Well, I don't. That's a very expensive piano that my department paid for and I won't have it casually manhandled by anyone."

"Have you listened to the music, Joanne? He's not manhandling anything. He plays beautifully."

"Maybe you think so but I'm putting a stop to it," Joanne said with a rising voice.

Michael heard a conversation occurring so he played just a few more measures and stopped. He and Helen looked over at the two staff members.

He whispered to his mother, "Now look what you've done. They're going to throw us out of here."

"Good. That's just what I was hoping for," Helen replied.

"You're not getting out of this place that easy, Mother," he said.

He recognized Amy as the two women walked over. He had seen the other gal before. He thought maybe she was the host of the evening events or something like that, but he didn't recall her name.

"Hello, ladies," he greeted as they reached the piano. "Hope you didn't mind me banging around the ivories for a few minutes."

Both women spoke at once, but Amy was determined to seize the conversation. Michael couldn't make out exactly what the other gal was trying to say but it didn't seem entirely pleasant. On the other hand, Amy was displaying that beautiful smile again—her hazel eyes held Michael's gaze.

"That was wonderful," she was saying. "I hope you didn't mind the two of us dropping in to listen."

Michael smiled at his mother. "So you're not going to expel my mother from the Village Green community for this infraction?"

Amy laughed. "Why would we ever think of such a thing?"

Helen pinched Michael on the leg. He put his arm around her and said, "Oh, I was just joking. This is a beautiful piano. Really, I hope it was okay that we played a few songs together."

Joanne was determined to have her say. This time, when Amy started to reply Joanne placed her hand on Amy's arm to stop her. "Actually, Mr. Telford. That is your name, isn't it?"

Michael nodded.

"Well, Mr. Telford, this instrument is very valuable. Our policy in the activities department has always been to permit only professional musicians to play it. We really can't have just anyone coming in here to bang on the keys, as you put it." Joanne finished with what she must have thought was a sweet smile, but the others could only describe as a sour one.

Helen beat Michael to the punch with a reply.

"Then I guess we're not in trouble then. My son here is a professional. He played in a band and he gives lessons too. We were just talking about setting up a time for Amy to have a lesson."

Michael almost burst out laughing at what Helen was saying. But he loved to see her being her old self again, even for just a few minutes. Her words had clearly confused Joanne Holly, who turned to Amy and said, "Is this true?"

Amy looked from Joanne to Michael, who was wearing a mischievous grin. He raised his shoulders slightly, which she interpreted to mean it was all right with him if she went along with the pretense. She smiled and winked at him before turning back to Joanne.

"That is true. We were talking about lessons earlier this morning. Michael is a professional, so I guess everyone's complying with your rules, Joanne."

The activities director had enough of this conversation. She didn't like it that things were not going her way. "I see." Then turning to Michael, she added, "In the future would you be so kind as to schedule your use of my piano with my staff?"

Your piano, he thought. *Boy, we really stepped on some toes.*

"Certainly. Thanks very much for being so gracious."

That fell on deaf ears as Joanne turned to leave the gathering. No one spoke until she was safely out of hearing distance.

"I don't think Miss Holly likes you, Mother," he joked.

"I guess we better pack up and move back home then," she deadpanned.

Amy laughed with them. "You're not going anywhere, Helen. And you, sir, owe me a piano lesson. We can't very well forget that, after dragging me into that whopper you dreamed up."

"Me?" Michael said. "Blame this gal here."

"Okay, you two. Stop your bickering," Helen said. "Looks like you're going to start lessons together real soon."

Michael admitted to himself that the thought of sitting alongside Amy was appealing.

"Do I have to sign up to use the piano?" he asked.

Amy laughed. "I'll take care of Miss Holly."

The two of them discussed their work schedules and agreed to start a few days later with a half hour lesson. After Amy left, Michael walked Helen back to her apartment.

"I hope you're proud of yourself, Mother," he said, just before leaving.

"What ever do you mean, son?"

He shook his head. "You know exactly what I mean."

"Hey, you're the piano teacher, not me."

There was no winning with her today. He could see that. He gave her a kiss and headed out.

That evening Michael returned to share dinner with Helen in the main dining room. Although the food was good, she ate little of her meal.

"I don't know how you do it, Mother," Michael laughed as he put his napkin down. "You eat less than a bird."

"I don't need a lot to keep me going," Helen replied. "I'm full."

"Is that right?" Michael replied. "Too bad, because I see there's apple pie ala mode being served for dessert tonight."

"Well, maybe I could squeeze in some apple pie."

Michael laughed. "Why doesn't that surprise me?"

"Listen, Buster," Helen smiled back, "you worry about yourself. Now find our waiter and order some dessert before they run out."

After dinner they walked past the auditorium where chairs were being set up for the concert.

"Let's go see the park," Helen said.

Michael knew Helen meant the courtyard and gardens, so he gladly steered her out down the hallway for a walk in her park. Helen agreed they would return to the auditorium after their walk to listen to the music.

The courtyard was framed by the doorway from which they had just come. The yard was bordered on the left by Building Five, a three-story structure which held Helen's apartment. The building was almost a hundred feet long. To the right was Building Three which held Henry's apartment. Both of the buildings featured bay windows in the hallways overlooking the courtyard. The ground-level units all had patios adjoining the gardens. The next two levels had balconies overlooking the yard as well.

At the rear of the yard was a large fountain. Beyond the fountain was a parking lot servicing the two buildings.

The courtyard featured a ten-foot wide sidewalk that ran down the center all the way to the fountain at the rear. The sidewalks branching off the main walk led to the patios and side entryways for the adjoining buildings. Park benches were scattered throughout the yard, along with several large trees that offered shade for the residents. The landscaping was remarkable. The entire area looked like a park and offered a wonderful sense of beauty and peace to the residents.

Michael was impressed with the time and effort that the staff took to keep this area attractive. And he knew that this was not the only courtyard on the site. The facility held 300 residents in seven buildings. There were two other courtyards similar to this that ran between the other buildings, along with a magnificent expanse of lawn featuring huge shade trees that led from the street to the main entrance of the facility.

They walked down the path and found an empty bench. From there Michael could see the windows of Helen's apartment and he pointed them out to her.

"Isn't this a beautiful place to be?" he asked.

"It is beautiful, dear," she agreed. "It's not like home, but it is nice sitting here in the park."

Michael was pleased to hear her refer to the courtyard as a park. For a few minutes they sat watching squirrels run through the yard.

After a while, Henry came walking through the courtyard. Michael rose as Henry approached and greeted him.

"Hello, Henry."

Henry paused and stared, not unkindly, trying to place Michael and Helen.

"I'm Michael Telford. This is my mother, Helen. We spoke this morning about the day's activities. You told me about tonight's concert."

That rang a bell with Henry, and he smiled. "Yes, of course. Please forgive an old man's memory lapse. Good evening, Michael. And good evening to you, young lady," he said as he turned toward Helen.

Helen smiled. "Good evening. Care to join us?"

"Well, thank you," Henry responded, as he sat on the bench next to theirs. "It's a beautiful evening for a walk, isn't it?"

"It is," Michael responded. "We had a nice dinner and were just enjoying the evening breeze before the music begins."

"This is my favorite part of the day. I like to sit out here when it cools down in the evening," Henry said.

Henry looked over at Helen's wrist and saw that she had a tag with her room number attached to her key bracelet. Michael noticed Henry's observation, and said, "Thanks for your advice on the extra tag with the room number on it. It's been a help already."

"Not at all," said Henry. "We all need to stick together when we're consigned to a place like this."

"Well, we're trying, aren't we, Mother?"

Helen smiled but said nothing.

"So, what line of work are you in, young man?" Henry asked.

"I'm on the faculty at the University of Cincinnati," Michael replied.

"Excellent. A professor, are you?"

Michael turned to Helen, raising his eyes slightly, as if to say, 'What's the answer to that, Mother?' It had been a joke between them for almost twenty years. His mother thought the title 'Professor' was a little pompous, so she liked to call him 'Perfessor' instead, just to make sure he didn't get a big head.

Helen saw Michael's smile, got the message, and spoke up, "Michael teaches English at the university. I'm very proud of him."

Henry nodded in return, as Michael smiled. She just couldn't bring herself to say that word.

"How long have you lived here, Henry?" Michael continued.

"I'm told it's been around eighteen months. But it feels longer," he replied.

"Do you have family in town?" Helen asked.

"I have a daughter who lives here, or rather here in town. My wife died several years ago. My daughter lived with me in my home for a few years after that, but eventually she convinced me to move here."

"Does she still live in your home?" Michael asked.

"Oh yes. She'll never give it up. It was always my favorite place in the world, and I believe it's hers now, too." Henry replied.

"Do you miss your home?" Helen asked. Michael looked over at her, surprised but pleased that she was finally engaging in conversation with someone.

"Oh, I should say so."

"Tell us about it," Helen urged, again surprising Michael.

"Well, it's an old two-story home, surrounded by trees, with a long driveway that sweeps under the pines. The trees form a kind of canopy over the drive, so that it feels like you're driving through the woods when you head up the driveway."

"It sounds beautiful. It reminds me of our old home in New York."

"It is beautiful, Helen," Henry replied.

Helen pictured her former home briefly before saying, "I miss my home, too."

"I'm sure you do," Henry said. "From time to time, I think about lying down again under the pine trees. I wish that could happen again."

Henry looked at his watch. "Say, it's almost seven now. Are you going to hear the music?"

"We sure are," Michael replied. "Let's go in."

Together they headed back into the building and over to the auditorium. When they arrived, the room was filling with residents, and the singers were setting up on the platform. They found seats near the front, and enjoyed the old songs, laughing as they sang *"When you wore a tulip, a sweet yellow tulip, and I wore a big red rose."*

After the performance, the activity director thanked the duet and wished everyone a good evening. The smile she had pasted on for everyone changed slightly when she observed Michael and Helen walking by. He decided to thank her effusively at the doorway. Helen held her laughter until they had exited.

"You just can't let things go, can you?" she said.

Henry chimed in. "It looks like you've met the dreaded Miss Holly already."

"Yes, we had the pleasure this morning," Michael said. "She was displeased that we were playing the piano back in the auditorium."

"Did she suggest it was her piano?" Henry asked mischievously.

That made the three of them cackle as they walked past the nursing station to the elevators servicing the upper floors. Once reaching the third floor, Henry wished Helen and Michael a good evening. After first taking one more look at the room number on his wristband he headed off down another hall. Helen and Michael returned to her room.

"That was lovely, wasn't it?" Helen said

"It sure was, and it was nice talking with Henry, too."

"He's an interesting man. Maybe we'll see him again tomorrow."

CHAPTER 5

The next month passed relatively peacefully. Michael didn't visit every day, but he was a regular. Tom and Mary each made it a practice to visit regularly as well, so that Helen had at least one visitor every day. Each of them continued to look at photographs with Helen on their visits in an effort to preserve her memory. Still, Helen continued to display memory loss and confusion—not on a large scale, but enough that each of her children could see the decline.

Meanwhile, the piano lessons with Amy were becoming a standard weekly event. She had a natural ear for music, and was progressing well. Michael was really enjoying their time together. He thought Amy felt the same way.

Mixed with the lessons each week was general conversation. They kept it pretty light, each wanting to learn more about the other, but with neither pushing too hard. Michael learned that Amy had been married once. It had been a difficult marriage for her and did not last long. She had a daughter from the marriage that she was raising. The father seemed to be out of the picture completely.

Michael told her about his position at the University. After a few weeks he even talked one day about Lainie and her death. Amy had been attentive and empathetic. He appreciated that she didn't feel threatened by his memories, and even encouraged him to tell her stories of his prior relationship. He hadn't asked her out for an evening yet, but he was beginning to feel that each of his lessons with her was almost like a date.

In early October, posters announcing an Autumn Dance for all residents and their guests began appearing throughout the facility. This was an unusual event, and Michael could sense that many of the residents were very excited about it. He had heard some of them talking about wearing a costume to the dance. Helen agreed she would attend the dance with Michael, even though she was not one of those residents excited about the evening.

Mary purchased a new sweater for Helen for the big evening. After dinner Michael escorted Helen to the dance. He was surprised to see a stocked bar and a live band on hand for entertainment. The tables quickly filled with the regulars, many of whom were all dolled up for the dance. Michael found a table for four tucked away in a far corner and settled Helen in before setting off to get a glass of wine for each of them.

Michael had just returned to the table with two glasses of wine when he spotted Henry entering the room.

"Mother, there's Henry. Should I ask him to join us?"

"Sure, go get him."

As Michael was walking across the room, Henry saw him and smiled. Michael waved for him to join them, and Henry ambled over, after first stopping at the bar for a Manhattan.

"Good evening, Helen," he said as he pulled up a chair.

"Hello, Henry. Glad you could join us."

Henry looked at Helen's glass of wine and raised his Manhattan in a toast.

"I have a feeling more than a few of the folks in here are not supposed to have alcohol, but here's to the management for ignoring the rules for the night."

"I'll drink to that," Helen said, raising her glass and sipping her wine.

"Have you noticed the group of gigolos talking to the staff over by the band?" Michael asked.

The three of them turned to gaze at a group of fifty to sixty-year-old men in nice attire standing to the left of the bandstand. Some of the men were wearing a coat and tie; the rest were in sweaters.

"Are those hired dancers for the night?" Helen asked.

"A prize for the lady," Michael said, smiling at her.

Henry laughed. "So they brought in ringers to dance 'cause we men are outnumbered, is that it?"

"I believe so," said Michael. "There they go."

The band started playing an old standard, "Smoke Gets in Your Eyes." As the music began, the ringers scattered across the room and began to approach the older ladies, inviting them to dance.

The three of them laughed as they saw some of the residents blush, but get up nevertheless for a trip around the dance floor.

"Well, isn't that something?" Henry said. "Gigolos at Village Green. I wonder if they'll all get up and do a striptease number later."

Michael laughed while looking over at his mother for her reaction.

She was smiling and shaking her head. "We can only hope," she replied, sending Henry off into a long, hearty laugh as they listened to the old song.

When the band launched into an old Glenn Miller arrangement, Helen spoke up. "This brings back memories."

"It sure does," replied Henry. "You recognize this one, Helen?"

"Yes, I do. It takes me back to our dancing days when we were young."

"Where did you and your husband like to dance?"

"Valley Dale was our favorite spot."

"Valley Dale?" asked Henry with surprise. "In Columbus?"

"Sure. Tom and I grew up in Columbus."

Henry sat back with a smile. It was his turn to shake his head. "I danced at Valley Dale a few times back in my day."

Michael looked over at Henry. "Mother has talked about Valley Dale for as long as I can remember. She and Dad were regulars there."

"Well, I lived here in Cincinnati, so I didn't get up to Columbus often, but I loved it when I did go. I remember being there one summer evening to hear the Tommy Dorsey Band. That was one of the hottest bands in the country then. There were a lot of big bands that passed through that place in those days. They must have paid a mint to get that orchestra to play in Columbus, but they made their money back, because the place was packed."

Helen took a sip of wine, and while looking intently at Henry, let a huge smile spread across her face.

"That was in July of 1939," she said.

It was Henry's turn to be surprised again. "Don't tell me you were there."

Helen smiled. "I was there all right. That was the night Tom asked me to marry him. I remember that night like it was yesterday."

Helen looked out to the dance floor. Michael and Henry could sense she was revisiting the memories of that evening.

"Tell us about it, Mother," Michael urged.

After collecting her thoughts, she began to tell her story.

"The dance floor was packed all night, but we didn't care. I don't think we left it for more than ten minutes the entire evening."

"Did you know Dad was going to ask you to marry him that night?"

"No, not for certain, but," she said with a wink, "I was hoping it might happen."

Now Henry was caught up in the story. "So what happened?"

"You remember who was singing with Tommy Dorsey that night, don't you, Henry?" Helen asked.

Henry smiled. "A very young Frank Sinatra."

"Frank Sinatra was there that night?" Michael asked with surprise.

"Sure, he was," Henry answered. "And Jo Stafford was singing with the orchestra that night, too."

Helen looked over at Henry. "She and Frank sang 'Blues in the Night' together. Do you remember?"

Henry nodded with a smile. "You've got a good memory, Helen."

They listened to the music for a few measures, before Helen resumed.

"What song do you remember best from Frank Sinatra that night?" she asked Henry.

"Boy, he sang a lot of them. But the one I remember most was 'Always.'"

"I'll be loving you ... " Helen sang, *"always."*

"I always loved that slight pause before he sang the word *always*," Henry said. "You sang that line just as I remember it."

"Aren't you sweet," Helen said.

"I always thought Frank Sinatra was a master at phrasing. When he was silent for just a moment it just added so much more to the song."

"You are a fascinating man, Henry Taylor," Helen said before turning her attention back toward the orchestra.

Michael was stunned at how talkative and open his mother had become.

After hearing a few more measures of music, she turned back to her son and asked, "Do you remember your father humming that song at odd times as you were growing up?"

"Yes, I do. That and 'Beautiful Dreamer.'"

"He loved that, too," Helen said. "Whenever he would hum 'Always' I would try to get his attention, just catch his eye. And when I did I'd always be rewarded with a big smile. He was remembering, too."

"What was he remembering, Mother?"

Helen looked back to Michael and to Henry as well. "He was remembering that at the end of that song he sank to one knee on the dance floor of Valley Dale and asked me to marry him."

Michael looked over at Henry and found him smiling away. Then he turned back to his mother and put an arm around her shoulder.

"I never knew that story. That must have been quite a romantic evening."

Helen's eyes were moist. "That it was. Your Aunt Louise was standing right behind me when it happened, and she saw it all. She was as touched as I was."

Helen then turned to Henry. "I may have some memory issues from time to time, but that night is fixed well in my mind. I'm glad you were there that night."

Henry shook his head. "So we were together that night, at least at the same show. Isn't that amazing?"

"It sure is. I remember how crowded it was all night and how the girls were just screaming when Sinatra would step up to the microphone. We got there early and found a table for four at the edge of the outdoor dance floor. Tom was anxious to get just the right table. We didn't know for sure whether the band would set up on the outdoor stage or the indoor stage, so Tom and his best friend Joe, who was dating my sister, Louise, planned to split up when we arrived to get two tables, one in and one out, just in case."

Helen sat back with a smile, reliving the memory.

"It was a good thing they played outside that night or the crowding would have been even worse," said Henry.

"That's right. I heard later there were almost 3,000 people there that night. Valley Dale could hold a lot of dancers if they had both dance floors open, but that was a full house."

Michael loved seeing his mother so engaged in conversation with someone else and so clear in her recollections. He offered to get them fresh drinks and they each readily agreed. When he left the table they were just beginning to talk about some of the other big bands they had seen over the years.

Standing near the makeshift bar was Amy in her nurse's uniform. She smiled as Michael approached.

"Care to join me for a drink?" he asked.

Amy laughed. "Thanks, but I'd better pass. I'm still on duty."

"Good duty tonight, I'd say, hanging out in a dance hall."

She smiled again. "This is fun, isn't it? The staff is rotating in and out to make sure everyone is doing okay, and to have a little fun ourselves."

"I have to tell you," Michael said, "I'm surprised there's an open bar here."

"That was a big issue for discussion when this event was planned. Joanne Holly was strongly opposed to having any alcohol served. Does that surprise you? The administrator finally ruled that we could offer drinks. These are adults, after all, as the residents' council kept reminding Miss Holly over the last few months. We're trying to keep our eye on those whom we know should refrain from alcohol. But this isn't a prison now, is it? It's a dance hall."

"My mother and Henry are having a wonderful time talking about the good old days with the big bands. It turns out that they were at the same show in Columbus the night my mother and father were engaged."

"Oh, that's great," Amy said. "Where are they? I want to say hello."

"Let me refresh their drinks first, and I'll walk you over."

Michael collected the drinks for each of them, including a Seven-Up for Amy, and led her over to their table.

Henry started to rise when he saw Amy approaching, but she quickly waved him back to his seat.

"Hello folks. May I join you for a spell?" she asked.

"Of course, dear," Helen replied. "Michael, did you bring a glass of wine for Amy?"

"The lady's on duty tonight, Mother, so she's having a soft drink," Michael said as he sat down. "I was telling Amy about the two of you being at Valley Dale on the night you were engaged."

Amy jumped in. "That is such an incredible coincidence."

"As it turns out, we think we were both there at Valley Dale on at least two other occasions," Henry said, smiling at the ladies. "Isn't that right, Helen?"

Helen took a sip of wine and nodded. "What a small world."

"So who was playing those other nights?" Michael asked.

"One night we're sure we were both there was for Guy Lombardo and the Royal Canadians. We think he only played there once. It may have been even more crowded than the Tommy Dorsey night," Helen said.

"Did he play 'Auld Lang Syne'?" Michael asked.

Henry and Helen both smiled at Michael like he had asked the simplest question.

"Of course he did," Helen said. "That was his trademark, wasn't it, Henry?"

"It certainly was. I remember it well."

"And what was the other show?" Amy prompted.

"Perry Como with the Ted Weems Orchestra," Henry said. "We remember that one because it was a cool evening, kind of unexpected, and it was just before the war, in the fall of 1941."

"That was one of the last shows we attended at Valley Dale," Helen said. "Once Pearl Harbor was struck the big bands stopped touring like they had been. That was the end of an era."

"These are wonderful stories," Amy said. "I hope you two keep sharing them and let me hear some of them again. I'm afraid I have to head back to the nurse's station now, so if you'll excuse me ... "

"Nonsense, young lady," Henry interrupted. "You'll join me in a dance first."

Henry slowly stood up and held out his hand.

"Well, how can I say no to that invitation?" Amy smiled.

She took Henry's hand and led him out to the dance floor. Michael and Helen watched as the number ended only a minute after Henry and Amy began dancing. When the music stopped, Henry walked over to the bandstand and said something to the band leader, who nodded his head. Henry then looked back toward Michael and Helen and waved for them to come out to the dance floor just as the band leader announced that the next selection was a special request.

"I wonder what this will be," Michael said, as the band began to play the opening notes of Frank Sinatra's hit.

"Oh, my goodness," Helen said. "He asked them to play 'Always'."

"Well, what do you think, Mother?" Michael asked. "Shall we take a spin to your old favorite?"

Helen beamed and took Michael's hand. "Let's give it a try."

Amy and Henry offered huge smiles as Michael and Helen reached the dance floor.

"I wonder who made this special request," Michael said.

"Amazing coincidence," said Henry, as he resumed dancing with Amy.

Michael and Helen began to dance as well.

"What a night that must have been for you and Dad. I never heard that story before."

"Well your father and I had a few private stories that were just ours," she said as they toured the floor. "He was a wonderful dancer."

"Something like me?" Michael asked, as they bumped into Henry and Amy.

"A little smoother, I'd say," Helen smiled. "But I'm not complaining."

After a few more steps, Michael felt a touch on his left shoulder. He turned to see Henry with his left hand extended and his right hand just off Michael's shoulder.

"May I cut in?" Henry asked.

Michael laughed. "Well, of course."

"Why don't we trade partners?" Henry suggested.

Michael turned to Amy who shrugged her shoulders as if to say, "It wasn't my idea."

Michael watched as Henry and Helen glided away on the dance floor, before turning to Amy.

"They're good. Look at them," he said.

"Shall we try to keep up with them?" Amy asked.

"I'm game if you are," Michael said as he placed his hand around Amy's waist and took her hand.

They each noticed a few residents eye them as they danced together.

"Do you feel like we're being sized up by the old-timers?" Michael asked.

Amy laughed. "I'll hear about this tomorrow for sure."

"Not that I'm complaining, mind you," Michael said.

"Well, thanks for that," Amy smiled in return. "Tell me more about yourself, Michael. You're here so often. How are you able to make the time?"

"Let's see. What about me? Well, you already know I teach in the English Department at UC. I have a home near campus where I try to hone my piano skills now that you are progressing so well."

"Do you think I'm progressing? I'm not so sure."

"Are you kidding? You're doing very well."

"How many classes do you teach each semester?"

"It varies, usually two or three though."

"But you still have time to get out here pretty often."

"The chair of my department dealt for a long time with aging parents, and he's been very good about allowing me to jump out here regularly during the day."

"You have a brother and sister I see often, too."

"Yes, Tom is the oldest. He's nine years older than me. Mary came next. Then me. I'm the baby of the family."

"And do you all have families, too?" Amy asked.

"Tom and Mary each have families. Tom and his wife, Janice, have three children. Mary and Bill have two."

"I've seen what I guessed were some of their children here a few times," Amy said.

They grew silent as they continued to dance. As the song ended they could see Henry and Helen were still talking at the other end of the dance floor.

"Look at those two," Michael said. "What a great idea this evening has been. I haven't seen my mother talk to someone outside of her family like that for a long time."

"They are having fun," Amy agreed. "This is a great evening for all the residents. I wish I could stay longer, but I'm afraid I have to walk back to my post now."

"How about I cause a major scandal and walk out with you?"

Amy smiled. "Are you leaving already?"

"No, I'll come back. I'll just walk you back."

"I won't turn you down. But you're right. This will be more fodder for the breakfast crowd tomorrow."

They walked out of the auditorium and headed up the main hall toward the assisted-living nurse's station. It was quiet in the halls. Usually there would be some residents walking around, but tonight they were all at the big dance.

Amy broke the silence as they neared the nurse's station.

"I hope you don't think I'm prying, Michael. You've told me about your brother and sister's families. How about you?"

Michael stopped at the end of the hallway, just shy of Amy's duty station, then turned to Amy and smiled.

"No family for me, outside of my mother and my siblings."

"That surprises me," Amy said. "Have you always been single?"

Michael smiled again. He wondered where this was going, and how much of his past he was ready to reveal. *Why not,* he thought.

"That's right. I told you already that I was almost engaged once. But things happened and marriage wasn't meant to be. I've never found anyone since."

"I'm sorry to hear that," Amy replied. "But that was a long time ago, wasn't it?"

Michael was surprised that he was talking about this subject, but, he felt comfortable talking to her. He was really starting to feel a connection.

"It has been a long time. Twenty years actually."

"Twenty years?" she said with astonishment.

"I'm slow to recover," he said in a droll tone.

Amy smiled. "I can see that."

"What about you? How old did you say your daughter is?"

"She just turned eleven. She's my angel."

"I bet she is. What's her name?"

"Corinne."

"Corinne. That's a beautiful name."

"If you're around next Sunday you'll get a chance to see her. Her piano teacher is hosting a little recital with her students for the residents. It'll be simple, but the folks here love seeing the children."

"I'm sure they do. I'll check it out if I'm around here Sunday."

One of the other nurses came around the corner and saw the two of them.

"Joanne Holly is looking for you, Amy," the nurse said. "She's at the nurse's station now. Is it okay if I head down to the auditorium to see the dance?"

"Sure, Linda, I'll head back now," Amy replied.

After the nurse left, Amy thanked Michael for walking her back to the nurse's desk, and added, "I better go see what Joanne wants. It was nice talking with you, and dancing, too."

"Thanks, Amy. I enjoyed it, too."

They held each other's gaze briefly, and before Amy could walk away, Michael kissed her very gently. After the kiss he stood back to see her reaction. She smiled, placed her hand around his neck, and kissed him again. When their kiss was over she tapped him lightly on the chest and said, "I hope that's a preview of coming attractions." Then she stepped around the corner to get back to work. Michael remained where he was standing for a minute. It had been a long time since he felt like there could be a connection between him and another woman. He had always compared any woman he dated to Lainie, who had been gone so long now. He knew that wasn't healthy, but he had never gotten past it. Maybe he could now.

When Amy reached the nurse's station Joanne was clearly steamed.

"I just want you to know that I think your behavior in the auditorium tonight was unseemly."

"What are you talking about?" Amy asked.

"Dancing with the son of one of our residents, that's what I'm talking about. It was totally improper."

"That's funny," Amy replied lightly before grabbing some charts and walking away, "I thought it was delightful."

She could feel the temperature rising behind her. *It's probably a good thing she didn't see us just a minute ago,* she thought as a big smile spread across her face.

After Michael returned to the auditorium he found Henry and Helen chatting away at the table. "Where did you go off to?" Helen asked him.

"I just walked Amy back to the nurse's station."

Henry and Helen both looked at each other and smiled.

"Okay, you two. That'll be enough."

"Who said anything?" Helen laughed.

"She's a nice young woman," Henry said.

"I get the message," Michael laughed. "Now can the two of you steer yourselves back to your rooms after the music stops?"

"We'll be fine, Michael," Helen said. "Why don't you head on home. It's getting late."

"Okay. Henry, it was nice talking with you again."

"Same here, young man. Good night."

"Good night, Mother," Michael said, kissing her on the cheek. "No more booze for either of you tonight. You've reached your limit."

Helen shook her head dismissively. "Kids. What can you do with them? Good night, Perfessor."

Michael shook his head and smiled. "It's Professor. Try to remember that," he said, as he walked away from the table leaving the two old-timers the opportunity to talk some more about the good-old-days.

The following Sunday afternoon Michael stopped out to see his mother. On his way to her apartment he saw a number of young children huddling with parents in the auditorium. The girls all had pretty dresses, while the boys were as groomed as well as any young men are these days, he thought, meaning long pants, polo shirts, and real shoes instead of sneakers. Another good sign, he noticed, was no baseball hats. The group stood out to him. Then he remembered that today was the piano recital that Amy had told him about. Her daughter was going to play.

Michael entered the auditorium and found Amy with her daughter Corinne off to the side. Amy was talking quietly with Corinne.

When Michael approached, Amy looked up with a broad smile.

"Well, hello, Michael," she said. "You remembered."

Actually he didn't, Michael confessed to himself, but he chose not to admit his memory lapse, and instead took full credit for having walked into the room.

"Here I am. And who is this young musician?"

Amy turned to her daughter, beaming with pride.

"This is my daughter, Corinne. Corinne, this is Mr. Telford."

"Nice to meet you, Corinne," Michael said, as he extended his hand.

"Hello," Corinne said meekly.

Corinne was the spitting image of her mother, Michael thought. She was a cute young lady, with short, dark hair, like Amy's. For the recital she was outfitted in a green, plaid dress, and a matching plaid headband. She looked nervous, just like he would have expected any youngster would be at the prospect of playing piano before a bunch of strangers.

"So I hear you're going to be playing piano today." Michael said.

Corinne was a shy one, and merely nodded her head affirmatively.

"You know, I play the piano, too," he added.

Corinne's eyes widened a little. "Are you my mom's teacher?" she asked.

"Yes, I am. How old are you, Corinne?"

"Eleven."

"That's when I started taking lessons. So tell me, what song are you going to be playing today?"

Corinne looked at her mother as if she needed permission to continue to talk to this stranger.

"You know the title, Corinne. Go ahead," Amy urged.

"Clair de Lune," Corinne spoke up.

"My goodness," Michael said emphatically. "That's an ambitious piece for a young lady. Good for you. It's one of my favorites."

"I don't know all of it yet. I just play a little."

"Any part of 'Clair de Lune' is still something to be proud of," Michael said.

He turned to Amy. "This looks like a big production."

Amy smiled. "There's going to be almost thirty students here, so you probably don't want to sit here for all of them. Corinne's playing near the end."

"Well, I certainly don't want to miss that. I'll leave you two alone now so you can get ready. It was nice meeting you, Corinne. I'll look forward to hearing you play."

Corinne smiled back at Michael. "Thank you," she said shyly, and grabbed her mother's hand.

Michael left the auditorium. *Amy's right, I sure don't want to hear that many young pianists, but it would be fun to hear a few.* He remembered his early days of piano lessons and how proud he was when he learned a piece. He had resisted lessons early on, but his mother had insisted he keep at it. Now he looked back on the lessons with fond memories. He played consistently through high school, then let it go during his college years. But since then, he had enjoyed playing in his home a few times a week for twenty minutes or so each session.

He found it ironic that he was going to watch Amy's daughter play piano at the recital. It was at that age that he first met Lainie, and at an event just like this one. Lainie's mother was forcing her to take lessons as well. He and Lainie met at a recital where each of them was expected to play one small piece. They were seated next to each other waiting to be called to play. He remembered that Lainie was very calm, and that she noticed his anxiety right away.

"Be still," she ordered him.

When Michael looked over at her in surprise, she asked him innocently, "Why are you afraid?"

"I'm not afraid," Michael huffed back at her.

"Well, then, do you always fidget like that?" she asked, before adding, "It's okay to be nervous. You'll be good today."

The young Michael was struck by Lainie's reassurance. Her little pep talk began their friendship, which developed and deepened steadily for the next ten years. Thanks to Lainie he was still playing piano.

Before his mother had started to need him more, he often played during the week in one of the piano studios at the music conservatory that was part of the university. He'd slip in during lunch time and find an empty studio and pass the time for a half hour playing the songs he had memorized with Lainie over the years. One summer right after college, the two of them found a studio with back to back grand pianos. They played tunes together several nights a week, talking afterwards of how they should put an act together and tour the world. He would have loved that.

He didn't think of her so often anymore, but for a long time she had been in his mind every day. Michael wondered if meeting Amy and Corinne at the recital was a good omen. He wanted to believe that it was.

He found his mother in her room watching television. "Good afternoon, my lady," he greeted her.

"Oh, Michael, I'm so glad to see you," she said.

More and more, it struck Michael, she greeted him as if she had been sitting there for hours waiting for him to show up.

"How're you feeling today?" he asked.

"Oh, I'm fine now. What are you up to?"

"I just thought I'd stop out for a little visit. Maybe force you to take a walk."

"You're going to wear my legs out one of these days," she said.

"You're all bark and no bite, lady. Now, let's get a move on."

"Okay, boss. Where we headed?"

"Let's walk down to the auditorium. There's a piano recital down there. A whole bunch of kids whose parents are forcing them to take piano lessons now have to show off for a bunch of strangers. Sound familiar?"

"You loved it, and you know it, young man."

Michael laughed. "Maybe I did, but I'll never admit it to you."

On the way down, Michael told Helen that Amy's daughter was in the recital.

Helen turned to face Michael directly. "Now I see why we're going."

Michael smiled and shook his head. "Don't get any ideas now, Mother. We're just being polite."

"I saw the two of you dancing the other night. You were a handsome couple. I think Amy would be a nice young woman for you to get to know."

"I'll remember that. In the meantime, let's enjoy the music and keep the matchmaking to ourselves, shall we?"

"Sure," Helen said, with a wicked little smile. "No need to be so sensitive. I hope I didn't touch a nerve."

"Be good, Mother," Michael replied, as they walked into the auditorium where the recital was already well underway.

They took a seat near the back and listened to a half dozen children take turns playing their pieces. Michael thought that a few showed a moderate degree of talent and interest, but that the others were there because their parents were requiring them to play. *Of course, that's how I started,* he thought. It wasn't until he was sixteen that he finally began to enjoy playing, and with that sense of enjoyment came a real advancement in his proficiency.

Next up was Corinne. Michael pointed her out to Helen, who clapped a little more enthusiastically when the child was introduced. Corinne took a brief bow to acknowledge the applause then settled in for a few measures of "Clair de Lune". Michael was impressed with her playing. The music was halting in a few places, as he would have expected from a youngster, but in passages she was quite certain of herself. As far as reading the music went, she was one of the few who played flawlessly. *That's always a good sign,* he thought.

At the conclusion of the short piece Corinne took another bow to friendly applause, then returned to her seat.

Michael saw Amy put her arm around Corinne and give her a big hug. That was nice to see.

After three more players the concert mercifully came to a close. Punch and cookies were set up and the families began to mingle with all the guests. Amy looked around the room and spotted Helen and Michael, then shepherded Corinne over to say hello.

Once Amy had introduced Corinne, Michael offered his hand in congratulations. "Well done, Corinne. I was very impressed with your playing. How long have you been at it?" he asked.

"Two years," she said softly.

"Well it sounds like you've been practicing a lot, because you played very well. Isn't that right, Mother?"

Helen jumped in with her congratulations as well. "That's right. I've always loved the piece you played, Corinne. Michael used to play that, too."

Amy was beaming at her daughter.

"How about I get a picture of the two of you on this special day?" Michael asked. "I'll print it out for you this week, Amy."

"Thanks, Michael; that would be great."

"Michael tells me you're doing real well on your piano lessons," Helen said.

"Oh, he said that, did he? He never tells me," Amy smiled.

"What kind of a teacher are you anyway?" Helen said to Michael. "I hope you've been telling Amy how well she's doing. You tell me all the time."

After posing for the camera, Amy suggested to Corinne that she get herself a glass of punch. Corinne happily took her mother up on the notion.

Amy then turned to Helen and Michael. "Thank you both for coming. Corinne's a very shy young girl, but I know your compliments meant a lot to her."

"She's a beautiful young lady," Helen said. "I'll go look after her at the punch line, and leave you two alone."

Michael shook his head at Helen as she walked off.

"What was that about?" Amy asked.

"I believe my mother fancies herself a matchmaker."

Amy laughed. "I see. I told you people would talk when they saw us dancing the other night."

"Well, let them talk, I say. It gives them something to do," Michael said, as he lounged against a corner pillar in the auditorium.

"It gave Joanne Holly something to do," Amy said.

"I've been wondering what she wanted with you the other night. Can you tell me?"

"She thinks it was scandalous that we were dancing together."

"I see. What's her position on kissing?"

Amy burst out laughing.

"Are you worried about her?"

"Not at all. She's not my supervisor, and what business is it of hers anyway? I think the only thing she can possibly do is cause us problems using the piano."

"Well, we can't let that happen. You're my prize student."

"Thanks, Michael. I appreciate that. Maybe we better get back over to your mother and Corinne before she starts figuring out a match for my little girl," Amy joked.

Michael smiled and shook his head. "You're right. No one's safe when she's in that mind-set."

Once they finished their punch, Michael and Helen said good-bye and walked over towards the Tea Café, which was located just off the main lobby. Both were silent as they walked.

Nearing the café, Michael suggested they stop for a cup of tea.

"Don't ask if you don't mean it," Helen said.

After ordering, Michael remained silent, staring off across the room.

Helen let him have his silence for a short while, before finally speaking.

"Old memories?" she asked.

Hearing her voice brought Michael out of his reverie and back to the here and now. He looked over at his mother and smiled.

"Yes," he said. "Memories from a long time ago. But I'm guessing you know that already."

"I think I do," Helen said. "But why don't you tell me about it anyway."

Michael grinned again. "Well, I was thinking about the first time I met Lainie."

"I thought so," Helen said. "Go on."

"You remember, too, don't you? You dragged me against my will when I was just a kid to a recital just like the one we saw this afternoon. I remember I was as nervous as a cat, waiting to play. We had to line up off stage and sit while we waited our turn. Lainie was sitting right next to me. I'm sure I was bouncing up and down on the chair, rocking my feet, shaking my hands, anything I could think of, because I was afraid to go out there. Meanwhile, Lainie was as composed as a professional. Occasionally she would hold out her hands and pretend she was playing her piece. Then she would take a deep breath, put her hands on her lap, and relax. She did this two or three times while I was acting like a Mexican jumping bean. Finally, after she had played her piece in her mind for the third time, she turned to me and ordered me to be still. Those were her first words to me. 'Be still.'"

"Did you listen to her?" Helen asked.

"I did. I never expected her to say a word to me at all. When she did order me to be still I was surprised, but I did calm down for a spell. Once I stopped fidgeting she asked me why I was so nervous. Of course I denied the very idea, which caused her to break into the biggest grin and eventually start laughing. That made me laugh too, and both of us continued until our teacher, Mrs. Ramsey, walked over and told us to stop playing around and concentrate on what we were there for. We both stopped laughing right away, but when Mrs. Ramsey walked back to the edge of the curtain to watch who was playing, Lainie looked at me again and we each burst out laughing. Boy, I remember that clear as a bell. That was the moment that sealed our friendship forever. The two of us, little ten-year-olds, joining together to laugh at a preposterous adult."

Helen smiled and nodded her head. "I didn't know about you and Lainie being so disrespectful to Mrs. Ramsey," Helen said, while continuing to smile, "but I did know about Lainie setting you straight that day. She told her mother about this strange, but nice young boy who sat next to her backstage and her mother told me the story the day you two graduated from college. We were sitting with Lainie's family during the commencement that day, and her mother and I just chatted away all through the ceremony."

Michael took a sip of tea, then began to stare off into space again.

Helen gave him another minute, then said, "Michael, I'm glad you have such good memories of Lainie. But wouldn't she want you to have another life? Isn't that what she told you at the end?"

Michael nodded, and turned back to his mother. "Yes, she did say that."

"But you don't seem to want to heed her words, do you?"

"I've tried, Mother. It's not exactly like I stopped dating altogether after she died. I don't know. I guess I've never had a moment with anyone quite like the one Lainie and I had at that recital. Someday maybe."

"It looked like you and Amy were enjoying each other's company the other night when you were dancing," Helen said, as she gave Michael a big grin and raised her eyes.

Michael shook his head and laughed. "You'll never quit, will you?"

"She is a sweet girl. You have to at least admit that."

"Okay. I admit that. And I did enjoy dancing with her the other night."

"And I noticed you walked her back to the nurse's station that night, too. How was that?"

"Are you going to ask me next if I kissed her good-night?"

"Would you tell me if you did?"

"Drink your tea, woman. I'm not talking to you anymore."

"Okay, boss," Helen laughed. "The tea's cold anyway. Let's head back up."

The following Wednesday Michael arrived for his visit shortly before noon, but did not find Helen in her apartment. On a table by the door lay a note. Michael picked it up and recognized his mother's handwriting. The note itself said simply, "*I am home.*" Nothing more was written on it.

"I am home," he read aloud. *So it's come to this,* he thought, as he gazed at the small piece of paper. *She has to look at a note to remind herself where she is.*

After finding her in the dining hall he joined her for lunch. Afterwards they walked back to the apartment, and once there he picked up her note.

"I see you've been making some notes for yourself," he said.

"What do you mean, Michael?"

"Well, here's one that says '*I am home*'. When did you write this?"

"Oh, I wrote that yesterday, I think. You know, sometimes I have trouble remembering where I am. I thought that might help."

He was momentarily speechless.

"Good idea, Mother. Maybe we can make a few more notes to help you."

When she didn't respond, he looked back to see her staring out the window.

When she was finished, she looked back to Michael, and asked, "Why can't I remember anymore?"

"You remember lots of things," Michael said, trying to reassure her and hoping she would not pick up on the sorrow in his voice. "You told us all about the night of your engagement just a week ago. Your memory is not all bad. The doctor says it's just your brain playing tricks on you once in a while. But don't worry, there are lots of people around here to help you remember."

Helen didn't respond. What could he say, short of agreeing with her that her memory was rapidly vanishing. In the past they had tried putting signs around the house to remind her about taking her medicine; they had kept a scrapbook of pictures on the coffee table so she could look at it each day; they regularly informed her of the adventures of her grandchildren; for a time they had even drilled her regularly with questions about her past. All these efforts had been no match for the relentless tide of her advancing years, lapping at her memory. *What do I say to that? What should our next idea be?* He settled for the moment with simple reassurance.

"You know all your family, and all your friends. I know you get confused about a few things, but you still are operating pretty well."

Helen looked over at her son. "Thanks for trying to make an old lady feel better, Michael."

That did sound pretty lame, he thought.

"Say, why don't we look at a few photographs?" Michael suggested, trying to brighten her up. He picked up a frame from the sofa table. "Check this out. Do you remember this one?"

It was a photo from four years back. That afternoon the family had gone to the race track. Helen's goal at the track was to cash a couple of winning tickets. It didn't matter how much she won. What mattered was picking a winner and presenting the ticket to the cashier. Near the end of the day she decided she just had to cash in one more winner to make the day complete. The second-to-last race had only five horses running, so she figured the smart choice would be to bet on each horse, and that's what she did. The photo showed her holding all five tickets just before the race began.

"That was at Churchill Downs, wasn't it?" Helen asked.

"You're right. See, you're still remembering things real well. I remember when we all found out what you were up to in that race. Do you see all the tickets you're holding? You bet on every horse that race."

"I remember that day, and how all of you made fun of me when I showed you my bets. And I also remember I cashed a ticket at the end of the race."

"Well, you're right about that. You couldn't help but have a winner, could you, what with betting on every horse."

Just like on the day of the race, Helen turned up her nose to Michael. She was still confident in her own mind that she knew what she was doing, and that as a result one of her tickets was a good one.

"I believe you won $3 on $10 worth of bets."

"Who's counting? I picked a winner, didn't I?"

"That you did, Mother. You've never looked for the big strike, have you? It's just the small victories that work for you."

"That's right. Now put that picture down and take me for a walk."

CHAPTER 6

Over the course of the next month, Michael continued to visit his mother regularly. His lessons with Amy continued. He found himself looking forward to that alone time with Amy more and more. At the same time, Henry and Helen were becoming good friends too. Henry usually would join them to listen to the music in the evening. Occasionally he and Helen would sit together for dinner in the assisted-living dining room. Clearly there was no romance between them, just a pair of confused older folks sharing some time together.

One evening Michael walked with Helen down to the main dining room for dinner, but had to leave for an evening class at the university. Henry was just taking a seat in the dining room as they entered, and when he saw Helen he walked over and invited her to join him for the evening meal.

Helen gladly accepted, and Michael left for the evening.

"How are you getting along these days, Helen?" Henry asked after they were seated at a dining table.

"It's not home, is it?" Helen replied.

"No, I'm afraid it's not. It seems like once you're here all your old friends are afraid to come around. Don't get me wrong, it's wonderful having family visit. But I wish some of my old neighbors and friends would visit. How about you, Helen? Do you hear much from your old friends?"

"No, I don't. A couple of gals from one of my old bridge leagues came out a few weeks after I moved here, but since then it's just been my kids."

"Did you have a lot of good friends before you moved here?"

"I had one good friend for a long time, but she died a few months ago," Helen said.

"I'm sorry to hear that," Henry said. "What was her name?"

"Frances Miles. We were bridge partners and good friends for a long time, particularly after my husband died."

"Tell me about Frances."

"Well, let's see. When I think about Frances I usually find myself focusing on the later days when she started to have trouble."

"What kind of trouble was that?" Henry asked.

"Trouble with remembering how to play the game we knew so well for so long," Helen said.

"Frances was losing her memory?"

"Yes, she was."

"Was that hard for you to be around?"

"It scared me."

"I know what you mean," Henry said. "I watched my wife go through that process. But tell me about your experience with your friend."

"At first there were just simple mistakes, ones we could laugh off. She might forget whose turn it was to shuffle the deck, or what the last bid was. Frances would laugh with us when it happened, but I could see she was embarrassed.

"One afternoon when we were driving home after Frances had a rough afternoon, she told me that she was starting to feel afraid that something was wrong, and that she was having a really hard time concentrating any more. Her doctor said that getting a little confused was a normal part of the aging process, and that she should try to calm down. He gave her some pills for her nerves."

Henry laughed. "Sometimes all these doctors want to do is tell you that you need something for your nerves."

"Isn't that the truth?"

"So what happened after Frances started taking the nerve pills?"

"They didn't help. Things just got worse. She seemed to lose track of the game more and more. One day she failed to follow suit. The lead was diamonds, which Frances held in her hand, but when the play came to her she put down a heart, which was trump, and took the trick. Then she led a diamond of her own. When Frances played the diamond everyone stared at the table, not knowing what to say. I remember that I was wishing someone would start talking again and take the focus away from what had happened, but nobody spoke. Finally, Frances picked up on the silence in the room and asked if she had done something wrong. I didn't want to embarrass her anymore, so I told her I had misplayed. I apologized to the other two women at the table and told them they had won that hand and suggested we start a new game."

"That was very gracious of you, Helen," Henry said.

"You know, my first instinct when those things happened was to protect her, and not point out that she was confused. I wrestled with that, because I thought that if it was me, I would want to know. But there were times when I did tell Frances she was mistaken, and no more had the words come out of my mouth then I felt I was not being a good friend."

"I know what you mean. I had the same experiences with my wife. At first I pointed out every instance of confusion to her because I couldn't understand why she was making so many mistakes. Then when I understood that she couldn't help herself I tried to humor her by ignoring her confusion or acting as if nothing was wrong. But throughout the first few years she would sometimes have very clear days when she had no confusion, and even knew that she was ill and had been making mistakes. On those days she knew she would be sinking back into some other world, and she would ask me to fight to keep her here, not to humor her when she made mistakes."

"Is that what you did?" Helen asked.

Henry smiled at Helen, then sat back and stared across the room, recalling those days. Helen let him reflect on the old days while she sipped her coffee.

Finally, Henry broke the silence. "I struggled with that notion for years. I tried to honor her request for a while, but it became too painful watching her grow even more confused when I would point out that she was living in yesteryear. And eventually, she sank so deep that I couldn't bring her back at all anymore."

"Deep into the darkness," Helen said.

"What's that, Helen?"

"I look at it like a person is sliding into darkness. You know, like the curtains are being drawn in your room, and you're all alone while the light is filtered out. Frances and I talked about it in those terms. It scared her, and me, too. I wondered then if that's how I was going to wind up. Little bits of confusion at first, then more and more as time goes by."

"And what do you think now?" Henry asked.

It was Helen's turn to offer a rueful smile, before shrugging her shoulders and saying, "Hey, I'm here, aren't I?"

Henry smiled while reaching across the table to pat Helen's hand. "You're not alone, Helen. We're all experiencing something similar. Who would have ever thought we'd live to be this old anyway?" he laughed.

"You're right about that. My parents died in their fifties, and I thought they were old then."

"Do you ever think about dying, Helen?" Henry asked. "I know that's a sensitive subject, so you don't have to answer that if you don't want to."

"I'm afraid," Helen said. "I've always believed there's a heaven, but still I'm not ready for it. That's not exactly right. Some days I feel like I am ready. Anymore I'm just so tired. But I'm afraid of what it will be like. I know it's coming, but it scares me."

"I understand what you're saying. The day is approaching for both of us, and I think mine will be here before yours."

"What are you saying? Are you sick?" Helen asked.

Henry nodded.

"Is there anything that can be done?"

"No," Henry said. "Not in my opinion anyway."

"What do you mean by that?"

Henry smiled. "What I mean is that I've gone through the operations, the chemo, the radiation, all of it. It gave me a few more years. I'm glad of that, but, you put it so well before, Helen. Hey, I'm here, aren't I?"

"I'm so sorry, Henry."

"Thank you. Please don't let this news be a burden between us."

"Okay. But can I ask you something now?"

"Certainly," Henry answered with a grin. "We've held nothing back so far tonight."

"Are you afraid?"

Henry paused before answering. "I know I'm afraid, but now I'm just about ready to embrace it."

"How do you embrace something like that?"

"Good question. I guess for me it means choosing a time and place to die."

"You can do that?" Helen asked

"I don't know for sure, Helen, but can you keep a secret?"

"I sure can."

"I'm not ready to go at this very moment. But it's coming soon, maybe in a few months. And when I recognize the time, I hope to leave this joint and pick a place of my own choosing to lie down for the last time."

"Do you know where that would be?"

"Yes, I do," Henry said. "There's a favorite spot of mine at my old home. It's at the base of a big, old spruce tree that's at the top of a grove of trees. I spent a lot of afternoons reading and daydreaming there after my wife died."

"And you're just going to go there and lie down and die? I don't understand how you'll be able to do that." Helen said.

"Have you ever daydreamed about dying, Helen?"

"Yes, I have. It scares me, but I do from time to time."

"Are there people with you in the end in your daydream?" Henry asked.

"Sometimes I'm alone, sometimes Michael's with me, sometimes all three of my kids."

"I have similar dreams," Henry said. "Sometimes my daughter is with me, but mainly it's just me. And I've decided that's how I want it."

"You don't want your daughter around at the end?" Helen asked.

Henry shook his head. "No, I don't. I know if I asked her she would want to be present. But I think that when the end comes I'll want to be alone."

Now it was Helen's turn to shake her head. "I don't know how you're going to do that. Neither of us gets around that well anymore."

"I agree. I'll need a little help when the time comes. We'll just have to wait and see."

The dining room was nearly empty. Neither of them had touched their food. Helen looked at both plates, then smiled at Henry. "If we keep eating like this it won't be long for either of us."

Henry's laugh was full and caused Helen to join in.

"What do you say we go see if there's some music playing tonight, Helen?"

"Sounds good to me. Do you know how to find the auditorium?"

Henry smiled and patted Helen's shoulder as he helped her up from her chair.

"We'll find the way."

CHAPTER 7

Two evenings after the dinner, Michael and Helen came upon Henry and a young woman walking in the courtyard. They stopped to say hello, and Henry introduced them to his daughter, Jackie. She was an attractive woman, tall with long, auburn hair. Her outfit was conservative, and clearly expensive, but her jewelry was simple and understated.

After exchanging greetings, Michael and Helen left Henry to continue his conversation with Jackie, and walked back inside to the auditorium. Michael settled Helen in a chair for the evening concert and made arrangements for a nurse to see her back to her apartment after the music.

As he was approaching the front door of the facility on his way to the parking lot, he happened upon Jackie again. He greeted her once more, and they walked toward their cars.

"I've really enjoyed spending time with your father. He's an interesting man," Michael said.

"Well, thanks for all your kindness to him. He talks about you and your mother every time we get together. I'm glad he's found some friends here at last. It's ironic, though, that when he had more of a grasp with his mind he made very few friends. Then, as his health deteriorated and his memory began to sag, he started talking and meeting other people."

"I've seen his memory lapses. But I didn't know he had some health issues. Is he being treated well here?" Michael asked.

Jackie paused before relating her story. She described how her father had been diagnosed with terminal cancer. He'd been treated for the past four years with surgery, chemotherapy and radiation. Two years ago the doctors thought he was cancer-free, but six months ago it had returned. The doctors wanted to be aggressive again, but Henry had refused to go through all the treatment again, and the doctors were now saying that it could be over within the next six months.

Michael was stunned. "He seems all right whenever I see him."

Once they reached the parking lot, Jackie slid behind the wheel of a silver Jaguar. Their conversation over, she started up the powerful machine and drove away.

It wasn't until two weeks later that Michael ran into Jackie again. She and Henry were enjoying one of the last warm November nights of the year.

"It's a beautiful evening, isn't it?" he offered as he and Helen came upon them on their evening stroll. "I hope this weather holds till Thanksgiving."

"Do join us. We were just talking about Thanksgiving," Henry said.

"Care to sit for a spell, Mother?" Michael asked.

"Sure. These old legs could use a rest," she replied.

"It's nice to see you again, Mrs. Telford," Jackie said.

"Well, thank you, young lady. It's nice to see you, too," Helen replied with a smile.

"Let me ask you a question, Professor Michael," Henry began. "A hypothetical if you will. Suppose you had the opportunity in your chosen field to attend, oh, a seminar, with some of the great minds in the world, people you admire considerably. Let's say the editor of a fine literary magazine, for example."

"He loves the *New Yorker*," offered Helen.

"Exactly, Helen. Thank you," Henry said with a smile. "So we have the editor of the *New Yorker*, and perhaps a great writer and thinker like William F. Buckley, and maybe John Updike and some other outstanding people, all assembled together for a seminar limited to just a few attendees. What would you think, Professor?"

"Well, what can I say? It would be a tremendous opportunity. A very difficult one to pass up," Michael replied, certain there was more to this question. "But tell me, are there more facts to consider with this hypothetical?"

Jackie laughed, nodding her head, and said, "An interesting question you raise, Michael."

She turned to her father and raised her eyes. "So why not lay out all the facts in your little hypothetical, Dad?" she suggested.

Henry smiled at her and continued. "I think we've laid out enough facts to support Michael's position," he said, and turning to Helen, asked, "So, how does the evening find you, Helen? In good spirits?"

Helen nodded her head and smiled, adding, "It's a wonderful evening for a walk."

At the same time Jackie spoke up. "I'm glad you're feeling well this evening, Mrs. Telford. It is a beautiful evening. Would you mind though if I insist my brilliant father return to his hypothetical?" she asked.

"I hope Michael hasn't caused some misunderstanding with his answer," Helen replied, looking to each of the three.

Michael was intrigued at Jackie's persistence, and both he and Jackie reassured Helen that this was just a friendly conversation. When Jackie turned back to her father, Henry appeared slightly ruffled at the thought of continuing the conversation. He had lost control and that did not suit him well. Nevertheless, he loved his daughter and would not choose to interrupt her now.

"So, Professor, if I may," continued Jackie.

"Please," Michael nodded again, turning quickly to his mother and winking.

Helen raised her head slightly, smiled, and shook her head side to side as if to say, "Don't get a big head, Buster."

Michael turned back to Jackie.

"Suppose," she began, "this incredible seminar with Mr. Buckley and company was set at a wonderful resort. Let's say San Diego."

"Sounds good," Michael said.

"Okay. So far, so good," Jackie agreed with a nod. Then, turning her head toward her father, she said, "And what if it was scheduled for the week before Thanksgiving, so that it ended on a Sunday evening, four days before the holiday? Now might that have some impact on your decision?" she asked, turning her eyes back to Michael.

Now he could see what they had walked into.

"You know, Jackie, I remember now why I've never liked hypotheticals," he said with a smile.

She smiled in return. "Exactly." Turning to her father, she nodded. "So why don't you tell them the whole story, Dad, instead of just a piece or two?"

Henry shook his head and, smiling, turned to Helen. "Did you ever think your children grew up to be just a little too glib for your taste, Helen?"

Helen caught on quickly. "Tell me about it," she said, jabbing Michael in the arm. "The old perfessor here needs to be reined in once in a while."

"I have the same problem with this young lady," Henry said.

"Okay, you two. We get it," Jackie said. "Now, Dad, let's hear the full story."

"My, but you are a persistent one," Henry said, casting his eyes on his daughter with a smile. "All right. Suppose, Michael, you were involved in the world of science and a seminar of great minds was scheduled, as it happens to be, in three weeks in San Diego, running for a week, and ending a few days before Thanksgiving. San Diego, remember. A city renowned for one of the most beautiful climates in the country. A place you've never been before. And suppose"—Henry leaned forward, touching his daughter's knee with his right hand—"you have the opportunity to join a few friends who have the great idea to remain in San Diego and its environs for another week of

R&R after the seminar. Some much needed and well-earned relaxation time over Thanksgiving," Henry concluded, sitting back again.

Michael and Helen also sat back and pondered the dilemma.

Finally, Henry said, "Oh, come now, Michael, surely you see the opportunity is not one to be passed up."

Helen spoke up, and displaying some of her old wisdom, looked at Jackie, and said, "It's always hard to think of being away from home over a holiday, but it doesn't make it wrong if you choose to be away when something special comes along."

All three looked at Helen. *She is more of a professor then I am,* Michael thought.

"You know, she's a smart lady, Henry. One thing that Mother and my late father always encouraged us to do over the years was to explore opportunities. At the risk of walking into a buzzsaw here, it sounds like something wonderful might be awaiting you, Jackie."

Henry smiled and nodded. But Jackie spoke first. Turning back to Michael and Helen, she admitted, "It is a great opportunity to learn. And I wouldn't be honest if I didn't say I am sorely tempted to stay in California for another week. But, I just can't see not being with Dad on Thanksgiving Day, and," she continued, looking at her father, "he refuses to get on a plane to join me."

Henry jumped in. "Now that would really be relaxing, wouldn't it? Entertaining the likes of me on your trip."

"You know I'd love it, Dad," Jackie pleaded.

Quiet descended over the four of them, as they all sat back again. Eventually Helen broke the silence.

"Henry, my daughter, Mary, is hosting Thanksgiving dinner for my family. She does every year. She's a wonderful cook and has a lovely home. My sister, Louise, usually joins us from Columbus, but she's already said she's not feeling up to it this year. That leaves an extra place setting. Would you consider joining us on Thanksgiving?"

Henry smiled. "Well, thank you, Helen; that is a most gracious invitation." He turned to Jackie. "What do you think?"

Jackie's eyes were misting over. Henry put his arm around her and drew her close. "It's okay, Jackie. I want you to go."

"Are you sure, Dad?" she asked. "I feel terrible."

"Go, young lady. I've just gotten an invitation that I feel duty-bound to accept."

Jackie looked up at her father again, smiling through her tears, and nodded her head.

"Good girl. Thank you, Helen," Henry continued, turning back to Helen. "I would be honored to join your family for the big day."

"Great," said Helen, turning to Jackie again, hoping for another confirmation from her.

Jackie looked over at Michael and Helen. Wiping a tear from each eye, she smiled. "How sweet of you to offer to share your family day, Helen."

"Don't you worry. We'll take good care of your father," Helen said.

"Okay. I guess I'm going to San Diego. Come on, Dad," Jackie urged. "Let's walk some more. Your old bones need a little workout."

"Kids," Henry shrugged, looking at Helen. "Always think they know what's best for you."

"Try having a perfessor in your family," Helen shrugged back.

The two old-timers laughed at their humor. Jackie and Michael exchanged glances, each shaking their heads.

"Get moving," Michael ordered. Turning to his mother, he smiled, "And that goes double for you, lady."

They all rose and bid one another good night, then the two pairs headed off in separate directions through the courtyard.

CHAPTER 8

The day before Thanksgiving Michael met Amy for another lesson. They practiced for almost a half hour, and then sat at the piano and chatted for another ten minutes. After the small talk was over, they sat in silence for a moment. Michael was surprised that he was a little nervous about what he wanted to say next.

"I was wondering," he began, then paused again.

"Yes, what were you wondering?"

He smiled, feeling a little more relaxed. "I know this is short notice, but I was wondering if you might like to join my family for dinner tomorrow. With your daughter, of course."

Amy was touched by the invitation. She gently placed her hand on Michael's arm. "I would love to be there…"

Hearing the first words of her response, Michael jumped in. "Really? You can?"

Amy squeezed his arm. "I'm glad you're excited about the prospect. I am too. But I was going to add that I have to work tomorrow, so I'll have to say no."

"You have to work on Thanksgiving?"

"You know we can't shut down on the holiday. Folks like your mother need us. I had a choice this year of working Thanksgiving or Christmas, so I chose turkey day. If I can only have one of those days off, I want it to be Christmas."

"Well, that makes sense," Michael admitted, looking a little crestfallen.

"Hey, there's always next year. I'd be happy to keep the holiday open if I knew another invitation was in the wings."

Those words restored Michael's smile. "I like the sound of that. Let's play one more upbeat number before we call it a lesson. What do you say?"

"You're on, mister."

*

Thanksgiving morning heralded the beginning of winter. The warm Indian summer nights had disappeared. Dinner at Mary's was always at three o'clock, a time none of the family ever dined otherwise, but a tradition on this feast day. And festivities, including cocktails, began at one.

Michael arrived at Village Green at 12:30. Mary had laid out her mother's Thanksgiving outfit on her visit the night before. Helen had mismatched the buttons and buttonholes on her blouse, and had fixed her favorite brooch on her jacket upside down. Michael smiled as he entered.

"Here, now, let me give you a hand," he offered.

"Thanks. I don't know why these buttons give me so much trouble these days."

Michael refastened the blouse and corrected the brooch. "You look great, Mother," he complimented.

"Thanks. All set?"

"Yes, we just have to walk over and meet Henry now."

"Oh, is Henry coming to Thanksgiving?"

Michael stopped. No matter how often they occurred, these memory lapses still came as a surprise. They had just spoken yesterday about Henry coming to dinner, but clearly Helen could no longer be counted on to remember a conversation from a few hours ago. Michael resisted showing impatience. He never wanted to show impatience or frustration to his mother, but it was difficult for him to understand how she could forget things so quickly.

When he spoke, it was in a tender way. "Mother, don't you remember? You invited him a few weeks ago."

"I don't know, Michael. Sometimes I wonder about myself."

"It's okay. We're going to have a good day. Everyone in the family is going to be together for you. Now let's go get Henry and get things started."

Henry was dressed in a grey, herringbone blazer, with black pants and a maroon checked tie. He was waiting for them outside his apartment, clutching a bouquet of fresh flowers. As Michael and Helen approached he stood and greeted them.

"Happy Thanksgiving, folks," Henry said.

"Happy Thanksgiving to you," they replied in unison and laughed.

"Helen, I want to thank you again for this invitation. These are for you," Henry said as he extended his arm with the flowers.

"Well, they're lovely. We'll use them as the centerpiece on the table today. Thank you, Henry." Helen smiled as she inhaled the sweet fragrance.

"That was very kind of you, Henry," Michael said. "Let's go have some dinner."

The three of them set off at their regular slow pace toward the elevator and Michael's car in the parking lot. As they passed the nurse's station on the first floor, Amy looked up to see the trio passing.

"Well, what's going on here? Are you two leaving us today?" she asked as she clasped Helen's arm and gave her a gentle squeeze.

"We're off to my daughter's house for Thanksgiving," Helen said.

"Oh, what beautiful flowers, Helen," Amy replied. "You look wonderful in your dress today."

"Thank you, Amy," Helen said. "These flowers are beautiful, aren't they? I'm going to put them on the dinner table today. Henry gave them to me."

Amy turned to Henry and winked. "You are such a gentle-man," she said.

"Well thank you, young lady. And what are you doing for Thanksgiving?" Henry asked.

Amy shrugged. "It's my turn to work on a holiday, so I'll be having some turkey in the main dining room when I get a break."

"Oh, I wish you didn't have to work on the holiday," Helen said.

"Well, it's part of the job. I'm not complaining. Now you three get moving before your dinner gets cold. Enjoy those flowers, Helen," Amy winked.

"Okay," Michael said as he began to usher his charges along. "I still wish you could join us."

Amy turned to Michael, another beautiful smile spreading across her face. "I'm so glad you asked," she said, as Helen and Henry resumed walking toward the door.

"I'm glad to hear you say that. Another time, perhaps. How about a rain check? Let's not wait till next Thanksgiving."

"Rain check it is," Amy said, smiling as she took Michael's arm and turned him toward the door. "Now you better catch up with those two."

"Yeah, you're right. A couple of crackerjacks they are. Well, have a nice dinner tonight if you can. And I'll hold you to that rain check," Michael said turning away toward the door.

"See that you do, mister," Amy offered back and waved as Michael walked off to catch up with Helen and Henry.

On their arrival at Mary's home, the family made a big fuss over Helen and Henry. Tom and his wife Janice, along with Mary and her husband, Bill, ushered the elderly couple into the living room for pre-dinner drinks. Helen's five grandchildren were all home for the holiday as well. They were excited about seeing their grandmother, and when they had her out of earshot of

Henry they had great fun asking Grandma if she really liked this handsome man she had brought to dinner.

"Oh, you kids just go on now," Helen said. "He's a nice man and you're all just jealous that he didn't bring you flowers."

The grandchildren loved her spark, and they all agreed with her. "Now, help your mother find a vase and put the flowers on the table," she told Mary's oldest daughter, Cindy.

After settling her mother down in the living room, Mary offered to give Henry a tour of the house. He accepted enthusiastically.

Mary walked through the first floor of the home with Henry, showing off the family mementos and photographs. In the study, Henry's eye took in a photograph of a younger Michael with an attractive young woman.

"Who's that with Michael?" he asked.

"That's Lainie. Michael's one true love, at least so far," Mary said.

"And where is Lainie?" Henry asked.

"She died almost twenty years ago after a brief illness."

"Oh, my goodness. And Michael hasn't gotten over it?"

"I don't think so. They were a wonderful couple, ready to get engaged. Michael just never recovered from losing her. And then when our parents began getting older he devoted more and more of his energy to them. It's been wonderful for mother, but at a cost to Michael's personal life."

The tour completed, Mary and Henry rejoined the family while the final touches for dinner were completed.

At dinner, Tom and the grandchildren drew Henry into the family conversation. The grandchildren talked of their college experiences and their majors. They drew out of Henry that he had been the owner of a manufacturing firm, and had sold the company twenty years ago. After the sale he had lived comfortably in retirement. Henry told them that his wife had suffered from early dementia and had died ten years ago. His daughter Jackie was divorced, and moved back into the family home after her mother died. He told them that he had no grandchildren, and that was something that saddened him.

Eventually, Tom turned the conversation to stories of Thanksgiving dinners in years past.

"Do you remember when Mary cooked the turkey an extra four hours?" Tom teased.

Michael joined in, "Yes, that was the year of dryness. There wasn't enough water in the city taps to restore us after that meal."

"Thank you, boys," Mary said. "I see you're eating pretty well this year."

"It's not bad," Tom said.

Henry spoke up, "Mary, this is perhaps the finest Thanksgiving dinner I've ever had. Thank you for all your hard work."

Mary was pleased with the compliment. She smiled and thanked Henry, and then turned to her brothers with a smirk. "It's nice to have a gentleman at the table."

Michael smiled back, and asked, "Mary, why don't you tell us all about the time that the toilet overflowed upstairs and water began dripping through the ceiling onto the table while we were enjoying one of your fabulous Thanksgiving meals?"

"Oh, that was so gross," pined Pat, Mary's youngest daughter.

"How about you, Henry," Mary prompted. "Care to share any stories about Thanksgiving misgivings?"

"I love hearing these stories," Henry began. "It's good to see that other families have had their share of unusual experiences on holidays. I confess that I was party to a bit of a disaster one year. I decided once—over opposition from my wife and daughter I must say—that I would cook the turkey on a gas rotisserie grill in the yard. Oh, they warned me. That's for sure. 'It'll never cook,' they said. 'Something's going to go wrong for sure,' they insisted. Turns out they were right."

Henry paused and took a sip of his wine. He looked around at the table. Everyone was listening intently. "What a good crowd for storytelling this is," he continued. "Well, anyway, I insisted that this would be the best turkey ever. So I rigged up the rotisserie, and started the grilling. So confident was I that the grill was in order, I went into my study after starting the grill and just left it alone. I read for a few hours, then nodded off for another few. I suppose four hours had passed since I had begun the grilling when my daughter Jackie came in to the study to ask how the cooking was coming. I told her everything was just fine. She could count on the turkey being ready in two more hours, just like the cookbook said. 'Aren't you going to check on it, Dad?' she asked me. 'There's no need, Jackie, but just to humor you I'll take a look with you.' So we walked outside, and the first thing I noticed was there was no sweet, roasting fragrance in the air. I lifted the grill cover and, much to my embarrassment, the turkey was as white as it had been when I had first put it on the grill. The fire was out, and the fuel tank was empty. I had forgotten to refill it that week. With it being Thanksgiving, there was no place to go to get another tank of fuel. 'It looks like it needs more time,' Jackie told me, in one of the understatements that she would love to bring up to me regularly over the next twenty years. Well, of course, there was nothing to do except take the turkey back indoors and beg my wife's indulgence. She shook her head at me as if to say she knew all along this would happen, and then put the turkey in the oven. Dinner was served that evening at 10:00 p.m."

Laughter erupted around the table.

"Ten o'clock!" Tom exclaimed. "Oh, I bet they did like to remind you of that adventure, Henry."

"That they did, Tom," Henry conceded with a smile. "But enough about me. How about you, Helen? Any good stories to share?"

Tom joined Henry in encouraging Helen to tell a story. "How about it, Mother? Tell Henry the one about your eyeglasses and the mashed potatoes."

Helen shook her head at her oldest son. "No one wants to hear that story. It's too old, and it's not even funny if you ask me."

That drew everyone's attention. Soon even the grandchildren were urging Helen to tell the story.

"Oh, I don't know why you brought that up, Tom," she said, then broke into a smile. "But if I must."

"Yes, you must, Mother," said Mary, patting Helen on the arm to encourage her to continue.

"Well, there was a time when I was not especially fond of wearing eyeglasses, even though I couldn't see very well without them. So one year, just before Thanksgiving, I purchased a lorgnette that had my eyeglass prescription."

"What's a lorgnette, Grandma?" asked one of Tom's children.

"It's a fancy pair of glasses that have no temples. They have a spring or something by the nosepiece, and they just sort of pinch your nose to stay on."

"Those were quite the fashion back in the day," Henry said.

Helen smiled over at her friend. "Yes, they were. But they were expensive. My father was shocked when he heard what I had paid for them. Anyway, I wore them for the first time on Thanksgiving. I was dating your father at the time," she continued, as she looked at Mary, who was still holding her hand.

"He was invited to Thanksgiving dinner, which was a sure sign in those days that we were serious. He loved the glasses, and told me that I looked beautiful in them. Anyway, I was feeling pretty good about myself as we settled down to dinner. Halfway through the meal, your father asked for some more mashed potatoes. They were sitting just to my left. When I turned to pick up the bowl, the glasses slipped off and landed right in the middle of the bowl of potatoes."

"Ouch," said Henry. "I bet that was a little embarrassing."

Helen smiled at the memory. "Well, there was no way to hide it. I couldn't just pick them out of the bowl and put them back on. They were covered with my mother's finest mashed potatoes."

Everyone laughed at the thought of Helen's predicament.

"What did Dad say?" Tom asked.

"Your father was a perfect gentleman, unlike you two boys with all your stories today. He took the glasses from my hands and cleaned them himself. Sometime later when we were engaged he asked me to wear them again on our wedding day."

"Did you have mashed potatoes at the reception after your wedding ceremony?" Tom asked with a mischievous grin.

"No, we didn't. And that's enough of that story," Helen said.

After dinner, pumpkin pie was served. Helen bragged about the fact that she was always in charge of the pies since the year she had stopped cooking, and this year had been no different.

"This pie is delicious," Henry said. "Did you make this yourself, Helen?"

The family paused to see what Helen would say. She hadn't cooked a pumpkin pie for over a decade, choosing to have Tom pick up two pies each Thanksgiving from the local bakery.

"Don't you concern yourself with how these pies were baked," Helen responded, just as the family thought she would say. It was her regular line in the face of questions year after year about when she had found time to cook the delicious pies.

Michael laughed and shook his head. "Boy, this is good pie, Mother," he winked at her.

"Just eat, Michael," she said.

After the plates were cleared the family retired to the living room for coffee. Once they were settled, Mary remembered that she had failed to offer the minced meat pie, another Thanksgiving staple.

"Would anyone like another slice of pie?" she asked. "Mother, how about you? It's minced meat."

"Oh, I shouldn't," Helen said.

"How about just a small one?" Mary asked.

Helen shrugged. "Get behind me, Satan, and push," she said.

"What does that mean, Grandma?" Pat asked.

"Oh that's a golden oldie, Honey," Helen said. "It means I'll have another slice of pie."

Once they completed their second round of pie, the family spread out through the living and dining rooms and began to talk with each other in smaller groups. Michael joined Henry in the living room, where they found a quiet corner with two comfortable chairs.

"This has been a very pleasant day," Henry said. "You have a wonderful family. It's easy to see that you all really care for one another. And that's a real joy to be around."

Michael sat back in his chair and pondered Henry's generous words.

"Thank you, Henry," he said. "We've celebrated Thanksgiving Day as a family all my life. I can't ever remember not being here with my parents and my brother and sister, and now their children on this holiday. I think it's my favorite holiday of the year, because I know that I can count on everyone being together. At Christmas we always try to meet up with one another at one time, but often enough one or the other of us is away with other family commitments. Our parents always understood that, but we all knew that they longed for one day of the year in which they could count on everyone returning to the fold. And that day happens to be today."

As Michael finished speaking, he realized that he had just spoken about the day where he could always count on everyone in his family being together. He regretted using that phrase because Henry was without his daughter. Michael was afraid he had just insulted their guest.

"I hope you took no offense at what I just said, Henry. I'm sure you miss having Jackie with you today. I should've been more thoughtful in my remarks," Michael added.

"Nonsense," Henry countered. "I do miss Jackie, but I know you meant no disrespect. On the contrary, Michael, I'm pleased to hear your thoughts, and I applaud when anyone is candid with me. I used to like Thanksgiving Day as well. For a number of years, my brother, who is now gone, would join us. But he stopped being part of the day many years ago, and once my wife became ill none of the holidays seemed to matter a great deal to me anymore."

"I'm sorry to hear that," Michael said. "I know it was difficult for all of us the first few years after Dad died. We felt like we didn't have a right to really enjoy the day, but on the third Thanksgiving after he was gone, Mother did something that helped us appreciate the day again."

"Now this sounds like an interesting story," Henry said. "Do tell, please."

"It all revolves around the opening toast at dinner. In the past it had always been my father who gave the toast, and then Tom assumed the role after Dad was gone. On that day, however, just as we sat down at the table, Mother took a spoon to her crystal goblet to command everyone's attention and held her glass up before Tom could take charge of the table. It was a real surprise to all of us."

Michael sat back and crossed his legs. He glanced across the room at his mother, who was sitting on the couch with two of her grandchildren, looking at a picture album.

Henry looked across the room to see Helen as well, then turned back to Michael, patiently waiting for him to continue.

"Do you remember her toast?" Henry asked.

Michael nodded. "I sure do. I was just thinking it's hard to believe that my mother was so astute in those days."

"She's a different lady now, Michael, but there is still a lot going on in her brain that makes her the same person that she was ten years ago. I don't know if that makes any sense to you, but it does to me. I know I can get forgetful and lose my way around, but even when I do get lost, somehow I realize that I've lost my way, and I feel like I'm still in control in some way. The day when I don't even realize I've gotten lost, that's the day that will scare me. I just hope I slip away before that day reaches me."

"Boy, we sure have slipped down a dark road in this conversation, haven't we?"

"That we have. Now, tell me about your mother's toast."

Michael proceeded to describe how Helen had tapped her glass for quiet. It was the only time he ever remembered her proposing a toast. After everyone turned to her she raised her glass and said, 'To all those here, and all those who've gone before us. To my mother and my father, whom I miss so very much, and to my grandmother and grandfather, whose passing was so very hard for my mother to accept, and to your father, the most wonderful man I've ever known. A man who would want us to remember him, and a man who would not want us to live in mourning for the rest of our days. These past few years have been difficult ones for us all when the holidays have come around, and Thanksgiving has been especially hard. So today please join me in remembering good days past, and pledging more good days to come. Here's to all of us, together again, happy that we are all here. Let's make this day a memorable one.' Then she raised her glass a little higher and took a sip of wine. Most of those gathered around the table had tears in their eyes, including some of the grandchildren.

"What a remarkable story," Henry said. "I can just imagine what that moment was like for all of you. That day has stayed with you and I suspect will remain with you all your days, Michael."

Michael nodded. "It gives me a lot of pleasure to recall that time, and even more so in the last few years as I've watched her peace of mind slipping away."

"I remember when my father died," Henry said. "It's been over forty years. It was awfully difficult for me to accept. So many more things happened to me in my life after he was gone. So many times there were events that I wanted to talk to him about, or get his impressions on. Sometimes that longing for a good conversation with him, and the opportunity to get some advice, even years after he was gone, was harder to take then the days around his actual death."

"Boy, you are right on that account," Michael said. "A lot of things have happened in my life since Dad's been gone. I sure wish he was around for me to share a word with."

"Tell me about your father, Michael," Henry said. "What do you remember about him?"

Michael paused for a minute to reflect, then said, "He was the lord of the manor."

Henry laughed. "And I take it he was a good lord of the manor."

Michael joined him in laughter. "Yes, he was a man of principle, honest as the day is long. He wasn't a big man in size, but he possessed a powerful voice that more than made up for his stature. He had a good laugh, too. I used to love to do something that would make Dad laugh."

"I bet that happened a lot," Henry said.

"Often enough to satisfy me," Michael agreed.

"And in his later years?" Henry asked.

"Dad always had his wits about him, even to the end, but he did change over the years with his illness. Where I had always gone to him for advice, in his last few years he began to rely on me and ask my counsel."

"I suppose it was an honor to have your father seek counsel from you. That's something you should be proud of and treasure. I hope you do."

Michael smiled. "You're figuring me out today, Henry."

Henry sat back in his chair, stretching his arms over his head. "Perhaps I am, young man. I hope you'll excuse an old man for probing."

Michael smiled again. "What do you say to an after dinner drink? Would you care for a glass of cognac?"

"I think some cognac would be the perfect way to top off this dinner," said Henry.

"I'll drink to that," said Michael. Then looking across the room at his brother, he said, "Oh, bartender. Cognac, please."

Tom laughed, and much to Michael's surprise, got up from the couch and poured cognac for the three of them.

After settling back in their chairs with their drinks, Henry turned again to Michael and said, "Tell me about yourself, Michael. I take it you've never been married."

Michael pursed his lips and shook his head no. Henry wasn't sure what that might indicate, so he continued.

"Afraid to walk down the aisle, or have you just not found the right one yet?"

This time Michael offered a slight smile.

"I did find the right one once, but that was a long time ago."

They sat in silence gazing at nothing in particular. Henry was waiting for Michael to continue, but after a minute he decided to press a little further.

"It would appear that what happened a long time ago still weighs heavily on you."

Michael let the remark hang in the air. He had spoken to Amy briefly about his past, but not in great depth.

"Sometimes it's hard to shake things off," he said.

Henry nodded in agreement.

"Mary took me around the house earlier. I noticed a photograph of you and a young lady from many years ago. Care to tell me about her?"

"I was almost engaged once," Michael said. "Many years ago."

When Michael paused again and stared back off into space Henry chose to steer him back.

"What was her name?" he asked.

"Loraine. But she liked to go by Lainie."

"That's not a name you hear often. Loraine. I knew a Loraine once back in the forties. She was a looker."

Michael smiled. "Maybe our two Loraines were related then, because mine was a looker, too."

"What happened to Loraine?"

Another pause, but he was finding Henry's probing to be oddly reassuring. He began to describe how he and Lainie had known each other since they were children, but had only begun dating half way through college. When they were seniors they knew they would be married some day, and had even window shopped for rings. Lainie always told Michael that when the time came to pick out a ring he should be sure to select something very clean and simple, and very expensive too. Henry liked that. Michael actually found a ring that he thought was just right, but he never purchased it. After college the two of them went off on a vacation together, wandering around Florida, then Nassau, and finally in New Orleans. They decided on that trip that when they returned home they would find an apartment and get a couple of part-time jobs just to have enough money to live, while they decided what they wanted to do when they grew up. That's how Lainie liked to put it anyway. But three weeks after they returned from the road trip, Lainie got sick. The two of them had spent the day together looking at cheap apartments, but she was feeling run down. When Michael took her home she felt like she had a high fever. Two days after that she was in the hospital; after a day of tests, Lainie learned she had leukemia.

"How long did it take?" Henry asked.

"Three months."

Henry shook his head, sensing the grief that Michael still carried after twenty years.

"You were with her all that time?"

Michael nodded. "Her parents and I took turns sitting at her side until the end. She was never alone in that hospital for a single hour. You know, a simple thing like just being there with someone till the end has always seemed to me one of my proudest achievements. Does that make sense?"

"Of course it does."

"She died in September, and ever since I've been ignoring her final wishes."

"Why would you be doing that?"

"Because I'm just not as strong as she was, I guess."

"She wanted you to find someone else to love, I suppose. Is that it?" Henry asked.

Michael smiled. "Did you study psychology or something, Henry? You always seem to be a step or two ahead of me."

"No," Henry laughed. "I just have a touch of wisdom from my old age. You know the saying, 'Too soon old, too late smart.'

There really is something to that theory. Who knows, maybe you'll get smart someday, too."

Michael laughed with him. "Maybe so."

"So why do you still find yourself at odds with Lainie's wishes?"

"She told me that her death could offer me two lessons. Lesson one is that life is fleeting. Don't let it pass you by."

"And lesson two?"

"Don't get attached to anyone, because someday they'll go away."

"I like lesson one a whole lot better," Henry said.

"Well, everything I've ever read says lesson one is the right choice to make," replied Michael. "But after Lainie I just never looked for anyone to be close to again."

"It sounds as if life paused after Lainie died."

Michael nodded. "I've always rationalized that the right person has never come along."

"But this time, maybe, the right person has come along."

Michael smiled. "Maybe she has. I've just been a little too busy to resolve that question."

"Your mother has told me about the piano lessons. And as a matter of fact, so has Amy herself."

"I can believe my mother would blab, but Amy spoke with you about us?"

"She's a fine young woman, and it's easy to see she's interested in you. Care to hear a little free advice?"

"Sure."

"Don't let someone like Amy dangle too long. You could lose her. And I think that would be a shame for both of you."

Michael considered the advice quietly. "I'll remember what you say, Henry."

"I enjoy talking with you, Michael."

"Same here. You're an easy man to open up to."

"Perhaps I'll do the same for you one of these days," Henry replied. "But in the meantime, what do you say to another cognac?"

"Sounds good to me," Michael said, and started to reach for Henry's glass.

"Allow me this time," Henry said before turning to Tom across the room and shouting, "Oh, bartender."

That drew a laugh out of everyone, but still resulted in Tom topping off their drinks again.

At eight o'clock the party was winding down, and Michael suggested they head back to Village Green. On the ride back Henry bemoaned the fact that he was returning to Village Green rather than to his beloved home.

"Oh, don't fuss now, Henry," she said. "I understand what you're saying. It's just not home, is it?"

The question hung unanswered in the air, and the three of them drove in silence the rest of the way.

CHAPTER 9

It was only a week before Christmas when Michael received the call from Amy.

"Your mother may have fallen this morning," she said. "We found her on the floor in her room earlier. She's with us at the nurse's station now. Her blood pressure is high. I think you should come on out."

He left his meeting at the university and came straightaway.

When Helen saw him enter the nurse's station, she spoke immediately. "Oh, Michael, I'm so glad you're here. Let's go home."

"Well, this is home now, Mother. But maybe we should go for a ride to the hospital and see the doctor."

Michael had spoken to Dr. Canton, his mother's physician, on the way out to Village Green, relaying the news from the nursing staff. Dr. Canton had advised Michael to take Helen to Christ Hospital to be examined.

Amy already had a wheelchair from the nursing station standing by. Together she and Michael wheeled Helen out to the car.

After they placed Helen in the car and closed the door, Amy turned to Michael. He could see she was shaken. "I don't really think the fall hurt her," she said, "but the high blood pressure worries me." Amy placed her hand on Michael's arm. "Will you call me when you know something?"

Michael placed his hand on Amy's. "Sure I will. It's really nice of you to want to know."

Amy gave him a little smile and a nod of her head and turned to go back in. Michael climbed into the car, and began the twenty-minute trip to the hospital.

"I don't want to stay at the hospital, Michael. We're just going to see the doctor, right?"

"We'll start with him seeing you, Mother. But before that we need to talk about what happened this morning. Did you fall down?"

"What are you talking about? I didn't fall down. Where do you hear these stories?"

"The nurses found you this morning on the floor next to your bed. Do you remember that?"

"Michael, are you making this stuff up?"

"I don't think so. But we'll get you checked out anyway."

At the hospital her blood pressure was high and her pulse was spiking. The emergency room physician suggested that more tests were needed. She was admitted that evening for what they hoped would only be a day or two, but instead turned out to be two weeks.

Although she was receiving the best of care, somehow the hospital stay began to weaken her both in mind and body. She displayed little energy and had to be coaxed to take a walk for some exercise. Even the visits from her grandchildren, home from college for the holidays, did little to raise her spirits. When she learned that she would still be in the hospital over Christmas she was especially disappointed.

Michael had volunteered to spend Christmas Eve with her, so that Tom and Mary could be with their families that evening. It was a cold, winter night, but brightened by a full moon. Michael arrived at Helen's room at 7:30. He found her lying in bed and staring at the wall on the other side of the room. To her right was a television and radio set. Further right was a window that looked onto the downtown city skyline.

"Oh, Michael, it's so good to see you," Helen said, as he entered her room. "Let's go home."

"No, Mother, we need to stay here for a while," he replied, pulling up a chair to sit next to her. "We need for you to get a little stronger first."

Michael suggested they look at the skyline and try to identify landmarks. Helen sat up for a spell and joined him in looking out at the city. She enjoyed hearing Michael guess at various buildings, but she didn't feel up to guessing herself and eventually grew tired.

Michael tuned the radio in to the local classical station, which was featuring Christmas carols all evening, and returned to his chair at Helen's bedside. He helped adjust Helen's bed so she could lie on her side facing him, her back to the window.

"Why don't we talk about some Christmas memories and listen to music?" he suggested.

"If that's the best you can do," she deadpanned.

They sat together and listened to the sacred music of the evening. "Silent Night." "Adestes Fidelis." "It Came Upon a Midnight Clear." All her favorite Christmas songs were pouring out of the radio behind her. As the hours passed, Helen's good spirits returned, making for a pleasant evening together. Michael had brought some photos from holidays past, which sparked memories and conversation about old Christmas gifts and celebrations. They laughed together about some of the funnier incidents that had occurred around the holidays.

One of the old photos showed Helen posing next to Santa Claus.

"Do you remember this one, Mother?" Michael asked.

"Well, that looks like Santa Claus with a good little girl," Helen said with a chuckle.

"I don't know about the good little girl, but that's Santa all right. Do you remember that trip?"

It had been just a few years ago when she had flown with Michael, Mary, and Mary's daughters to New York City just prior to Christmas to see the sights of New York, and experience the Rockettes at Radio City Music Hall. It was her last great travel adventure.

"I'm not sure where this was taken," Helen said.

"That was in New York, Mother, when we went with Mary to see all the decorations. It was about five years ago."

"Oh, yes, now I remember. That was a wonderful trip."

Michael recalled that his mother had loved the idea of traveling, but as the hours went by in New York she had grown increasingly nervous about being away from her home. She tired easily on the trip, but she had enjoyed the show and the holiday trimmings.

"Santa was walking through the hotel lobby when this photo was taken," Michael said. "I remember how happy he was to pose for a picture with someone even older than he was."

"Okay, funny boy. You can put that picture away now," Helen replied.

Around nine o'clock the nurse brought in ice cream and cake to celebrate Christmas Eve. That was a pleasant surprise, and prompted a few more stories. Helen recalled an early Christmas when Tom Jr. got into the spiked egg nog. She started laughing as she said, "He slept well that night."

After a few more stories they grew quiet again and listened to a recording of a medley of carols. As the long piece ended, Helen sighed and said, "That must be beautiful out there. Is there a big crowd?"

Michael smiled. *Boy, that's a lovely dream. An orchestra playing tonight for Mother right outside her window.* But rather than dwell on the beauty of her imagination, he corrected her. "Mother, there's no orchestra outside the window. The music is coming from the radio. The speaker is right behind you."

It was a harmless error on her part, one of many he had corrected her on over the last few years. But that evening he had no more said the words when he sensed he had somehow broken her spirit. Where she would generally smile and shrug off her mistakes, this time he could see she was embarrassed by what she had just said.

"Oh, I feel so foolish," she said with a crestfallen look. "I really thought there was an orchestra out there."

Michael was heartbroken that he hadn't played along with her this time, instead of pointing out her error. So many times in the past he had gone along with her when her mind had wandered. *Why didn't he just say, "Yes, it is beautiful out there," and agree with her imagination?* He had always tried to balance humoring her lapses with bringing her back to reality. This time he had misjudged, as the sorrow in her eyes so clearly demonstrated to him.

He tried to soften it. "It's an easy mistake, Mother. If I wasn't sitting here facing the window all night I would have thought the same thing."

But her embarrassment would not be so easily relieved. Her little smile told him that clearly. "Don't kid a kidder, Michael," she said softly, tears forming in her eyes. "I really thought there was a band out there. Sometimes I know I'm starting to lose my marbles."

"You're doing fine, Mother," he said. "We all get confused from time to time. You just can't let it get you down."

"Easier said than done," she replied.

They sat in silence for another minute.

Finally, Helen wiped the tears from her eyes and asked, "What am I doing here in the hospital?"

He told her how she was found in her room almost a week ago, and how her blood pressure had been unpredictable. "You've been here for a week now," he added.

"Oh, Michael, you're full of baloney tonight."

He wanted to ease her anguish, but didn't know what to say. They grew quiet again, as the music still played in the background.

Then she asked, "Will I get my mind back?"

Michael sat quietly, considering her question. *I'm afraid it will never be the same again,* he thought, *but I can't tell you that.*

"You still have your mind, Mother," he tried to reassure. "You just get a little confused now and then. It's not so bad."

"Oh, I think it's bad," she said. Helen paused before speaking again.

"Why don't they leave your mind alone and let you fight all the other problems?"

Well, there it is, Michael thought. *She really has captured the heart of the matter.*

"I don't know, Mother," he said. "I know it's not fair. You're trying real hard. We just need to work together on your memory. You're going to be fine if we keep working on it together."

She smiled at him and patted his hand that was resting on the edge of her bed, giving him another one of her 'don't kid a kidder' looks. Her touch felt good to him, but still he could tell she was upset about imagining the orchestra outside her room, and he felt awful about having contradicted her pleasant image.

By then it was 10:30, and time for him to leave. He told her he would be back to visit on Christmas Day. As he put on his coat to get ready to leave she called him over to her bedside.

"Michael," she summoned.

Michael walked back to her bed, leaned over and took her hand. "What is it, Mother?" he asked.

She looked him squarely in the eye and said again, "Let's go home."

"We'll go home soon, Mother," he said, squeezing her hand and leaning over to give her a kiss on the cheek. "Now get some rest while Santa Claus is busy delivering his presents."

"Maybe he'll bring me a band this year," she said, smiling meekly again.

Michael wanted to smile with her, but her wish almost moved him to tears. He struggled to keep them in, and returned a weak smile of his own.

"That would be a great idea. I hope that's what Santa brings you. Sweet dreams, Mother. Good night."

"Merry Christmas, Michael," she called out as he stepped into the hallway.

Driving home that Christmas Eve he was haunted by how his insistence on pointing out she was wrong about the orchestra had caused her so much pain. He wished that he had not corrected her, or, better yet, that she had been right all along. He remembered the little joke she made just before he left when she suggested that maybe Santa would bring her a band this year. *Wouldn't that be something,* he mused. *And wouldn't it have been something if she had been right tonight, and there had been an orchestra just outside her window? What a Christmas present that would be.*

Two days passed, and Michael was still troubled by the events of Christmas Eve. It was strange how her mistake and his correction were so troubling to him. So many times before she might have been slightly embarrassed when her confusion was pointed out. But those instances didn't linger with her or him. This one did. He wondered how he could possibly make amends, and somehow make things right.

CHAPTER 10

A week into the new year, Helen was discharged from the hospital with instructions to temporarily reside at Well Care, the skilled-care unit at Village Green. The goal was to recover further at Well Care for a few weeks, then return to the assisted-living apartment.

But Helen's memory was even more disturbed now than it had been before her hospital admission. It seemed to Michael that the hospital stay had zapped much of the strength and vitality that his mother possessed. Now she was really looking and acting older.

There would be no arguing with her, he thought, *if she called Well Care an old ladies' home.* It was a clean, respectable facility. The staff seemed to consist primarily of care-driven professionals. But the whole ward where Helen was assigned was depressing, no matter how much the staff might try.

For the first three days of her stay, Helen had a double room to herself. But on the fourth day a roommate was assigned. The patient was a ninety-year-old woman who could barely communicate. Fortunately, most of the day the woman slept, but when she was awake she would cry out for what sounded like some family member. The nurses would try to calm her, but generally to no avail. Each time she would cry out, Helen would look around and want to find someone to help. The whole scene began to confuse Helen even more. Michael tried to find another room, but none was available. For three days the confusion continued. Finally, at the beginning of Helen's second week in the facility, a private room opened and Helen was moved.

On her second day in the private room, Michael decided to check on Helen's apartment after he had finished his visit with her. He had not been back through Village Green and the assisted-living area for nearly two weeks. He was glad when he came across Henry walking down the hallway on the third floor.

"Henry," Michael called from down the hall as he saw him approaching the elevator. Michael's good feeling was quickly replaced, however, by a sense of shock at how worn Henry looked. Michael asked if Henry would join him for a cup of tea in the tea room on the main floor, and Henry agreed.

After they were seated and had ordered their tea, Henry asked about Helen. "I've wanted to visit your mother, but I'm afraid I've been feeling a little under the weather and haven't had the chance to get over to see her yet. How is she, Michael?"

"I think she's taken a turn," Michael said. "A turn in the wrong direction. I can't wait to get her out of skilled care and back to her apartment, but I'm not so sure when that is going to take place. The hospital stay seems to have taken a whole lot out of her."

"I'm sorry to hear that. I know it's easy for someone's spirits and mental condition to sink during a long hospital stay. And I can only imagine what it must be like to have to endure the skilled-care facility. How about physically, though? Do the doctors have her health issues under control?"

"That seems to be the one good thing," Michael said. "She has some new medications now. Her heart rate is stable and her blood pressure is staying within the norms. But it seems like the darkness is settling in on her, and that's so hard to see."

Each of them sipped their tea in silence for a few minutes. Finally, Michael spoke again. "And how are you, Henry? You look awfully tired today."

Henry smiled. "I have been tired, yet I feel like I am amazingly clearheaded lately. Still, old age seems to be catching up with me and I'm feeling a little rundown. Don't tell anybody I said that, though, because I don't want anyone getting any ideas about moving me over to skilled care."

Michael nodded and smiled. "Don't worry. Your secret is safe with me."

"I'm glad to hear you say that. I feel like I can trust you and speak of matters that ought not to be shared with others," Henry said.

Michael had been wanting to talk to someone about Helen's hospital stay and the incident on Christmas Eve with the Christmas music. He wondered whether Henry would be a good person to share this story with, and concluded that he was.

"Speaking of secrets," Michael began, "something took place in the hospital that has really bothered me, but I haven't felt comfortable talking to anyone about."

"I'm all ears, son. Tell me what's been on your mind," Henry prompted. "Perhaps we should have another pot of tea, while you bring me up to date," he added as he signaled to the waitress for some fresh tea.

"Thank you, Henry. I appreciate the fact that I can speak with you in confidence."

"Not at all. Perhaps you will do the same for me down the road."

Michael wondered whether there was more to that last comment from Henry than met the eye. But he decided not to press the matter and instead to concentrate on his own dilemma.

"Let me tell you a story about Christmas Eve," Michael began.

"Another holiday story," Henry said.

"Yes," Michael said. "Another adventure on a holiday. This one has me vexed though. I took the Christmas Eve evening shift at the hospital with Mother. For much of the evening it was actually one of the most pleasant Christmas Eves I've had in a while. There wasn't any fuss about opening presents. We relaxed together, just the two of us, and swapped tall tales. Around nine o'clock, the nurses brought in some ice cream and cake, so we had a little party, too. And throughout the evening there was beautiful music coming from the classical station on the radio. We would talk for a while and let the music drift into the background. Then we would grow silent for a spell, and give the music our full attention. Sometimes we'd sing with the carolers. Sometimes we'd just be silent and listen to the sounds of the orchestra. Both of us were drifting in our thoughts, I'm sure. Thinking of days gone by. But it was a really nice evening and the music was the constant theme that ran throughout the night."

"Sounds like a delightful evening," Henry said.

"Well, it was," Michael continued, "up to a certain point. Mother's room had a large window. There was a courtyard below alongside the parking lot. Beyond the parking lot, there are some two-family homes that adjoin the hospital property. Above and beyond those homes you could see part of the downtown skyline. Earlier in the evening we had looked out the window and tried to figure out some of the locations from the buildings and the lights we could see in the distance. But, back to the music. That's where my story lies. Around ten o'clock, the radio program played 'Adestes Fidelis', with just the music only. It was beautiful. When the song began, we found ourselves captured by the music, so we were both silent for the entire length of the piece. Mother was on her side, facing me. I was sitting in a chair next to her bed. Behind her were the radio and the window looking out toward the city. I can still hear the music. It was so calming to me. And it had that same effect on Mother, too. So calming in fact that when the piece was finished, Mother seemed to lose herself again. At its conclusion, she looked up to me and said, 'That must be beautiful out there. Is there a big crowd?'"

Michael paused in his story, taking another sip of tea. When he didn't immediately continue, Henry spoke up. "I take it we've now reached the point in the story that has been troubling you."

Michael smiled, and nodded his head, affirming Henry's remark. Then he continued. "I had two choices to make when she asked that question, and I believe I made the wrong one." Michael grew silent again.

"So your mother thought there was an orchestra right outside her window, did she?" Henry asked.

Michael nodded affirmatively again.

"I see. Well, it's best if I not conjecture as to what your response was. Let me just say that you're among friends here," Henry said.

Michael took another drink of tea and placed the cup back on the saucer. Then he looked back up at Henry and smiled. "Well, there's the rub, isn't it? How does a person deal with someone whose mind is slipping away? I've humored her at times, and played along for a while with her ideas. That night, however, I thought it best not to play along with her imagination, but to bring her back to reality. Now I regret doing so."

"So you told her there was no orchestra outside the window, and that the music was coming from the radio."

"That's right. I told her there was no orchestra, and no audience. Once I said those words she realized the very idea of an orchestra playing outside her window on Christmas Eve was a foolish one. She tried to laugh it off at first, but her eyes betrayed the embarrassment she was feeling, as well as the doubt that I think is now firmly lodged within her as to whether her mind will ever be clear again. Then the most amazing thing happened. For a minute she had all of her wits about her to the point where she knew for certain that her mind was acting up. Her mind was confused, but during the confusion suddenly her mind cleared up so that she knew she was in the middle of confusion. Does that make any sense?"

"Yes, it does, Michael. I know what she's experiencing. Maybe I'm not as far along as Helen, but I have my moments of confusion as I have told you, and then right in the middle of one I sometimes become aware that I am confused. I have to ask myself then, if I'm aware that I am confused then why am I confused at all? It's a vicious circle. It will take a better mind than I possess to figure out the human brain, and how those of us who watch a loved one struggle should deal with it."

"Well, I'm not dealing with it too well right now. I can't help but think that I should have told her there was an orchestra outside that window, even if there wasn't. I just keep wishing I would have agreed with her, rather than deprive her of that sweet thought and, in return, cause her to feel pain at the idea that her mind is slipping away. So for the last few weeks I've been thinking a lot about how I could try to make it right."

"I see. Short of hiring a symphony orchestra to play just outside her window, what kind of ideas have you come up with?"

Michael smiled. "Well, that seems to be the only thought that has crossed my mind."

Henry sat back and stared at Michael. "So that is the only thought you've been pursuing," he said.

Michael smiled again.

"That's a pretty ambitious idea you're carrying around, Michael. An interesting one, I'll grant you, but a highly ambitious one for sure. You know, I hired a band once to play at my home. I'd always wanted to have a party where an orchestra played under the stars and a dance platform would be set up."

"Did you pull it off?" Michael asked.

Henry paused to revisit the old memory. Michael took another sip of what was now a cool cup of tea and waited.

When Henry came around again, he looked back at Michael and said, "Yes, I did pull it off. My wife at first thought I was crazy. I had warned her for a number of years I wanted to do this and she always told me, no, that's just a crazy notion. But there came a point when I decided it wasn't so crazy after all. My wife was in the early days of her mental confusion. So one summer evening, I arranged for a twelve-piece orchestra to perform at our home. I had Jackie take her mother out for an afternoon, so that the stage, lighting, and sound crews could come onto the property and set up the stage, hook up the electricity, and lay out a dance floor. There was a lot to it, but it was all set up before Jackie and her mother returned home. When they did arrive, they saw the set-up and asked what I was up to. I told them they needed to put on their finest dancing clothes, because there was going to be a party tonight. I remember Jackie just shaking her head and smiling. I could read her mind. She was wondering which one of her parents was crazier than the other. When I told Jackie I knew what she was thinking, she just shook her head again and laughed. At that point her mother clasped her hands and smiled and said she'd always wanted an evening like this. Can you believe that? All those years, she told me it was a crazy idea. Then when I plan it, it's not so crazy anymore."

"How did the evening go?" Michael asked. But he already knew the answer to that question. He could see it in the tears that were beginning to fill Henry's eyes. "You don't have to answer that question, Henry. It must have been wonderful."

Henry nodded, then took a handkerchief from his pocket and dabbed his eyes.

At that point, Amy was passing by the tea café, and stopped at their table. "Well, if it isn't two of my favorite gentlemen. You two look thick as thieves in here."

Henry nodded at her, and said, "That we are, my dear. Just a couple of men swapping stories. Isn't that right, Michael?"

"That's right. Say, don't they have a sign out front that says no women allowed when men are in here?" Michael said, winking at Amy.

"I see now, and if that's how you feel, maybe it's time for this conversation to end," Amy said with a smile as she took Henry's arm. "Time for lunch, mister. You're coming with me."

"How are the piano lessons coming, Amy?" Henry asked as she helped him up.

"Not too bad. I've missed a few lessons with my instructor though, because Helen was in the hospital."

"So, Michael, are you ready to resume lessons again?" Henry asked.

Another matchmaker, Michael thought.

"Yes, I am. I was just going to ask my star pupil when we could start up again."

"Did you say star pupil or only pupil?" Amy laughed. "I didn't hear you."

"Star pupil, of course. I'm sorry about falling off the piano wagon. I'm ready to get back on now if you want."

"Sure I do. I'll catch up with you later and see what your schedule looks like. Meanwhile, let's get moving, Henry."

Amy began to help Henry up from his chair, but before leaving their table Henry turned back to Michael and said, "I think we were about done for the day, don't you think, Michael? Besides, I think you'd agree that an invitation from a pretty young lady like Amy should not be ignored."

"Well, thank you, Henry," Amy said. "I'm glad to see you have your priorities straight."

"You go along now, Henry. You're the lucky one this time to get the invitation. I'm still waiting for mine," Michael said, smiling again at Amy.

"I like the sound of that, too, Michael. I'll be back for you another day," Amy said, turning Henry toward the door and walking away toward the dining hall.

*

When Michael returned to see his mother a few days later he found Henry visiting Helen in her skilled-care room. *What a nice surprise,* Michael thought. It was good to see Henry out again. Henry and Helen continued to chat with Michael present for half an hour. When the conversation hit a lull, Helen asked Michael what was in the package he brought.

"I've brought a little book today," Michael said. "It's a memory book that talks all about you. I thought you might enjoy refreshing your memory once in a while, and this could help."

"That sounds nice," Helen said. "Let's have a peek."

Michael pulled out a book and the three of them admired the cover. It featured two photos. One was of Helen taken just a few months ago at Thanksgiving. The other was a shot of her from forty years earlier.

"What lovely photographs, Helen," Henry said.

"One of them is not too bad, but who's that old lady in the other?" Helen joked back. "Let's see what's inside. Michael, my eyes are a little tired today. Would you mind reading it to me?"

Henry stood and said, "This looks like a good place for my departure. I'll let you two have some private time."

Helen placed her hand on his arm and said, "Shush now, Henry. Stay a little longer and listen to this story with me, won't you?"

Henry smiled. "I'd be delighted."

Michael opened the book and began to read.

"Mother's Book. I am Helen Mary Telford. I was born in Columbus on January 5, 1912.

I live in Cincinnati in an apartment at Village Green. My apartment number is 5301.

I went to Christ Hospital a few weeks ago because I wasn't feeling well. Dr. Canton is my doctor. He told my son Michael to take me to the hospital.

Now I am staying for a while at Well Care. There are nurses here to help me get better. When I get stronger I will go back to my apartment where all my things are. My husband's name was Tom. He died six years ago. A picture of the two of us is on my night stand. We were married in Columbus, and lived together for almost fifty years.

I have three children. Tom Junior is the oldest. He's always been proud that he was named after his father. My daughter Mary is in the middle. She calls me every day. She lives nearby. My son Michael lives near, too. I have five grandchildren. I have a sister, Louise, who still lives in Columbus.

My friend Henry Taylor lives here at Village Green. I've lived here since last August. All my special things are in my apartment, like the lamp my mother gave me on my wedding day, and the silver clock that Tom gave me on our twenty-fifth wedding anniversary.

I need to keep working with the nurses to walk as much as I can with the walker so that I get stronger and can go back to my apartment. All my medical bills are being paid for by Medicare, so I have no bills. My apartment rent is paid with my Social Security money. I receive Social Security every month. Michael takes care of paying my bills. Michael reminds me that I have plenty of money in the bank and I do not have to worry about any bills. My savings came from money that my husband Tom and I saved after we paid for college for all three of our children. The money grew over the years, so now I have enough to be comfortable forever."

"That's all there is for now, Mother. Maybe we'll add a few more pages as time goes on."

Helen was pleased with the book. "You know, I'm going to keep this close by and read it every day. You said my bills are all taken care of. Is that right, Michael?"

"They sure are. It says so right in the book. You can check it out any time."

"It's a wonderful story, Helen. I'm glad you let me listen," Henry added, "but you look a little tired now. Perhaps I should go."

"I'm bushed. My mother used to always say she was born tired. I think I inherited it from her," Helen said.

"Why don't we let you rest, Mother? Henry and I will take a walk, and I'll stop back in a while to see how you're doing," Michael said.

"Promise?" Helen asked.

"Promise," Michael replied as be bent down to kiss her on the cheek. "Now get some rest."

Out in the hallway, Henry suggested they walk over to the sunroom in the main building. The room was bright, comfortably furnished, and to Michael's relief, empty. Once they sat down Henry told Michael how impressed he was with the memory book.

"What a terrific idea, Michael," he said. "Your mother really enjoyed it. You could sure tell that."

"Thanks, Henry. I don't know if she'll remember to read it again, but I just keep hoping there's some little thing I can do to make things better for her."

"You're doing that, son. That's easy to see."

"She did like it though, didn't she? That was nice," Michael said.

They sat for a while in silence, enjoying the warmth of the room. Eventually, Henry spoke up. "Something on your mind, Michael? You look like you're cooking something up over there."

Michael smiled. "I've been doing a lot of thinking and day-dreaming these last few days," Michael admitted.

"So out with it now," Henry demanded.

"There's been two things actually," Michael said. "First, I've been daydreaming about the night you had the band play at your home. I bet that was a sight."

Henry sat back and laughed. "Oh, yes, it was. I can still see the gleam in my wife's eyes when we had our first dance that night. What a thrill."

"I'm sure it was."

"And the second matter?" Henry prompted.

"Well, I wonder if I could do the same for my mother," Michael said.

"What do you have in mind?"

"Yesterday I came across a story in the newspaper about a wedding of a socially prominent couple whose reception featured a performance by the Symphony Orchestra, conducted by the maestro, Nicholas Shefsky. What a reception that must have been. Once I finished reading I started thinking again about Christmas Eve, and I began to daydream how different the evening would have been if there had actually been an orchestra outside. It's a crazy idea to think about the symphony performing on Christmas Eve, but then I began to wonder, why not some other night? I know this is going to sound crazy, Henry, but what if I could arrange for the symphony to perform a concert right outside her window, so that this time she would be right when she imagines that it must be beautiful out there?"

Both men sat quietly, each considering Michael's idea. Eventually, Henry broke the silence.

"Michael, first let me ask if you are serious about this."

Michael offered a sheepish grin. "I think I am."

Henry nodded his head. "Can I be candid with you, son?"

Here it comes, Michael thought. *Even Henry is going to tell me I'm crazy.* But he held back from speaking those thoughts, and said, "Please do. I value your advice."

"Very well then," Henry began. "Have you spoken with anyone about this? Your sister perhaps, or someone in the music business?"

"Nope. Just you."

"I see."

Henry pondered the matter before adding, "I have to tell you this idea is a whopper of an ambitious one, Michael. This seems like quite a major thing to do because of this sense of guilt you're carrying. Does it really mean that much to you, that you would try to pull off something like this?"

Michael nodded, unable to speak.

"The cost alone, Michael, will be excessive. I have some experience in these matters. Do you have any idea how much this might be?"

Michael recovered his voice. "I haven't done a lick of research yet. I don't have a clue. All I have is the idea."

Henry laughed. "Let me tell you something then. A lot of people will tell you this is one whale of a foolish notion."

Michael chose not to respond, letting the silence drift over them again. After a minute, Henry spoke again. "But I won't be one of them."

A broad grin slowly spread across Michael's face, followed by another across Henry's. "Now I'm not saying yet that this can really happen, Michael. The cost alone may be more than you can afford. And the idea of holding it right outside your mother's window is really going to be a tough sell. I don't know how you could fit everyone out there. All in all, young man, you've got your work cut out for you if you want to make this happen."

"I agree. The whole idea may be a long shot, but if nothing else, at least one good thing happened already."

"What's that?" Henry asked.

"At least you don't think I'm crazy."

Henry roared with laughter. "Michael, let's be clear. I do think you're crazy." Henry continued to laugh. "But I like crazy. Good things come from crazy, and this could be a wonderful thing."

"Thanks, Henry. That means a lot to me."

"So, where will you begin?" Henry asked.

"I guess it starts with the symphony first. I think I'll sound them out before talking to the activities department here. One step at a time."

"Care for some advice on that front?"

"I'm all ears."

"Give the activities director the courtesy of a heads-up on the project, if you get that far. But make your real pitch to the administrator of this place. That man impresses me. I sense he's the kind of guy that would work with you, rather than against you."

"Thanks, Henry. I'll remember that."

"One more thing. When do you propose this take place?"

"The sooner the better," Michael said. "I don't know how warm it has to be for an outdoor concert."

Henry sat back in his chair, closing his eyes.

Michael saw the old man grow quiet. "Are you all right, Henry?" he asked.

After a pause, Henry opened his eyes. Looking again at Michael, he said, "Fine, Michael. I'm fine. A little tired though. I was just thinking I wish I could be there when the weather warms again."

The remark stunned Michael. He stared at Henry for what seemed like minutes, while Henry sat back in his chair and closed his eyes again.

"Why wouldn't you be here when the weather warms?" Michael asked.

Henry opened his eyes again, and said, "We'll have to see how early spring comes, won't we?"

"Jackie told me that you're ill, Henry."

Henry smiled briefly. "I'm getting older every day, Michael. Let's just leave it at that, shall we?"

Michael wanted to talk about his health some more, but he had too much respect to dishonor Henry's request. "Sure thing, Henry. We'll leave it at that."

"Thank you, son. Keep me posted now. I'll be curious to hear about your communications with the orchestra. Now if you'll excuse me, I'm going to take a little nap."

"Get a good rest, Henry. I'll find you again as soon as I have more word."

Henry then shuffled off toward the elevator and his room. Michael headed back upstairs to look in again on Helen.

That evening, Michael began drafting a letter to the conductor of the symphony orchestra. He concluded, after deliberating for a day, that the letter should simply state that he would like to meet with someone about the possibility of the symphony playing a concert at an assisted-living facility.

After carrying the letter around for another day, he decided that it was time to act, and he put it in the mail.

CHAPTER 11

Two weeks after Michael had written to the symphony, he received a phone call from Carolyn Webster, who identified herself as the operations manager for the orchestra. She told Michael that Nicholas Shefsky, the conductor of the symphony, had received his letter and found his request to be quite intriguing. Shefsky had instructed her to contact Michael and set up a meeting.

That afternoon the staff agreed that Helen had recovered sufficiently from her illness to return to her apartment in assisted living. Michael and Mary packed up Helen's clothing and personal items and the three of them left Well Care for what they each hoped would be forever.

"I'm glad to be out of there," Helen said. She had refused to use the wheelchair offered her for the trip to her apartment. It was only two buildings over, but the winding walk through the maze of hallways would take ten minutes. Michael could see it was a matter of pride to his mother that she could walk out of the skilled-care facility rather than be wheeled out.

"Where to next, Michael?" she asked. Michael and Mary exchanged knowing glances. She already had forgotten they were headed to the apartment. They both knew they were fortunate to have been able to get her released from skilled care. They also believed that was the right course. Being in her apartment with her own belongings and some sense of privacy and dignity was important.

"We're walking back to your place now, Mother," Michael said. "Do you remember that you have an apartment here?"

She considered the question as they slowly traversed the hallways, but did not respond.

Once they reached the assisted-living building they came across two nurses talking to a resident in the hallway. They each greeted Helen warmly, welcoming her back to her apartment.

At the elevator near the nurse's station, Michael asked Helen if she remembered that her home was just upstairs.

Helen nodded grimly. "I remember," she said, lifting her left arm to show him the key ring that was back on her wrist again.

"I thought we were going home," she added.

"This is home, Mother," Mary said, as she took her mother's arm and guided her onto the elevator. "This is where you live now. Your apartment is decorated with all your pictures and furniture."

Helen looked at Mary as the elevator ascended. "Is this really my home now, Mary?" she asked.

This is so hard, Michael thought, as he watched Mary try to hold back her tears. *Their mother was the sweetest lady in the world,* Michael thought. To see what old age and dementia was doing to her, and to his brother and sister dealing with it, was sometimes too much to bear. But what could they do? They couldn't just give up on her. She was their mother.

"Hey there, lady," he said. "This is a great place. Come on now. Show us which way to go to your apartment."

As they stepped off the elevator, she looked left and right, and then set off in the correct direction. *That's a good start,* he thought.

"See, you've got it together," he encouraged. "Let's go check your place out."

Once inside she was glad to see her precious mementos. It was good that she recognized the place as her home.

After a half hour passed, Amy knocked on the apartment door and entered. Michael and Mary smiled as she entered the room.

"Welcome back, Helen," Amy said. "It's good to see you again."

"Thank you," Helen said. "Do you live here, too?"

"No, I work here, Helen. My name is Amy. I'm one of the nurses that will help take care of you when you need something. Do you remember me?"

Helen looked to Michael for the answer. He nodded briefly.

"Well, I think I do remember you now, Amy. I'm sorry I may have forgotten a few names and faces. Will you forgive me, dear?"

Amy sat next to Helen on the couch and patted her on the arm. "Of course. There's no need to apologize. There's so many names and faces around here. It will take a few days to get used to being back in your apartment. You've been gone almost a month now. We'll take it slow for a while and help you meet everyone again, okay?"

Michael admired how Amy went the extra mile to reassure her patient. It was good to see his mother treated so well.

"Now, I'm going to check your blood pressure and then I'll let you continue your visit with your family."

When the brief checkup was completed Amy stood to leave, and Michael told his mother he would be back tomorrow and would walk Amy out.

Once they were in the hallway Michael thanked Amy for the care she offered his mother.

"Well, thank you," Amy said. "That's very sweet of you to say. She's a wonderful lady. I'm so glad she was able to return to her apartment. I'm sure it's a great relief for you, too."

"Yes, it is. I'm not a fan of skilled care. I know it's a difficult challenge for the staff to deal with so many patients, so many of whom are helpless, but it just seems like it's easy for someone to lose a sense of dignity as a patient on a skilled-care ward. Back here she has plenty of nurses to check in on her. And she has some privacy, too. I know that would mean a lot to me if I was the patient."

Amy smiled and nodded. "I've worked briefly in a skilled-care facility. I have a lot of respect for the nurses who make it a career. It's difficult dealing all day with patients who need almost constant supervision. I couldn't do it. I'm very happy working with patients who have memory issues like your mother. That's enough of a challenge every day for me."

Michael smiled. "I don't know how you do it. It seems like a full-time job for us just dealing with Mother. Having a building full of memory-impaired folks has got to tax your patience."

"It does, some days," Amy laughed. "But today has been a good day, and once I return your mother's chart my shift will be over and the day will end on a good note."

As they neared the nurse's station, Michael paused. Amy did as well, sensing he had something to say.

"I know we've joked about dinner together, but would you like to have dinner with me some evening?"

A smile spread across Amy's face and, to Michael's eye, glowed. "I thought you'd never ask, Michael."

"Well, I am a little slow, I'll give you that," he said.

"I'd love to have dinner with you. You just let me know when."

"How does a week from Saturday look?"

"That would be fine. I'll talk to you later this week then," Amy said. "I'm looking forward to it, Michael."

"So am I. I'll see you soon."

Michael sat down with Carolyn Webster, the operations manager at the symphony offices the following afternoon. Carolyn was a young woman, wearing a dark blue suit. Her long hair was pulled back and held in place by a cream-colored ribbon. Reading glasses rested at the top of her head. She gave the appearance to Michael of being a no-nonsense person.

Her office was spacious and well organized, with two large windows overlooking a park across the street. Behind her desk was an oil painting of the symphony hall. At the far end of the office was a small conference table with six chairs. The walls around the table held photos of famous symphony halls from around the world.

Carolyn showed Michael to the table and offered him a chair.

"Mr. Shefsky will be joining us in a few minutes," she said. "We thought it might be a good idea if I began the meeting and got some initial information from you and then gave you some information about how we plan for private events."

"That would be wonderful," Michael said.

Carolyn proceeded to explain that the symphony is asked to perform at private events only a few times each year. A number of free public concerts are regularly offered, like concerts in the park, but events not generally open to the public are rarely held. Most of the requests are considered either to be inappropriate venues for the orchestra, or too expensive for the sponsor to bear. When Michael told her that he wanted the performance to be held as soon as possible, possibly in April, and that he wanted it held outdoors, Carolyn told him that would be absolutely impossible. The orchestra only scheduled outdoor concerts between the middle of May and the middle of September due to the unpredictability of the weather. She explained further that due to the fragile nature of the instruments, a hard and fast rule of the orchestra was that no concert can be held in temperatures under 62 degrees. Beyond that, the timing from an initial meeting like she was conducting now and the actual performance was typically nine months.

When she asked whether time was a factor in the planning, Michael was hesitant in his reply. He did not want to go into the entire story of his purpose for requesting the concert. He felt foolish enough even being in this meeting. They would never take him seriously if he told them the whole story.

"Let me put it this way," he said. "I want to arrange this for the benefit of my mother specifically. I'd like all the residents of Village Green, or as many as can be squeezed into the area where it's conducted, to be able to enjoy the music. But my primary reason is to do this for my mother. And she's not well."

"I'm sorry to hear that," Carolyn replied. "So time is a serious factor. Let me ask you about the site for the performance. Does it really need to be outdoors to fulfill your needs?"

Michael smiled. "I'm not making this easy, am I? I'm afraid that in order for this to achieve the purpose that I have in mind, it does need to be outdoors."

Carolyn smiled in return. She was a good fact finder, Michael thought. When he told her that he had no information about the dimensions of the performance area and that he had not even consulted yet with the staff at Village Green, she told him there really wasn't much further they could talk about except the cost. Michael confessed to being nervous about what that figure might be. She advised him that most outdoor concerts featured a pops orchestra, rather than the full symphonic orchestra, which meant there would be a maximum of 75 musicians rather than the normal 99. She couldn't provide an exact figure but she was able to estimate that the cost would be in the area of $35,000.

Michael nodded his head, thinking about the number. He hoped Carolyn was not able to observe the tremor that had just run through him. He certainly didn't want to expose the money fears he had. Thirty five thousand dollars! How in heaven's name could he ever raise that much money?

He took a deep breath, and asked, "And would there possibly be any other fees associated with the event?"

Carolyn informed him that a fee in that range would cover the cost of the orchestra and an assistant conductor, who would preside over the performance. That surprised Michael. He had always assumed that the maestro, whom he had seen perform and read so much about, would be conducting all the performances. But now he was being told that typically an assistant conductor handled all the performances at private events. Carolyn assured him that anyone who would conduct the orchestra would be fully qualified to do so.

"Mr. Shefsky does conduct at some performances outside of Symphony Hall. However, there would be an additional fee if he did so."

"Can you tell me what that fee might be?"

"No, I'm afraid I cannot discuss that with you. That is a matter that would be addressed by Mr. Shefsky himself."

Michael sat back in his chair and nodded his head.

"Shall we continue?" Carolyn asked.

In for a penny, in for a pound, Michael thought. *Why not?*

"Yes. I'd like to pursue the matter."

"Fine. This is just a preliminary meeting, Michael. We like to start this process off with a discussion like you and I just held. Typically we would follow up with a cost estimate for you, a site visit to be certain the area is suitable, and then a contract. But, as I said at the outset, Mr. Shefsky found your request to be very intriguing, and he asked that he join the meeting once we covered all the initial matters. So if you would be so kind as to wait here, I'll get Mr. Shefsky."

While he waited, Michael admired the photographs of the current orchestra and the past principal conductors that lined the office. The projected cost was already agonizing, but to be sitting in the symphony offices, and about to meet the conductor, was thrilling. For a moment he felt like an impostor who had no business being there.

In a few minutes Carolyn returned with Nicholas Shefsky.

"Good afternoon, Mr. Telford," the maestro said as he swept into the room and extended his hand. Carolyn entered just behind him. He wasn't as tall as Michael had imagined him. But his long, dark hair, swept back over his ears, with a touch of gray blending in, and his deep, rich voice gave him a commanding presence. Michael was impressed with the man immediately. He jumped to his feet.

"An honor, sir," he said as he shook the conductor's hand.

"Please be seated," Nicholas said as he took a chair opposite Michael. "Carolyn does a magnificent job as our operations manager. She filled me in on some of the points that you and she discussed this afternoon."

"She's been very informative. It's been a pleasure talking with her. So far at least anyway," Michael said with a smile.

Nicholas joined Michael in laughter. "We don't get many requests for performances for such an exclusive audience. The concert you propose would be attended primarily by the residents of a nursing facility, is that correct?"

"Yes, sir. That would be my desire. There are approximately 300 residents at Village Green. About fifty of those are in the assisted-living section, and the rest are in independent living. There are more residents who reside in the skilled-care facility. Some of them may attend, but I suspect that most of them would be unable to enjoy the concert."

"Carolyn tells me you wish to arrange for this performance as a tribute to your mother," Nicholas said.

"It's a long story, but, yes, if this can happen, it would be a gift to my mother. No doubt an excessive gift, but a gift nonetheless," Michael said with a smile.

"Sometimes wonderful gifts come at a high cost," Nicholas said. "Naturally, you will have to consider that in making your decision. Now I understand timing could present problems as well."

"Yes. I don't know whether the beneficiary of this gift will be around in nine months."

"I understand," Nicholas said. "My mother lived in a nursing facility for two years before she died."

"Did you perform at your mother's home?" Michael asked.

Carolyn looked surprised that Michael would ask such a personal question of the maestro. Nicholas merely smiled, surprised as well at the question, and said, "Not a full orchestra, as you have in mind, Mr. Telford. I did play the violin for my mother and the other residents. It was quite a moment for me. Still, I must confess that I always regretted the fact that I did not include the entire orchestra in the performance. Of course I could hardly ask everyone in the orchestra to donate their time now, could I?"

"No, of course not," Michael said.

"Why don't you think things over, Mr. Telford," Nicholas suggested. "Give Carolyn a call when you're ready. Your idea is a noble one, but I hope I'm not offending you when I say that it just might not be a realistic one in light of the cost. Nevertheless, if you decide to proceed, we'll meet again."

Nicholas rose from the table and extended his hand again to Michael. Michael rose from his seat and took his hand. "I look forward to hearing from you, Mr. Telford," Nicholas said as he left the room.

"Unless there are any more questions, I'd be happy to escort you out to the lobby," Carolyn said.

Michael nodded his head and Carolyn led him from her office through the photo-lined hallway to the lobby, where several people were waiting for appointments.

"Thank you for your hospitality, Carolyn," Michael said. "I'll be in touch soon."

As Michael drove away, he remained stunned by the cost that had been projected. He knew it would be expensive, but $35,000 as a start point—and God only knows what other fees might pop up—was a hard number to swallow. He realized he had been naive, but he never imagined that he would have to come up with that kind of money.

He wrestled with the idea all evening, torn between his desire to make it right for his mother and the need to have some financial stability. He tried to consider ways to raise the money for the orchestra. He knew there would be no inheritance from his mother to speak of. His salary at the university had been enough to keep him afloat, but not enough to make him a wealthy man by any stretch of the imagination. The only real savings he had was invested in a retirement plan he opened early in his career at the university.

The next morning he pulled out his financial records. His last monthly statement showed that he had almost $60,000 in the retirement plan. *Not a lot of money*, he thought; just enough to help offset the small teacher's pension and Social Security he would receive when he retired some day. That afternoon he called his retirement account representative to ask about the availability of the money and the tax implications from an early withdrawal. His financial advisor was shocked to hear that Michael was even considering withdrawing the money. When he learned what the funds would be used for he couldn't help but offer Michael a lecture on the folly of such a use of his savings. Nevertheless, he calculated that after penalties and taxes Michael would net $35,000, just enough for the concert, but at the cost of depleting all his retirement fund.

He arranged to meet with the activities director at Village Green on the following day. Joanne Holly had been in that position at the facility for twelve years, longer than any of the other senior staff members, including the administrator. In the five months since his mother had resided at the facility Mrs. Holly had always given the impression to Michael that she was a busy, busy woman; too busy, in fact, to offer much time for anyone. Michael had grown to believe that Mrs. Holly sometimes felt she was in charge of the entire operation at Village Green. He already had a chip on his shoulder because of his belief, shared by Henry, that very few activities were designed primarily for the assisted-living residents other than the musical programs offered in the evening. When he combined that chip with his resentment that she had suggested Amy's dance with him was improper, his attitude as he approached her was not positive. They met on a Wednesday afternoon in Mrs. Holly's office.

"What can I do for you today, Mr. Telford?" Mrs. Holly asked, all business as usual.

Oh, my mother is fine, thanks for asking, Michael was tempted to say, but he thought it best not to get off on that bad of a foot. Instead, he jumped right into it.

"I met a few days ago with Nicholas Shefsky and the operations manager at the symphony orchestra."

"Well, that must have been very interesting for you, Mr. Telford. I'm afraid I only have a few minutes for this meeting, so if you'd be so kind as to enlighten me, I would really appreciate it."

Michael smiled. *She really is an imperial one, isn't she?* he thought.

"Thanks for giving me a few minutes, Mrs. Holly. I'll get right to the point. I spoke with the symphony about the possibility of arranging a private concert to be held outdoors in the courtyard between the assisted-living buildings."

Mrs. Holly made no attempt to stifle a laugh. "Oh you did, did you? And did you think to perhaps secure the approval of this facility before planning such an event?" she asked. Then quickly dropping her smile, she added, "You seem to have a habit of using this facility for your own benefit without asking anyone for permission."

Michael chose to ignore the reference to the piano playing. "Actually, I thought you would be quite pleased at the thought that such a major event could possibly be held on the grounds here," Michael responded.

"You can't be serious, Mr. Telford. I have been planning activities for the residents for over a dozen years. I take my job very seriously. And I must say that I don't appreciate anyone attempting to schedule any type of event without clearing it through my office first."

Michael thought it best to try to calm her down a bit and, distasteful as it may be, appeal to her ego. "Mrs. Holly, I went to the orchestra first just to see whether the idea would even be possible. I thought that was the proper place to begin. It turns out that it is possible. Once I learned that, I immediately contacted you, because I know you are the go-to person around here when someone wants to get something accomplished." *That ought to calm her down,* Michael thought. But he was wrong.

"Mr. Telford, if you had followed proper protocol and begun with this office, you would not have wasted your time meeting with the symphony orchestra. The idea of hosting a major orchestra, and in the courtyard between the assisted-living units as well, is preposterous. The logistics of such a concert would tax our resources too heavily in terms of staff and budget. We can't afford to pay for those types of expenses. The setup, the running of electrical wires to support the event, the seating, and the security alone could easily cost $10,000. I don't have the budget for such an event."

Michael remembered the advice that Henry had given him, which was to skip Mrs. Holly and go straight to the administrator. He knew this meeting was not going to achieve anything other than to make Mrs. Holly even angrier with him, so he decided to end it abruptly and cut his losses.

"Well, thank you for your time, Mrs. Holly. Always a pleasure talking with you. I won't keep you any longer," Michael said as he stood.

Her victory in this skirmish apparently secured, Mrs. Holly fell back on her charm. "Anytime, Mr. Telford. And if you have any other ideas for activities, please don't hesitate to come to me first for a discussion."

Michael smiled and left her office, then immediately headed down the main hallway to the administrator's office. Carl Fowler had impressed Michael earlier with his compassion and his commitment to the care of all the residents at the facility. But Michael didn't envy any administrator having to come into a new environment and deal with existing staff members like Mrs. Holly, who were entrenched in their positions.

Michael caught a break when Carl spotted him just outside the office as a meeting was breaking up. They had greeted each other a number of times in the hallway over the last few months, so Carl knew that Michael was a regular visitor.

"Well hello, Michael," the younger man greeted, as he stood in the doorway of his private office. "You just can't stay away from this place, can you?" he added with a smile.

"No, I can't," Michael smiled in return. "But at this very moment you are just the man I was looking for."

"Is that right? Would you like to come in and talk for a few minutes?" Carl offered.

"Thank you. I certainly would," said Michael as he stepped into the office.

"Please have a seat. So what can I do for you today, Michael?" Carl began.

The difference in atmosphere between the opening of this meeting and the one he had just held with Mrs. Holly was palpable.

"What a magnificent view you have. I think if this was my office, I'd be tempted to sit and stare out the window most of the day," Michael began.

The trees outside Carl's office were in winter hibernation, but the grounds were still meticulously maintained. Michael stared at the yard and imagined seeing an orchestra on stage.

Carl's voice brought him back to the present. "Truth be told, and let's leave it between us if you will, I do like to sit back and stare out the window a few times a day. I'll admit to that," Carl said.

Michael turned his gaze from the window to Carl. *Why beat around the bush?*

"When I look out the window into that courtyard, I can imagine seeing a symphony orchestra performing a concert for all the residents on a beautiful, spring evening. That would be something, wouldn't it?"

"It's a beautiful thought, Michael. I don't think that the courtyard is large enough, but you could not find a prettier setting for a concert. I'll give you that. But I'm sure you didn't come in here to talk about the symphony orchestra, so what is it that I can do for you?"

Michael displayed a very large grin, and held it in place long enough that Carl's intuition kicked in.

"Or is that the reason you came in here?" Carl asked.

"You've read my mind, Carl."

Carl smiled. "Well, you don't exactly have a poker face right now, Michael. So tell me what's up."

Once again, Michael refrained from telling the story of Christmas Eve, but he filled Carl in on his grand idea, and followed that with a description of his meeting with Nicholas Shefsky at the symphony. He concluded with a description of his ill-fated meeting with the activities director just a few minutes earlier.

Carl smiled when he heard about Michael's encounter with his staff.

"Well, not to say that I agree with Mrs. Holly, but she does have a point about such an ambitious project. There's no question that it would tax our staff and financial resources to support it. And the purpose for all this is simply to please your mother? Do I have that right?"

"Well, attendance certainly wouldn't be restricted to just my mother. I think the concert would be beneficial for all the residents," Michael said.

"I'm sure it would be," replied the administrator. "Look, I'm willing to work with you, and I can assure you that Mrs. Holly would be cooperative as well, if you really are able to go forward with this. She is correct, however, that it would be a lot easier to have it indoors in our entertainment room. That would reduce our workload and expense considerably. Why must this be outside?"

Because that's the only way to make things right, Michael thought. *Was there anyone besides Henry that he could tell the full story to?* Carl Fowler was a gentleman of the highest order, but Michael still could not bring himself to discuss the real reason behind the concert. He was afraid that a full explanation would make him look like a bigger fool than he was already sounding. So he could offer no good reason for an outdoor concert, other than that he thought it would be more enjoyable for everyone if it was outside.

"Carl, I know this is a crazy notion. I honestly don't know if I can even pull it off financially. If I can, then I'll include all of your costs into my budget as well. I'm not looking for anyone's finances to suffer from this, other than my own."

Michael then turned toward the window and the view of the courtyard. "Imagine an event like that right out there. I can see it there, Carl. Can you?"

Carl turned to look out the window as well. "You are a dreamer, aren't you, Michael?" he said. "All right. I'll dream a little further with you. You make a decision on whether you really want to go forward. When you decide, you let me know. I'll do my best to find a way to help make it happen."

"Thank you, Carl. That's all I could ask. I really appreciate it."

"You're welcome. In return, how about promising me one thing as well," Carl asked.

"What's that?"

"Promise me you'll come to me first with your next, may I say, imaginative notion, rather than starting with Mrs. Holly," Carl said, smiling.

Michael laughed. "That's an easy promise for me to make. It's a deal."

After the meeting Michael was still undecided on going forward. Even though Carl Fowler didn't oppose the notion, Michael sensed that no one seemed to think the idea was any good, except for Henry. And the cost was something that would devastate his finances. As he walked to his mother's apartment for a visit, he hoped to come across Henry, and update him on what was happening. There was no sign of him, however. Helen surprised him shortly after he arrived at the apartment when she asked about Henry. Her memory of him was intact today.

"I haven't seen Henry for several days. Where do you suppose he's been?" Helen asked.

"Why don't we take a little walk and maybe we'll come across him today," Michael suggested. He still liked to take her regularly for walks to reacquaint her with all the landmarks within Village Green. As they passed outside the nurse's station, Amy emerged. "Well, hello, you two," she nodded with a smile. "It's good to see you walking around, Helen."

"You know Michael," Helen replied, while affectionately patting him on his arm. "He thinks I forget my way around so he's always trying to shore me up."

"Well, Mother," Michael smiled, "you have taken a few wrong turns before."

Looking at Amy, he continued, "We're just off on a little adventure, enjoying the sights."

Amy held his gaze, "It's good to see you, Michael. It's always nice to see folks walking around with a smile on their face."

"By the way," Michael said, "we haven't seen Henry Taylor for a spell. Is he okay?"

Amy's smile quickly faded. "No, I'm afraid Henry has been very ill for the past week. He hasn't left his room, and hasn't wanted to see anyone. Sometimes it's all I can do to get him to let me in just to perform a quick check-up."

Michael was alarmed. Stepping between his mother and Amy, he softly asked, "Do you think he's dying?"

Amy whispered back. "You know I'm not allowed to tell you about Henry's condition, Michael. I can only say that there might not be too many more opportunities for visiting him."

"What are you two whispering about?" Helen asked. "Is something wrong with Henry?"

Amy turned back to Helen, "He's not been well, Helen, and he's resting in his room."

"I'll go visit him tonight, Mother, and let you know what I find. How's that?" Michael suggested.

Helen nodded her approval.

"Now you two get moving," Amy scolded. "Don't let me catch you standing around here again."

"You heard the nurse, Mother," Michael smiled. "Let's get moving."

"All right," Helen responded, "But don't wear these tired old legs to the bone, Michael. Let's head back to the apartment."

As they headed back upstairs, Helen looked pensive to Michael.

"Are you okay?" he asked.

"Will you check on Henry today and let me know? It doesn't seem right that he's all alone in his room."

"I'll go today, Mother."

"Will you come see me again after that?" she asked.

He smiled. "Of course."

CHAPTER 12

After settling Helen down at the apartment with one of her favorite game shows, Michael walked over to Henry's apartment.

He knocked softly before calling out, "Henry, it's Michael Telford."

The door opened, and Michael found himself looking into the tired eyes of Henry's daughter, Jackie.

"Hello, Jackie," Michael said, offering his hand. "Is everything all right?"

Jackie motioned for him to step back into the hallway. She stepped out as well and closed the apartment door softly.

"I don't think we should talk in there," Jackie said.

Just down the hall they found two wing chairs. Michael could see that Jackie was very tired. "How are you doing, Jackie?" he asked.

She offered a wan smile. "It's nice of you to ask, Michael. I'm awfully tired. It's hard to see him slip away and not be able to do what I really want to do with him."

"What do you mean?" he prompted.

"Dad is dying, Michael," she answered, tears streaming down her face. "And I can't help him anymore." With those words she began to let the anguish pour out through her tears.

Michael leaned forward and rested a hand softly on her back. "I'm so sorry, Jackie," he said, and then sat quietly while she wept.

In a minute Jackie began to calm. She sat up, fishing through her jacket pocket for a tissue to dry her eyes. She smiled at Michael. "Thank you for sitting with me," she said. "This has been so hard."

"Well, I've only known your father for six months, but in that time he's always been a pleasure to be with. I know my mother feels the same way."

"You two have been wonderful to Dad," she smiled in return, tears still in her eyes. "Sometimes I think he won't shut up about the two of you," she laughed. "It was so kind of you to have him for Thanksgiving. I know I never really thanked you for that, but I have remembered it. That was so sweet. He really enjoyed the day, spending time with your family."

Michael smiled, and when he remained silent, she continued. "He needs to go to hospice now, Michael, but he won't hear of it. I've actually had a hospice nurse in yesterday and today. He's dying," she cried.

Michael took her hand. "Is there anything I can do?"

Jackie looked up, "I wish there was," she replied.

"Can I go in to see him?" Michael asked.

Jackie patted his hand in return. "Sure you can. I think it would be good for him, and maybe good for you, too, Michael."

Silence returned again as they both looked down, lost in their thoughts.

Jackie was the first to speak again. She offered a small laugh, and looked up. "Are you planning some kind of concert out here, Michael? It's one thing he keeps talking about that makes no sense to me. He keeps talking about a symphony, and how he remembers how much he enjoyed having an orchestra play for my mother. I can't tell if he's serious about this concert idea, or if he's making something up in his mind."

Michael smiled in return. "Well, it's a long story, Jackie. But I will tell you Henry isn't making it up. If anyone has made something up, it's been me."

Jackie smiled again. "Well, that's good to know. I was afraid he was getting delusional on me. I'm going back home for a rest. I'm worn out. I hate to leave because I'm afraid I won't be around when the end comes."

"I understand," Michael offered. "You say he's refusing hospice?"

"He'll see the hospice nurse," Jackie replied, "and he'll let the staff nurse in, Amy especially, but he won't leave the room. He says he refuses to die in hospice or in a hospital. I'm surprised the staff here hasn't ordered him out. Sometimes I think he's got some of them wrapped around his little finger, but it doesn't matter now. He's not going anywhere, and there's nothing I can do about it."

"I'd be happy to visit," Michael said.

"Thanks," she replied. "I'll be back tomorrow morning, unless they call me sooner."

As Jackie rose, Michael patted her on the shoulder. She dabbed her eyes again with her tissue, smiled, and walked to the elevator.

Michael returned to Henry's door, knocked twice softly, then entered without waiting for a response. He walked into the bedroom, where he was shocked to see Henry's pallor. He looked years older, pale and worn, but he summoned the strength to offer a small smile and nod.

"Hello, Michael," he offered. "You're just the man I've been waiting for."

"Well, thanks, Henry," Michael replied, sitting down on the chair next to the bed. "I've just been talking with Jackie."

"Oh, you have now," he said slowly. "So I take it from your demeanor that you know the medical folks are of the opinion that the end is near for me."

Michael was moved to hear these words spoken so directly. He could only nod his head, tears beginning to form in his eyes.

"It's all right, Michael," Henry reassured him. "It comes to all of us. Your time will come someday, just like your father's did. Now it's my turn. Don't cry, Michael. I'm ready for it. In fact, I welcome it now."

"You do?" Michael asked in wonder.

"We're all going to die, Michael. You know that. I'm just glad that I'm aware of it, and that I've been able to have a clear mind these last few days," Henry said. "I've been waiting for you."

"You have?" Michael asked. "I didn't know until earlier today that you've been so ill, or I would have been here sooner. No one told me you were asking for me."

"Calm down, son," Henry soothed. "I spoke to no one about having you visit. But I figured you would stop by one of these days to help me along. And now you're here."

"Help you along?"

"Yes, that's what I said. I'm going to need your help in two days' time."

"What would you like me to do?"

"Nothing for now. Just promise me you'll be back two nights from now. Eight o'clock would be fine. I'll need you for about an hour. It would be wise if you did not speak about our appointment to anyone. If Jackie is here when you arrive just hang around until she leaves. Is that all clear?"

"It's all clear, Henry, but why the secrecy? What's going on? Are you all right?"

"I'm a little sick these days, Michael, as I believe you know, but I'll be better in two days' time when you arrive."

"Okay, Henry. I'll be back in two days. You're worrying me a little here, but I'll be back."

"Good man. I knew I could count on you," Henry said. "Now, why don't you get going? I'm pretty tired and I want to save up my strength for our next visit."

Michael was totally confused when he left. He had a bad feeling that Henry was up to something, but he felt he owed it to the old man to respect his confidence for the next couple of days.

He walked slowly through the hallways to his mother's apartment. Once there he found her with Amy, who was administering the evening medicines and helping her change into her nightgown.

"How is Henry?" Helen asked. "You were gone a long time. I was afraid you forgot to come back."

Michael smiled grimly at his mother, and at Amy, too. "He's very ill, Mother. I think his time with us is drawing to a close. So why don't you say a prayer for him tonight when you lie down?"

"I will, son," she said, and her memory issues quickly arose again. "I didn't even know he was sick."

"I know, Mother. You get some rest now, and I'll stop by tomorrow and talk some more."

"Promise?" she asked.

"Promise. Now let's get you under the covers."

He and Amy tucked her in and said good night. Back in the hallway, Amy spoke first.

"Sometimes the memory issues make it easier for someone like Helen to hear about a good friend dying."

"Yes, you're right," Michael said quietly.

"How was your visit?"

"It was short, actually. I met with his daughter for a while. She's gone home for the evening. She wants Henry to go to hospice or a hospital, but he won't hear of it. She's taking it hard, like you would expect."

"And Henry?"

"He seems stoic to me. Like he expects to stand up and embrace death," Michael answered.

"My shift ends soon. I think I'll go visit him then," Amy said.

"He seemed pretty tired when I left him," he said. "I think he was going to sleep."

"Well, that's good. Maybe I'll wait then till I come back tomorrow."

"Good idea, Amy," Michael smiled. "I know he likes you, like everyone does."

"Present company included?" she asked with a big smile.

"You can count on that," Michael said with another smile. "We're still on for Saturday evening, I hope."

Amy held his gaze and his smile. "We sure are. Now I've got more meds to deliver tonight."

"I hope I see you tomorrow then," Michael said.

"So do I, Michael. Let's make a point of it," she smiled.

Amy resumed pushing the medicine cart down the hall. Michael watched her walk to the next apartment, where she took up her chart, a cup of pills and knocked on the door before entering. Just before she stepped into the apartment, she looked back at Michael, still standing in the hall, smiled, and said, "Shush now. Get going."

Michael smiled, waved, and after Amy had entered the apartment, he turned back to the staircase to leave.

Michael decided to alter his routine when he arrived for his meeting with Henry two nights later. Instead of walking through the main facility and visiting his mother first he thought it best to park out front where he usually did, but walk around the buildings to the rear and take a back entrance and stairs to get to Henry's apartment. Henry wanted Michael to be quiet about this visit, which Michael found troubling, but walking around to the rear would at least partially comply with Henry's request.

Once he arrived on the floor he saw Jackie leaving her father's apartment. She looked even more worn and tired. Michael stepped back around the hallway until Jackie had reached the elevator at the end of the other hall. Once she was on the elevator, he proceeded to Henry's door.

He didn't knock this time, which was a first for him. He just opened the door at the appointed hour and walked in.

Henry heard him enter and called out. "Is that you, Michael?"

"Yes, it is."

"Good man. Come on back."

Michael entered Henry's bedroom and found him looking drawn and pale.

"Thank you for coming. I knew I could count on you," Henry began.

"I'm happy to be here, Henry, but what is it you're counting on me to do? It feels like there's some mystery going on here."

Henry offered a weak smile. "I need your help so that I can get out of here tonight."

Michael was astounded at the idea. "What are you talking about? Making a getaway?"

"That's exactly what I mean," Henry said with as much bearing as he could muster. "I want to go for one more walk, Michael," Henry continued, now with a firmer voice. "I've been waiting for the day, and now it's here. I want to take a walk, and I want you to help me make that happen."

"What do you mean, Henry? It's already dark outside, and a little chilly, too. You want us to go for a walk now?"

"Not us, Michael." Henry stated. "Just me."

"Henry," Michael said slowly, searching carefully for his words. "What are you planning here, and what is it you want me to do? I need to talk to the nurses first before I help you up and out for a walk."

"Now listen to me, Michael," Henry said again in a voice that seemed to be growing stronger in spite of his weak condition. "I mean to take my walk. It's important to me. I need to get out of this building one more time. And I need your help for that to happen. I'm not asking you to break any laws. I am asking you to help me quietly, but all I want is for you to help lay out my clothes for me first, and in a little while I'll want you to assist me getting to the staircase at the end of the hall. I've only got so much energy left. I need to save it for my walk."

"This doesn't sound good, Henry," Michael said. "Why don't I ask Amy to come up to help?"

"No, Michael," Henry strongly stated again. "It's your help, and yours alone, that I want. Jackie's gone home to rest, and I'm glad for that. I need a friend now to get my clothes, my hat and coat, and some shoes ready for me. I'd like you to lay them out for me right here on the bed. Can you do that for me, Michael?"

"Henry, I don't like this idea. I have to tell you that."

"I can see that, son, but I need you now. Don't let me down, please."

Hearing those words, Michael recalled the lunch visit with his father six years earlier, where he was asked by a dying man to not let him down. "Okay, Henry, I'll help."

"Good lad. Now we'll keep it simple. Just a clean, white shirt, some dark pants, and my black shoes. Lay them over here next to me."

Michael chose the clothing from the dresser and laid it on the bed, then went to the closet to fetch the shoes. As he returned to the bed with the shoes, he saw Henry trying to lay the clothes out under the blanket. When Michael approached, Henry looked up with a smile.

"I'll put these on after you're gone. No sense upsetting any of the nurses that might walk in on me now, is there?"

Michael smiled for the first time since he entered the apartment. "What are you up to, Henry?"

"Michael, I think it's best for you that there not be full disclosure this evening. Do you understand?"

Michael's smile slid away, and alarm crept into his voice. "Where are you going, Henry?"

"I want to take a private walk, Michael, like a man. I've walked all my life. Whenever I wanted to. Dawn, evenings, three o'clock in the morning. I've walked at all hours, and now I want to walk once more."

Henry took the shoes and tucked them under the covers. "Now get me my coat and hat, please."

Michael retrieved the items from the closet and watched Henry slide them safely beneath the covers.

"Now what?" Michael asked.

"Now, my good young man, I want you to say farewell and go look in on your mother before you tell her you're going home for the night. In an hour I want you to come back to my room and knock three times. I don't want you to come in. We'll say our farewells now. When you return just knock three times if there is no one about in the hallways. I will need some privacy, as you can imagine, to walk to the staircase."

"Will you be returning tonight after your walk?" Michael asked.

"You've been a good friend, Michael, and now a trusted one. It would not be wise for us to discuss anything more about my walk than what we have already. I'd like you to leave me now, quietly. Your help here this evening is something that you and I will keep between us. That's important to remember. Sound all right to you?"

Michael stared at the old man, who reminded him more and more of his long-gone father. "I want to say it's all right, but I have to tell you I have a bad feeling about this, Henry."

"Of course you do, son. And it's okay that you do. Just so long as you honor our agreement. You're committing no crime here. You've just had a little conversation with an old man."

"But how are you going to get out of here for a walk? You look so weak."

"I'm ready for it now, Michael. I've been planning this for a long time. You'd be amazed what a man can do when he sets his mind to it, no matter how sick he might be. I'll take my walk. Don't worry about that."

A silence fell over the room.

Henry spoke again. "Go say hello to your mother for me, Michael. You're a good man. Your father would be proud of the man you've grown to be. Take care of your mother. And don't give up on your concert dream. Make it happen, Michael. I know you believe it's the right thing to do. I think so, too."

With those words, Henry lifted his hand from the bed, offering one last shake. Michael took his hand. Henry's grip was not as strong as in times past, but Michael could still sense some reserve of strength.

"Thank you, Henry. I hope I don't regret what I'm doing for you tonight. Will I see you tomorrow?"

Henry smiled warmly, and slipped his hand out of Michael's grasp. "I think you know the answer to that, Michael. Now, off with you."

Michael fought to offer a smile to Henry in return, fresh tears again in his eyes. "Thank you for your friendship, Henry," he said as he turned toward the doorway.

"Oh, I almost forgot. There's an envelope with your name on it under the socks in my dresser. Will you get that out before you go?"

Michael opened the dresser and found the slim envelope. "What's this?" he asked.

"Something for you to open later. Maybe not for a few days. Give me a head start first."

Michael turned back to Henry and shook his head sadly. "Good night, Henry. I'll check on you tomorrow."

"You do that, young man," Henry nodded. "You do that. Now, good night and thanks."

Henry laid his head back onto his pillow.

"Good night, Henry," Michael said one last time, and walked out of the apartment.

As Michael walked toward his mother's apartment he kept wondering if he shouldn't notify someone about Henry's plan. Michael had feared over the last few days that something crazy was being hatched by Henry, but he really didn't think until now that Henry was going to simply march off, never to be seen again.

Much as Michael worried about the idea, part of him kept thinking that Henry was entitled to have him keep his word. Henry deserved to be able to take a walk when he figured that one more walk was all he had.

He found his mother getting ready for bed. It was quarter past eight, and she was tired. He helped her finish getting ready for bed, and once she crawled under the covers he sat on the edge of the bed to talk for a while.

"What do you think Dad was thinking when we walked him to the car on his last trip to the hospital?" he asked his mother.

"That's an odd question," she responded.

"I've been thinking about that walk recently. On my way here tonight it came back to me again. I didn't know that Dad was dying at the time. I wish I had. But I keep wondering what was going through his mind at the time."

"He didn't want to go. He knew what was lying ahead. And that day he wasn't ready to accept that his time was coming."

"You knew it all the while, didn't you?"

Helen smiled. "Of course I did. I lived with your father for a long time. I knew he was failing. I had suggested the hospital two days earlier, but he begged me not to take him there. So I waited. Finally, I began to cry because I was so worried, and he told me to call the doctor. After that I called you."

"I wish I had told him that I loved him when we were holding each other as we walked across the room."

"Michael, you can tell someone you love them in many ways. You don't have to use words. You told him. Just by being there and holding him you told him. He knew it all along."

Michael took hold of his mother's hand. "You're a wise old hen, aren't you?"

"I have my moments."

"Thanks for tonight, Mother," Michael said as he bent over to kiss her on the cheek. "I'll be back tomorrow to see you."

"Promise?"

"You can count on it. Now get some sleep."

Michael turned out the lamp in the living room and quietly left the apartment. At the end of the hall he found a sofa near a window overlooking the courtyard. It was quarter til nine, so Michael sat down to wait for his appointed time.

He wondered whether he had said enough to Henry, just as he always wondered about that day with his father.

He was pondering what his mother had just told him about demonstrating your love for someone without the need for expressing the words themselves. That was a comforting thought. Now he hoped that he was doing the same for Henry. Henry wasn't his father, of course, but he was a fine man that

Michael had learned to care about. He hoped that Henry could see that Michael's support tonight was an expression of love. *God knows, it's an expression of something,* he said to himself, almost laughing. *What in heaven's name have I agreed to do?*

A grandfather clock outside one of the resident's apartments struck nine bells, and drew Michael out of his reverie. He gathered himself and set off again to Henry's apartment.

When he reached the hallway on Henry's floor, he saw one of the nurses just finishing up her evening dispensing of medicines. He waited down the hall so that she didn't see him. After she had finished her charts, she took the medicine cart to the elevator and went down to the second floor to continue her work.

At that point no one was about in the hallway. Michael waited for another few minutes just to be sure the nurse hadn't forgotten anyone. The place was quiet, though, and he was certain the coast was clear as he walked down the rest of the hallway to Henry's door.

Once there he was sorely tempted to walk in and offer the old man one more hail and farewell. But he knew that was not what Henry wanted. He had already made his good-byes. It was time now to keep his word.

He looked around the hallway one more time. It remained quiet. He knocked three times, then walked down the hall away from where Henry intended to head. He was sure that Henry would not want to see him again, so he turned the corner at the end of the hallway. But curiosity forced him to stop there and wait. He peeked around the corner to see Henry quietly closing his apartment door. He was dressed in hat and coat, ready to go. Henry looked down toward Michael's end of the hall, and Michael ducked his head back. After a moment he chanced to peek again and saw Henry amble off toward the end of the hall. Once he reached the end of the hallway, Henry paused and looked back down the long hall one more time. He tipped his cap, as if he knew Michael was down there watching him, then opened the door to the staircase and slipped out.

Michael smiled to himself. *He knew I couldn't resist watching him leave. Okay, Henry. Hats off to you, too. Good luck.* Michael then headed off to the rear staircase at the other side of the building. *Best he be discreet this evening*, he thought. He didn't want to run into anyone else tonight.

CHAPTER 13

Once he was safely outside, Michael paused to sit on one of the benches at the back of the courtyard. He had parked his car near the front of Village Green rather than in the lot near his mother's apartment. He always enjoyed the walk through the grounds. Tonight he looked forward to it again, but he didn't want to hurry for fear that he might run into Henry coming from the other side of the building.

The air was brisk, as the sky was wide open, filled with stars and a bright half moon. It was a beautiful night to be out, he thought. He sat for ten minutes before beginning the walk around the buildings to the front lawn.

On reaching the front of the property Michael peered down the long drive that led to the street. He saw a cab turn in, then stop before pulling down the drive. He thought he could see someone silhouetted in the headlights of the vehicle. *Is that Henry,* he wondered? *Is that him?*

The rear door of the taxi opened and someone got into the back seat. The taxi sat for a moment longer before the driver backed out of the drive onto the street rather than drive up and turn around in the circle by the main building where Michael stood. Michael couldn't be certain, but he had a strong feeling that he had just seen Henry drive away in the cab.

Henry was pleased that the cab driver spotted him near the entrance to the property. He didn't want to be seen near the front of the building, but he was afraid the driver would miss him in the darkness. The driver found him, though, and Henry breathed a sigh of relief before opening the door and climbing into the back seat.

"Where to, sir?" the driver asked his passenger as the back door was closed.

"Not far," said Henry. "289 Knollwood Drive. It's off Carson Avenue in College Hill."

The driver looked in his rearview mirror. "Are you a resident here, sir?"

Henry laughed. "Oh, good heavens, no," he replied. "My sister lives here. I was just out here visiting for the day."

Henry was relieved that the driver chose to back out onto the main road rather than go up the driveway and pull around the front of the building. He thought he had seen someone at the top of the drive just as he had entered the car. He wondered whether Michael was out looking for him. He wouldn't doubt it. He had seen him peeking around the corner of the hallway when he had left the apartment. That wasn't surprising. Michael was a good man, but it was just as well that he didn't drive by anyone he might know. College Hill was only about fifteen minutes away. If he could just make it there without interruption, he would be fine.

The rest of the drive passed in pleasant silence. Fortunately, Henry did not have to keep up a conversation with the driver. He was already exhausted from dressing himself and exiting the building unseen. He had chosen to take the stairs rather than risk being seen coming off an elevator. That meant he had to exit at the rear of his building and take the long walk around. But he knew that was the only way he could get out on his own. Besides, he told Michael he wanted a final walk, didn't he?

They were nearing Carson Avenue and the turn to Knollwood Drive.

"How far down, sir?" the driver asked as he turned onto Knollwood.

"I'll point it out for you," Henry responded. "It's the second to last drive on the left."

As they reached a driveway a few houses up from his own Henry called out, "This will do me fine right here."

"This is 281 Knollwood, sir. I thought you wanted 289. Looks like that's one further."

Henry realized he had slipped up, giving the driver the correct address when he first entered the cab, rather than the house next door, which is where he wanted to quietly exit the cab.

"Forgive an old man, sir. It's 281. This is it right here. I'll just hop out at the driveway and walk up. What's the fare?"

"It's $12.80. No offense intended, sir, but that looks like a long driveway. Why don't you let me take you up to the house?"

"No, thanks, that won't be necessary. I need to finish my walk tonight," Henry responded, while pulling a twenty out of his wallet and handing it to the driver. "Here you are, sir, thanks for the lift."

The driver took the bill and reached into his pocket to make change.

"Keep it, my good man," Henry said as he opened the door and stepped out. "Thanks for your help."

"Good night, sir," the driver replied, idling in his vehicle as he watched Henry begin the ascent up the driveway at 281 Knollwood. The driveway turned to the right about twenty yards up. Once Henry reached that point and was lost from view, the driver put the cab in gear and drove off.

Henry had climbed the steep driveway until it turned away from the road. There he stopped to lean against a tree. He had looked over his shoulder once and had seen that the driver was still sitting on the road. So he had no choice but to keep walking until he slipped out of sight. He was exhausted now. He hadn't counted on walking so far up the wrong driveway. Now he needed to walk back down the driveway, then another hundred yards down the road to his driveway before beginning the ascent up his long, twisting drive.

He wanted to rest where he was standing, he felt so weary. But he knew that if he stopped now his evening would end here, so he summoned every ounce of his strength and set off back down the driveway. His pace was exceedingly slow. The temperature was low and he felt his legs begin to ache. Once he neared the roadway he paused to rest again. There were no street lights on the road to interfere with the view of the stars on this clear night. He tried to catch his breath while he gazed at the sky. Orion stood out brilliantly. He'd always enjoyed this time of evening, gazing at the stars. *I wonder if that's Jupiter over there.* A slight wind served as a reminder to him to keep moving. Now that he was at the roadway, he needed to walk as fast as his old legs would take him so that no one would see him. There would be no place to hide if someone came along. Fortunately, Knollwood was a quiet street, populated with homes that all had several acres of ground surrounding them. After another few minutes of walking, he made it to his driveway without another car driving by.

Once he reached the mailbox at the foot of the driveway, Henry paused to stare up the long, twisting lane. Here he was at last. Home. The grounds were quiet and beautiful. It had been well over a year since he had seen his home of fifty years. There had been many changes to it over the years, but it had always been his shelter, his refuge, and, in his mind, the place where he wanted to die.

After first taking another deep breath, he began the climb. Thirty yards up the darkened lane, a glade of pine trees began to parallel the drive, and he stepped off the blacktop onto the familiar bed of needles beneath the canopy of the white pines. Two steps further in he was enveloped by the darkness. The moon and star light did not penetrate these trees.

He was so tired now, but he kept climbing, looking for just the right spot. There was a particularly wide-based pine at the top of this stand of trees. It was a favorite of his. He had planted the tree himself almost fifty years ago, along with all the others he was now hiking past. This one, however, was the most majestic of all, in his view, and a favorite reading and pondering place for him over the years, particularly after his wife died.

Twenty more steps found him at his destination. *I don't know if I could have gone any farther.* It was even colder now. He bundled his arms around himself, leaning his head back against the trunk, so very cold. His shivering began, followed by a doubt. *Is this really what I wanted,* he asked himself. *Is it really time for it all to end? Here? Alone?*

The cold was quickly seeping into his bones. He stretched out his arm and gathered some more pine needles into a small pile, then slid further down the tree to lay his head on them. It was cold, but once he rested his head in his old familiar spot, he felt his doubts slide away. *I've dreamed about this moment,* he thought.

He could see his home clearly now. There were a few lights on inside. Jackie was probably there. His only regret now was the pain he knew he would be causing his sweet daughter. The only way he could justify that in his mind was to believe that, even in her grief, she would understand this was how he needed to go. He was tired of the nurses and the doctors. Tired of the hospitals. And tired of the nursing home. That was no way to live, and once he had been told by his physician that his days were numbered, he concluded it was no place to die either.

She'll understand, he rationalized. *She'll understand.* The cold was penetrating. It was getting harder for him to get a good deep breath. His lungs began to ache, and he could feel that he was about to slip into unconsciousness.

Before the darkness fully overtook him he looked back toward his home. As his eyes settled upon the house, he saw the living room lights go out.

"Good night, my sweet Jackie," he said softly, so softly even the breeze could not carry it aloft. Images from the past raced through his mind, and suddenly the cold no longer bothered him. He sensed some higher power waiting for him to complete his journey. He watched as the last light within the home was extinguished. Henry closed his eyes, and a few moments later the light within him was extinguished as well.

CHAPTER 14

Michael arrived at Village Green the following morning to find police in the hallway and general commotion all about. He came across Amy outside the nurse's station, visibly upset. She had just finished being interviewed for a second time by a police officer. "Henry is missing," she cried to Michael. "Sometime during the night one of the nurses went in to check on him and found his apartment empty. Michael, I'm so worried for him. You know how sick he is. Do you have any idea where he might be?"

My God, did he really go off and die? Even though he knew Henry was planning something, it was still a shock to think that he may be gone for good. As much as he wanted to tell Amy everything he knew, he was torn about discussing anything about last night. Instead, he chose to give an easy answer, since he really didn't know where Henry might be.

"I'm afraid I'd only be guessing," he said. "I'm so sorry, Amy. I know how close you are to Henry."

Michael felt sick in deceiving Amy. Yet, now with the police around, he wondered if he may be complicit in some crime by having helped Henry with his clothes last night. Fortunately, Amy didn't pick up on any of the feelings coursing through Michael's body.

"Thanks, Michael. I just hope he turns up soon. You better get up to your mother's apartment and check in on her. It seems like all the residents are already aware of Henry's absence. She may be, too."

Michael was glad to get away from the police scene, so he scurried off to the elevator. Just as Amy had predicted, his mother was already aware of the mystery. The story had circulated in the dining room at breakfast that morning.

Her first words were, "Did you hear about Henry?"

"Yes, I did," Michael said. "It sounds like there's a lot of people looking for him."

"Where do you think he went to?" Helen asked. "Back to his home?"

"That's a real possibility, Mother. I don't really know."

After talking in the apartment for an hour, it was time for Helen's lunch. Michael walked her downstairs toward the dining room. Once they reached the nurse's station they heard the news that Henry's body had been discovered. The police had questioned local cab agencies, and late in the morning had found the driver who had taken Henry from Village Green.

Amy met Michael and Helen in the hall outside the dining room, where she told them what she had just learned.

"The police believe Henry called for a taxi from his room, then walked out of the building and met the cab near the front entrance of the property. They say the cabdriver took Henry to his old street, but not to the right home. The driver was a little suspicious, but once he saw Henry walk up what he thought was the right driveway, he figured everything was all right."

Helen was distressed, and asked Michael to help her sit down. Amy looked at Michael to see if he wanted her to continue. Michael nodded to her to go on.

"For some reason Henry got out of the cab up the street from his home. Then he must have tried to find his way home. What happened next is hard to understand. Maybe Henry just became confused while he was walking. At any rate, he was found by the police on his property next to a large, old pine tree. He died sometime during the night. I can't believe it."

Michael had anticipated something like this, but the news was still chilling. He knew in his heart that Henry was planning to exit this life. But hearing the news aloud was a shock. He and Amy sat down with his mother.

"That poor man," Helen said. Then, with a flash of clarity, she added, "I wish this hadn't happened. But I know that Henry wanted to die at his home. Maybe he just decided it was time to get his wish."

Amy and Michael each looked at Helen in astonishment.

"Helen, did Henry tell you he was going to do this?" Amy asked.

"No, dear," Helen replied. "I didn't know he would choose last night to die, but I knew this was what he wanted to do."

Michael and Amy exchanged glances, before Michael asked, "When did Henry talk about this?"

"Oh, some time ago. I can't remember when. We talked about a lot of things at dinner time," Helen answered. She then looked over at Michael and began to cry.

Michael hugged her while Amy took Helen's hand.

"It's alright," Michael said. "He was a good friend, wasn't he?" Helen nodded.

"I think you're right about Henry, Mother," Michael said. "It's sad and it's hard to believe, but maybe this is what he wanted to do."

Amy couldn't buy into the theory yet. But she knew that she couldn't discount Helen's thought either.

"Why don't you two get a little something to eat," Amy suggested. "It will do you good, Helen. Michael, will you stop by the nurse's station before you leave?"

"Sure, I will," Michael said, as he helped Helen up from her chair and walked with her into the dining room.

The two of them sat at a quiet table in the corner and ordered soup and coffee. After their food was served, Michael asked his mother how she was feeling.

"I don't know, Michael," she said. "Part of me thinks this is what Henry wanted, so I guess I should be happy for him. But mostly I'm scared."

"Scared?"

"Yes. Henry knew what he wanted to do, and he did it. He was a brave man. I'm not that brave. I don't know when it will come for me."

"Mother, are you talking about dying? Did you and Henry talk about all this?"

Helen nodded. "We talked about a lot of things. He told me he was sick, and that he was going to find a way to go home to die."

"Have you told anyone about this?"

"Just what I said to Amy."

Helen studied Michael's face before speaking again. "Michael, you were here visiting last night, weren't you?"

Michael smiled and nodded his head.

"Did you see Henry last night? Did you help him?" she asked.

Michael looked at his mother closely, then reached across the table and took her hand.

"This is a delicate matter, now, Mother. Maybe I did see Henry last night. And maybe we shouldn't say anything further about that."

Helen stared into Michael's eyes. Then she smiled and said, "Henry wanted to be alone when he died. He told me that. And it sounds like he got his wish. I wonder how I'll feel when that time comes."

"Let's not dwell on that, right now. You've got more living to do."

"Michael, maybe this is a good time to talk about dying. I know you think I've got a lot more living to do, but I'm tired, just like Henry was."

"Do you want to be alone at the end? I thought you would want us all to be together like we were for Dad."

"I love having you all around. And I don't want to be lonely at the end. But I know you're not ready for me to go yet, so maybe when the time comes I'll just slip away when you're not looking. Would that be alright with you?"

"I can't believe we're talking about this now."

"It's okay, Michael. All of a sudden it feels good to talk about it."

After they finished their coffee, Helen said, "This whole business has worn me out. I think I want to rest for awhile."

"Would it be alright if I asked an aide to walk you back to the apartment?"

"That's fine with me. You go ahead and run on. Will you be back again later?"

"You know it."

Michael found an aide in the hallway who agreed to escort Helen back upstairs, then he headed toward the nurse's station.

"You wanted to see me?" he asked Amy as she came out of the office.

Amy motioned for him to walk with her toward the door. As he walked alongside her she said, "Michael, I've really been looking forward to our dinner on Saturday, but I'm afraid the funeral for Henry might be that day, and I just feel funny celebrating something in the midst of this tragedy."

Michael was disappointed, but he understood. "I know what you're saying. How about we postpone, not cancel. How does that sound?"

Amy smiled. "I like the sound of it, Michael. It's just a postponement."

Michael gently placed his hand on her shoulder as they paused at the exit. Amy smiled, touched her hand to his, then turned back toward the nurse's station.

As Michael neared the door at the front of the building he came upon Carl Fowler, who was just entering.

Michael paused as Carl walked in, shaking his head in disbelief.

"Carl, this must be a terrible ordeal for you."

Carl removed his hat and gloves. "What a tragedy. I just came from Henry's home."

"How is Jackie taking this?"

"As you would expect. Shocked and angry that we could have allowed something like this to happen."

"Are you being blamed for this?" Michael asked.

"When something like this happens, Michael, blame becomes a natural part of anyone's reaction."

"Surely you don't feel responsible for this though, do you?"

"Do I feel personally responsible? No, I don't. Did our facility somehow let Henry and his daughter down? Right now I feel like the answer to that is yes. I don't know what we could have done differently, short of insisting that anyone as ill as Henry be transported to hospice or a hospital."

"Do you think he just marched out of here to find a place to die?"

Carl grimaced, and then nodded his head affirmatively.

"I visited Henry in his room yesterday morning," Carl said. "Jackie had called me and asked that I try to convince her father that he should go to hospice. I tried, but to no avail."

Michael nodded his head. "What was Henry like at your visit, if you don't mind my asking?"

"No, I don't mind. I used to see the two of you huddled together in conversation from time to time. I knew he became one of your friends, too," Carl replied. "You know, it's a funny thing about yesterday. It was clear Henry was gravely ill. Yet I could still sense a fire within him. I felt he was determined to do something. At the time I thought he hadn't accepted that death was so near and he was determined to fight it. Now, I wonder if I misread him."

"Do you think now that the determination you saw was that he was planning to die on his own terms?" Michael asked.

Carl studied Michael closely.

"Exactly," he said.

A silence descended between the two. After a minute, Carl spoke.

"Is there anything you can add to this mystery, Michael?"

Michael offered a rueful smile. He could only imagine the pain that a good administrator like Carl must be feeling, and the questions that were going to be raised about his facility. Still, there was nothing he could say that would bring Henry back. He could see that Carl had drawn the same conclusion that Helen reached. Henry had decided to die at his home. What good would it do to betray the plan Henry had confided in him?

"I think Henry was prepared to die. And he decided that he would choose where his final breath would occur. That's as much as I can add."

Carl nodded his head, while still gazing strongly at Michael.

"Did you know he was fully dressed?" Carl asked. "Pants, shirt, sweater, hat, coat, gloves. He got fully dressed, in his condition, and somehow reached the front entrance to catch a cab. Yet there's no sign that he had any kind of help. How he did all that by himself," Carl paused for emphasis, "by himself mind you, is pretty difficult for me to comprehend."

Michael simply nodded his acknowledgment.

"You weren't by chance out here last night, were you, Michael?"

The question struck a chord deep in Michael's gut. *This is dangerous territory. Be careful now.*

"Yes, I was, as a matter of fact. I was out here around eight o'clock. I visited Mother for just a short while."

Carl nodded.

"There are a lot of police around here today, asking a lot of questions. Has anyone interviewed you, Michael?"

Michael swallowed, and felt like Carl and everyone else in the building had heard what sounded like a gulp.

"No. No one's asked me anything. I was just leaving when you came in."

Carl continued to stare at Michael before giving him a very tight smile. "Maybe you ought to scoot, Michael. I'm sure you have things to attend to elsewhere."

Michael knew then that Carl was somehow on to him. But he was going to let him off the hook.

"You're right, Carl. I have a class to teach this afternoon. I better get moving so I have time to prepare."

Michael walked out of the building, as Carl headed inside to face more of the music. As Michael walked across the grounds to his car, he reflected on how he had just failed to be honest with both Amy and Carl, two people he had great respect for. *Oh, Henry. You've stirred things up for a lot of people.* Michael got into his car and paused before driving off. Was he doing the right thing, not being honest with Carl and Amy? Aside from his worry about the police getting involved in his life, was it right to keep them in the dark? On the other hand, what good would it do? Henry was gone. *I've got no choice now,* he thought, and drove away.

✳

Funeral services for Henry were conducted Saturday morning. Michael and Helen attended. Each of them was moved by the emotional service.

A few elderly men and women that Michael took to be uncles or cousins sat with an inconsolable Jackie. The minister presiding had been a long-time friend of the family. His homily was very personal, filled with examples of many acts of generosity performed by Henry over the years.

At the reception afterwards Michael and Helen offered their sympathies to Jackie, who was still in shock, and devastated at the thought that her father had died in the cold so close to their home. She was convinced that he was trying to get to the house and had expired on the way. Michael didn't know what to say other than it was probably a mystery that would never be solved. Jackie nodded her head in agreement, then turned to give Helen a hug.

"I'm so sorry, sweetheart," Helen said. "I hope you don't blame yourself in any way. Your father died just where he wanted to be. That's what I believe. You didn't let him down."

Jackie stared intently at Helen, then hugged her again, before saying, "Thank you for saying that. You were a good friend to my father, and now to me."

"You have a lot of friends here for you now, Jackie," Helen replied. "We'll be heading out now. You take care."

Jackie smiled at Helen, then turned to Michael and shook her head. "You've got a wonderful mother here, Michael. You take good care of her."

Michael smiled before giving Jackie a hug, then took his mother's hand to leave.

"The poor girl," Helen said, as Jackie walked away to greet other friends.

"I'm afraid it would be easy for someone to take on a sense of blame, wouldn't it?" Michael said. "I guess it's pretty easy to believe that Henry wanted to get to the house itself and just couldn't make it. With her inside that night, she must feel awful."

"I know," Helen said. "But I'm not so sure Henry was trying to reach the house itself. Maybe he just wanted to see it again from the outside, and that's all he needed."

"You really have this figured out pretty well, don't you?"

"Well, I have watched a few mystery shows in my day."

The two of them knew few others in the room so they headed toward the exit. Near the door, a gentleman approached them. The man introduced himself as Daniel Baylor, Henry's long-time attorney, and asked Michael if he could have a private word with him.

Michael found a seat for his mother and stepped to the side of the room to speak with the attorney.

"I won't take but a moment of your time, Michael," Daniel said. "I just wanted to ask if you have in your possession an envelope given you by Henry."

Michael had forgotten about the envelope until this reminder. "Oh my gosh, yes, I do have an envelope. Henry gave it to me on his last evening at Village Green. I completely forgot about it."

"On his last evening there, you say?"

Michael didn't know Daniel Baylor, and that last remark raised caution lights in his head. He hadn't told anyone that he had seen Henry on his last evening. Michael chose not to respond to the comment and stood before the attorney waiting for him to speak again.

Daniel smiled slightly. He could sense the caution that had fallen around Michael, and respected it. After all, the circumstances of Henry's death were still uncertain, and apparently Michael was one of the last people to see Henry before he died.

"My purpose, Michael, was only to introduce myself. I knew that Henry had an envelope for you, and I wanted to be sure you received it. I'm sure his death has been difficult for you. I won't trouble you further today, but I would like to discuss the contents of the envelope with you in a few weeks if you'd be so kind."

Michael was really confused now. "I don't even know what's in the envelope," he said.

"Of course. I'll contact you in a few weeks and we'll talk then. Until then, thank you for your time," Daniel said, before walking off to greet another acquaintance.

When Michael returned to his mother she asked what the chat was all about.

"Mysterious conversation," he said, shaking his head, but he chose not to elaborate, even to his mother. "That was Henry's lawyer, and he was just introducing himself. Nothing important. Shall we go?"

Michael helped his mother to his feet and they left to return to Village Green.

That evening at his home Michael retrieved the envelope Henry had given him. Inside it was a letter from Henry. Michael sat down and began to read.

Dear Michael,

I hope this letter finds you in good stead, and well after my demise. It's better this way. Do not dwell on my passing, Michael. My time had come. At this writing I don't know whether my exit plan, if I may call it that, will be successful. But I suspect there's enough guile left in this old man to pull it off.

Perhaps you will have offered me some assistance in that regard. Present circumstances call for that assistance, but we will see what the future holds. In the event you have assumed a role in my adventure, such as helping me with my clothing, let me just say kudos to you, young man. Don't regret anything I asked of you.

I've so enjoyed our conversations over the last several months. I will miss them, but not enough to delay my departure any further. I'm just glad that we covered so much ground. Thank you for prompting me to revisit the night of the music and dancing at my home. Truly that was one of the greatest thrills of all my years. Money well spent, as they say.

Your music dream is a little different from the one I held, but a marvelous one nonetheless. I won't presume to suggest to you that your actions last Christmas Eve with your mother should not trouble you. Those are your feelings, and so they are real. Your suggested course of action in response to that evening is ambitious, as I have suggested to you. Forgive an old man, if you will, but I took the liberty of inquiring just how financially ambitious it might be. Turns out I have a few contacts in the world of arts.

It is my wish that you fill the courtyard outside your mother's window with sweet music, as you have conceived. It's the imagination that is the critical part of a great adventure such as you have devised. You are responsible for that. A good dreamer should be given the opportunity on occasion to realize the dream without regard to a host of strictures, such as financing, for example. I hope you'll tolerate my meddlesome behavior. At any rate, it's too late for you to debate me on the subject. So allow me to be part of your dream.

I have instructed a good and loyal man named Daniel Baylor to contact you after my funeral. He is a friend, and a credit to his profession, and he is someone you can trust, as I have. Daniel will be overseeing some of my finances in the years ahead. Jackie is a smart young lady, but she can use some help in the world of finance. Daniel has been instructed to meet with you to discuss your concert. He is not to be the planner, for that is entirely your role. He is simply to serve as a resource.

As a final favor to me, please accept his contact and his support. I would be much obliged. Think of me when the music begins. I'll train my ear in your direction, and perhaps my wife and I will have another dance together in some far-off distant land.

Make it happen, Michael.

Sincerely,
Henry Taylor

Michael put the letter down and stared off into space. *Was he serious? Was he suggesting that he's going to pay for the entire symphony? No, he couldn't mean that.* The thought was just too incredible to imagine. He sat there for an hour reading and rereading the letter, recalling his talks with Henry, and dreaming of the prospect of an evening of music.

It was almost three weeks before Michael received a call from Daniel Baylor, who identified himself again as Henry's attorney. Daniel requested that Michael come to his office to discuss a matter in connection with Henry Taylor.

Michael was intrigued, and made the appointment for later that week.

He arrived for the meeting at two o'clock. The attorney was prompt and invited him into the firm's conference room just a few minutes after the receptionist announced Michael's arrival.

"Thank you for coming, Michael," Daniel began.

"My pleasure," Michael replied. "What's this all about?"

"Before we begin, I have to admit I'm mildly curious. How well did you know Mr. Taylor?"

"I knew him reasonably well, but not for a long time. He was a resident at Village Green where my mother lives. That's how we met."

"Did you see him often out there?"

"Not as often as I see my mother, naturally, but probably a few times a week we would run into him, sometimes more. And this past Thanksgiving he came to my sister's home for dinner. We really enjoyed being with Henry. It was a sad day for all of us when we learned he was gone."

"Yes, it was, and a bit of a mystery, too, I'm sure you would agree," Daniel replied.

Michael moved in his seat. The caution light flicked on again in his head. He began to wonder whether this otherwise cordial meeting might be the beginning of an investigation into his role on the night Henry died. He hoped he didn't look nervous as he gazed at the attorney. He cleared his throat before speaking, and began to use measured words.

"Maybe it's not a mystery after all," Michael suggested. "Perhaps Henry decided he wanted to just stop living and he chose to lie down and die. I don't know how a person can know the moment is upon him but it seems like that was the case with Henry."

"I agree with your assessment, Michael," Daniel responded. "It does seem like Henry simply chose to die and where he wanted to die. I understand you were one of the last persons to have seen Henry that evening, besides the cab driver that the police located."

Here it comes, Michel thought nervously.

"Yes, I was," he stated firmly. "Is that what this meeting is about?"

The attorney sat back and smiled, realizing that his tone sounded a little aggressive. "Pardon me if I offended you, Michael. That was not my intention. No, I did not invite you here to conduct an investigation. Jackie Taylor is satisfied that no foul play surrounded her father's death, as are the police. I've asked you about Henry only because I knew him for over thirty years. I found him to be a delightful and fascinating man. I met with Henry just over a week before his death. He told me at that time that he was ill, but his mind on the day I met with him was sharp and focused. So even though I knew of his illness, his death was still a shock to me."

Michael felt the tension ease in his posture. He smiled at the attorney and said, "I know Henry had some memory issues as time passed, but on many occasions, and I have to say particularly the last time that I saw him, he seemed very sharp to me as well."

"His actions on his last day are remarkable to me," Daniel said. "Knowing Henry as I did, I don't believe there was any foul play either. He was a very intelligent and meticulous man. He often told me how much he loved the property that surrounded his home. If anyone could just pick a time to die and then find a method to get to the place he wanted, I have to say Henry would be that person. Still, it's hard for me to imagine. And it seems so lonely, too."

Michael sensed the attorney really was an old friend of Henry's, not just an advisor, but still he chose not to divulge all that he knew of the final hours.

"He was a remarkable man. I sensed that he wanted the end to come, but I didn't know that he was about to march off to die that night. It is a very lonely thought."

"Indeed," Daniel replied. He could tell that Michael was cautious with his words, but clearly someone who respected and cared for the attorney's old client. He was glad to see that, and chose to move on to a different subject.

"Thank you for telling me about your history with Henry," Daniel said.

"You're welcome," Michael replied, still uncertain as to where this meeting was going to head.

"I can see you will miss him, as will I and many others. I wanted to meet with you and learn a little about your relationship with Henry, and what you've related to me matches with what Henry himself told me in our last meeting."

The attorney smiled as he opened a leather folio and extracted a few papers and an envelope. "I understand that you like the symphony orchestra," the attorney began again as he shifted a few of the papers.

"Yes, I do."

"May I ask whether you have read the contents of the letter which Henry gave you on the night of his death?"

Michael chose not to answer, again suspicious about anything that might have occurred on the night of Henry's death.

Daniel smiled. "Again, please forgive me if my tone strikes you as aggressive. I mean you no ill will, Michael. On the contrary, I have very clear instructions to be of assistance to you. I merely was asking whether Henry informed you of that during his lifetime. I was not privy to his private writings."

The attorney smiled again. "So please relax," he continued. "You're among friends here. The fact that you seem to like the symphony is the real reason I asked you to come in."

Michael acknowledged that he had read the letter.

That admission drew another smile from the lawyer, who then said, "When I last met with Henry he informed me of the warm relationship he had developed with your family, particularly you and your mother. Sometimes an attorney like me might seem a little invasive with his questions and his manner. Henry gave me some instructions at our last meeting. When he told me what he wanted I did speak up to ensure that he was not being victimized by someone. Henry assured me that he was not, and I was confident that he knew what he was doing. Meeting you today strengthens that confidence. I believe you were a good friend to Henry. And I believe you are still uncertain as to what Henry has proposed. Is that the case?"

Michael nodded his head. "For a while I thought you were investigating Henry's death. Now I'm not sure what you or Henry have in mind."

"Well, let me tell you without any further ado. Henry confided in me some of the conversations he had with you."

"He did?" Michael asked with some surprise.

"I hope you don't judge Henry harshly at that news. The context of our discussions and his desires were all positive. And, I suspect, he did not tell me the content of all his conversations with you. He spoke very highly of you."

Michael nodded.

Daniel continued, "What Henry did tell me was that you had a desire to have the symphony play a concert at Village Green, and that your reasons had to do with your mother, and a desire on your part, one which Henry considered to be quite noble by the way, to perhaps make amends or attempt to make something right with your mother."

Michael blushed, as one of his most private embarrassments was raised before him.

"I don't mean to make you uncomfortable, Michael. I don't know all the facts about your reasons for desiring to bring the symphony out to Village Green. Henry told me enough to satisfy an attorney's demand for his rationale, but, as I said before, he was a man of integrity and chose to keep most of his conversations with you private. That was just another aspect that I admired in the man."

Michael sat back, took a deep breath, and let it out slowly. He was totally bewildered.

The attorney spoke again. "Michael, what Henry did tell me was that the idea of bringing the symphony to Village Green was yours, and in some way could be a major event in your life. That's as personal as Henry got with me, except to say that the cost may have been prohibitive to you, or at the very least would have had a devastating impact on your finances. I hope it's not too personal of a question to ask you if that is correct?"

Michael nodded his head affirmatively, at a loss for words.

"Henry asked that I meet with you after his death to address the symphony issue again. Specifically, he left me instructions to help you make it happen, and that's what I'd like to do now."

Michael could feel his mouth drop open. He looked into the attorney's eyes and asked, "What are you saying? Help with the symphony? That's a dream I've had, but the cost is so high. I told Henry that, but he and I never talked about him working with me to make it happen."

"That's what Henry told me," Daniel replied, "and he added that he had no intention of telling you this during his lifetime, for fear that you would turn him down."

"So what are you saying now?"

"What I'm saying, Michael, is that Henry was a man of some means. I don't know if you were aware of that. Henry didn't think so, and I suspect he was right. He was always cautious about discussing money. Nevertheless, he was very well off. During his lifetime he created a trust that primarily benefits his daughter Jackie. But the trust also contains provisions for other dispositions to occur at Henry's death to some churches and charities. The trust also includes a provision, one added at our last meeting, for a concert to be held at Village Green, to be paid by the trust, with an instruction to the trustee that all arrangements are to be conducted on behalf of the trust by you and me."

Daniel paused and smiled broadly at Michael.

"Henry wants your dream of a concert to come true, Michael. And I want to work with you to carry out his wishes."

"So are you saying that Henry's trust will pay for the concert?"

"What I'm saying is that Henry made provision for you to plan and carry out the concert at Village Green, and the trust will pay all expenses incurred with that event."

"But the cost will be over $50,000!"

"I've already spoken to the symphony office. It might be just over that figure. Regardless of the amount, Henry wants us to make it happen, and that is what we shall do."

"Does Jackie know about this?"

"She certainly does. She doesn't know all of the history behind the idea, but she is not concerned about it. She inherits a considerable amount of money and property and she has no problem with any of the charitable bequests or this concert."

Michael was stunned. "He really provided for the whole concert?" He sat back in his chair and stared out the conference room window to the sky.

Daniel remained silent.

"Why?"

The attorney continued to maintain his silence.

Michael spoke again. "Why would Henry care about the concert? Why would he agree to pay for it?"

Finally Daniel spoke up. "Henry and I talked about this at length. He believed in you, and wanted to be certain that the concert happened. He was an extremely generous man, as the other charitable provisions in his trust will attest. This is just another way that he wanted to help other people. In this case he knew the concert might be for your mother, but he saw how other residents could benefit as well."

"My God. I can't believe it. Henry..." Michael was lost in his thoughts, looking again at the skyline outside the conference room window.

Daniel brought him back. "Michael, perhaps we could discuss a few details."

Michael looked back. "Oh, certainly. I'm sorry. I'm having trouble comprehending all this."

"Who wouldn't?" Daniel replied. "When you're ready I'd like to begin discussing a plan to make the concert happen."

"Yes, yes, of course," Michael replied. "Where do we begin?"

"Well, I understand you've already met with the symphony, so I'd like to see you follow up on that end. I was also told that the activities director at Village Green was somewhat less than enthusiastic about the idea."

"She had some issues," Michael admitted. "But the administrator, Carl Fowler, is probably on board."

"Perhaps then you'll let me take care of that end. You decide when and exactly where on the grounds you want to hold the event and I'll see to it that Village Green embraces the idea to the letter."

Michael smiled. "That may be a tall task."

Daniel responded with his own smile. "Not to worry, Michael. I'll see that it all happens on that end. I believe that if Jackie Taylor asked Carl Fowler to host a concert in his living room he would do it for her now. I can assure you that the folks at Village Green will embrace the idea."

That bothered Michael. "Carl is a fine man. I would not want to use Henry's death as some kind of leverage in this situation."

Daniel raised his hands as if to offer peace to Michael.

"I did not mean to suggest that we would force Mr. Fowler into doing something he does not want to do. Jackie has made her peace with Village Green and Mr. Fowler. What I meant to say was that Mr. Fowler, as a compassionate administrator, would love to cooperate in a venture such as you have proposed, particularly knowing that Henry Taylor, or at least his trust, is somehow involved."

"I'm glad to hear that," Michael said.

"Why don't you let me know when you've had your next meeting with the symphony? Then we'll get together again."

Daniel rose and offered his hand as a gesture to conclude the meeting. Michael shook his hand warmly before speaking again.

"I really never imagined that Henry would provide for something like this. I'm overwhelmed. Thank you for having me here today. I look forward to working with you."

"I'm glad to hear that," Daniel said as he walked Michael out to the lobby. "Good day."

Michael walked out of the high rise building to the bustling city street. He looked to the sky and thought, *Henry, you crazy old man. This is really going to happen, isn't it?*

CHAPTER 15

Henry's death took its toll on Helen. Michael could see that it was too close to home, and that it reminded her that her time was drawing near. Her confusion over time and place became more pronounced. Though it didn't completely overtake her, it became almost a daily staple of her life now.

She would often remark that she had not seen Henry in a while and wondered where he was. Michael would bring her back to reality and point out that Henry had passed away. Each time Helen would be surprised to hear the news, then grow pensive. It seemed like she was forced to relive the experience of Henry's death again and again. Michael grew concerned that he would need to schedule the concert as soon as possible in the warm weather, or it might never happen for her.

Although Daniel Baylor had suggested he would deal with Village Green, Michael contacted Carl Fowler again and was reassured by the administrator that he would support any reasonable plan, including an outdoor concert. Carl told Michael that Henry's attorney had already informed him about Henry's trust. Carl suggested that additional security be hired and that overtime be offered to staff in order to have as many nurses and nurse assistants around as possible to help the elderly and infirm safely walk to the courtyard and enjoy the concert.

Michael was pleased that the administrator was already planning ahead. But when Carl suggested the cost to the facility could approach $10,000, Michael's first reaction was to blanch at the number and wonder how he was he going to come up with that money, then he laughed to himself. *My God,* he thought, *even with the prices going up, this event can happen, thanks to Henry's generosity.* Michael called Daniel Baylor to let him know of the anticipated costs, and the attorney instructed him to tell Carl to do whatever it takes to make things work. Any overtime costs would be borne by Henry's trust.

After the phone call, Michael smiled at Carl while shaking his head in wonder. Then he passed on that all of the Village Green expenses would be covered. They agreed to meet again after a date was selected with the orchestra.

Michael then contacted Carolyn Webster at the symphony and arranged to meet at the end of the week.

When Michael arrived for the meeting, he was greeted warmly by Carolyn in the lobby of the symphony building, and was led by her through the office hallways again. As they entered her office, Michael was surprised to find Nicholas Shefsky seated at the conference table.

"Hello again, Mr. Telford," Nicholas said as he rose from his chair when Michael entered the room.

"Hello, Mr. Shefsky," Michael replied, shaking Nicholas' hand. "I wasn't expecting to see you again today."

"Why don't we drop the surnames, what do you say?" Nicholas said.

"Fine by me. "

"Very well, Michael. When I heard that you had contacted Carolyn again and arranged to come in, I decided I wanted to join you for the second round of talks. I'm interested in your idea, and I want to see it happen."

"Well that's good to hear," Michael said. "I'd like to come to an agreement today and select a date."

"I understand that you now have the resources to afford this event," Nicholas said.

Michael smiled. "I do. I'm not sure that I could have afforded to do it myself, but a magnificent man has chosen to support the concert plan. So the cost is now within range."

"Well, that's wonderful news," Nicholas said enthusiastically. "Let's take the next step."

"Where shall we begin?" Michael asked.

Nicholas turned to Carolyn to take the floor.

Carolyn smiled at Michael as she began. "The orchestra will prepare the program and choose the selections for the performance. Generally the program would include light classical music with some pop show tunes and patriotic numbers. This audience, like most, will enjoy hearing the orchestra play some recognizable music. Most outdoor performances run sixty to seventy-five minutes, with one brief intermission."

"Can you give me an idea of what music you might choose?" Michael asked.

"Certainly," Carolyn replied. "We've been thinking about the prospective audience, and we like the idea of opening with 'An American Salute,' and then feature an older arrangement, such as 'When the Saints Go Marchin' In,' and close out the first half with some swing. 'Sing, Sing, Sing' is always a popular number. In the second half we might include the Overture to 'West Side Story,' some selections from 'Porgy and Bess,' and we would end with what we are certain the residents would love, 'The Stars and Stripes Forever.'"

"That all sounds wonderful," Michael said.

"Naturally we'll fill in more selections. But those I've mentioned would be popular choices."

Michael hadn't planned on participating in the musical selections. He was actually surprised that they were discussing the selections with him at all. But since they had indicated all the pieces had not been chosen yet he wondered whether it would be inappropriate for him to make one request.

Nicholas observed Michael looking pensive. "Michael, is there something on your mind? You look to be rather deep in thought," he said.

Michael turned back to Nicholas and smiled, "Just day-dreaming a little."

"If it has something to do with the performance, please share," Nicholas encouraged.

Michael smiled. *Why not. All they can do is turn me down.*

"I was wondering about including one selection," Michael said.

"Now what might that be?" Nicholas asked eagerly.

"It's an old religious song called 'In the Garden.'"

"Hmmm, I can't say that I'm familiar with that title. How does it go?"

Surprising himself at his lack of reserve, Michael began to sing the opening lines of the song. A song that was played at his father's funeral, as well as his grandparents, who died before Michael was even born.

"I come to the garden alone, while the dew is still on the roses, and the voice I hear falling on my ear, the Son of God discloses. And he walks with me, and he talks with me, and he tells me I am his own; and the joy we share as we tarry there, none other has ever known."

As he ended the first stanza, he was swept with emotion, and his voice faltered. He was remembering the day when the song was played for his father. He stopped, and tried to compose himself while Nicholas and Carolyn sat in silence.

Still fighting back tears, he continued. "Oh, my gracious. I'm sorry about that. It's not often I hear that song, but when I do it just takes me back to an emotional time."

Nicholas smiled, and said, "What little I heard sounded like the piece has a wonderful melody, but I'm afraid I'm not familiar with the music."

"Well, as I said, it's an old church song, but one that I've never actually heard played in any church I've attended except for my father's funeral. In fact, it's actually very difficult to find it included in the music books that the churches maintain."

"Is that right?" Nicholas said.

Michael smiled, and continued, "This may sound a little strange to you, but I like to look through the music books I find in churches and chapels to see what kind of songs sound like they'd work at a funeral. When I find one, I sometimes take the music with me. I don't know why I'm telling you all this now. The point is, it's very rare to find a music book that contains 'In the Garden.'"

Before Nicholas could comment, Carolyn muttered in a low voice, "Oh boy."

Michael turned to her. "Oh boy," he repeated. "Those words are generally not the harbinger of good news to follow."

Carolyn turned to Nicholas and directed her response to him. "I wouldn't be surprised if we would need a takedown for that piece."

Nicholas nodded in agreement. "I've never heard the name before. But I'm sure you're right, Carolyn. If it's an old religious song we'll probably be able to find a recording, but that could be all."

"It's been sung by a number of gospel singers. I know that you could easily find a recording of it," Michael said.

Carolyn and Nicholas were silent as each considered the issue at hand. Finally, Nicholas spoke up.

"I'm sure we could find a recording of a fine gospel singer. That's not the issue. The issue is whether or not we would need a takedown," Nicholas said.

"What's a takedown?" Michael asked.

Carolyn spoke. "Occasionally we receive requests for certain musical pieces to be included in a performance. The orchestra always considers requests, but can't guarantee that every one can be fulfilled."

"I understand. I didn't just assume you would agree to play 'In the Garden,'" Michael said.

Carolyn continued. "If a new or contemporary piece of music is requested, there could be copyright issues. Those types of pieces are called a rental. An old, religious piece would not likely be considered a rental, so I would not anticipate any problem there. The reason I said 'oh boy', however, is that a much more significant challenge arises with old pieces that have not been played by a symphony orchestra before."

"I don't know if an orchestra has played that piece before," Michael said. "I only know a lot of gospel singers have recorded it."

"Well, that's at least a start," said Nicholas. Turning to Carolyn, he said, "May I explain our dilemma here?"

"Certainly, sir," Carolyn demurred.

Nicholas turned back to Michael. "Michael, if the song is not to be found in an orchestral form, but there is a recording, we would need to have a staff arranger perform what we call a takedown. The staff member listens to the recorded piece and transcribes the music. That is the beginning of the takedown. After that, the staff would begin to arrange the piece, or orchestrate it. This is very time consuming. It can take anywhere from three to five months to complete an arrangement."

Michael interrupted, thinking that three months was doable, since it would be that long until the orchestra's outdoor season could even begin. "Okay. If it can be done in three months we're still in business," he said.

Nicholas indulged him with a smile. "I'm afraid there's more."

"Oh," Michael said. "I apologize."

"It's quite all right," Nicholas said. "Let me explain what would come next with such a piece. Once the piece is arranged for the orchestra—something accomplished in the three-to-five-month process I was describing—the music is then given to the concertmaster. The concertmaster then shares the music with the second violin, the principal viola, the principal cello, and the principal string bass. All of these extraordinary musicians must then begin to coordinate what we call the bowings."

"The bowings?" Michael asked. "What is that?"

"When the orchestra plays any piece, all the strings must be in unison so that they match. Every bow must move in the same direction on a piece. At any point where the violins, violas, cellos, and bass are playing, the bows throughout each section must match overall. If the violin bow is going down, then at that same moment so must the bows on the other strings. Follow?" asked Nicholas.

Michael nodded that he understood, and Nicholas continued.

"When the arranger has completed the orchestration, the music is presented to the concertmaster clean, meaning it does not contain what we call 'markings.' The process of coordinating the completion of the bowings can easily take another two months."

"I had no idea," Michael said.

"Once all the takedown, orchestration, and bowings are completed we need to present the piece to the entire orchestra for rehearsal. Realistically, the minimum amount of time you could expect to see us spend preparing this one piece would be six months. And that, Michael, is a very ambitious time table," Nicholas said.

Carolyn then added, "I should also point out that there obviously would be additional costs involved in the takedown process that would increase the orchestra's fee if we were to include this piece."

I don't know how much Henry set aside in his trust, Michael mused to himself, *but I bet he didn't include a takedown fee.* He smiled briefly, thinking of Henry and how what Michael originally thought was a simple idea was now becoming so complicated.

"Lost in thought again, Michael?" Nicholas asked.

Michael laughed. "Yes, that seems to be happening to me a lot lately."

"Let me ask you a question. Does this piece mean so much to you that you would want to have us include it in the program? I'm confident we can do it. But it would likely mean the concert would be at the end of the outdoor season, rather than at the beginning in May as you said you wanted."

Michael shifted in his seat and considered the question, thinking about how far this idea had progressed since the night of Christmas Eve. The performance would be wonderful without "In the Garden." He knew that, yet he had a strong feeling that adding this one, personal family touch was what he really needed. He didn't like the idea of waiting past May, but if that was the only way it could happen, then he would just have to will his mother to keep going.

"It is important to me," Michael said finally. "I know it may be asking a lot. It's hard for me to describe why, but including something so personal for my mother just feels like the right thing to do."

"Very well," Nicholas said. "An outdoor concert it will be, and we shall do our best to accommodate your request."

Nicholas stood and extended his hand. "A pleasure meeting with you again, Michael. I'll leave you now with Carolyn to work out the remaining details."

Michael knew there was one more significant detail to arrange that wouldn't take place with Carolyn. "May I have a word in private with you before you go?" he asked.

Nicholas was surprised at the request. He looked over at Carolyn to seek an indication from her what this private audience might be all about. Carolyn merely raised her eyebrows slightly to indicate she knew nothing.

Nicholas turned back to Michael. "Certainly. Carolyn, could you excuse us for a minute?"

Carolyn stepped out into the hallway, closing the door behind her.

Nicholas returned to his chair and sat. Michael joined him.

"What's on your mind?" Nicholas asked.

"It's about the performance, sir," Michael said, using a deferential tone. "Carolyn has told me that an associate conductor would lead the orchestra at the performance."

"That's right. Let me assure you that our associate conductors are among the finest in the world. You will be in very good hands," Nicholas said.

"I'm sure I would," Michael conceded. "But I feel a rapport with you after the two meetings we've had."

"That's very kind of you to say, Michael," Nicholas said with a smile. "I have taken a personal interest in your request because of the venue you have suggested."

"I understand that. And I understand that it's customary for an associate conductor to handle a performance such as this one. And I also understand that if you were asked to lead the orchestra at this performance there would be a private contract with you for your fee."

"All that is true," Nicholas said.

"I would like for you to lead the orchestra at this performance, if your schedule would permit it and you were so inclined," Michael said. "I don't know if I've breached protocol by speaking directly to you about this rather than going through Carolyn first. If so, then I apologize. And I don't mean to put you on the spot, either. If you need to think about it, I understand. Still, I would hope you could say yes."

Nicholas gazed deeply at Michael, a wry grin spreading across his face.

"Michael," he began, "you're right about the protocol."

Michael's face froze. *Oh no,* he thought, *now I've messed this up.*

Then Nicholas began to laugh.

"Your face locked up for a moment there," Nicholas said. "You're forgiven on the protocol issue, okay?" Nicholas laughed again.

Michael relaxed and laughed as well. "Thank you."

"Now forgive my possible breach of protocol, but I'm curious. At our first meeting the cost of the orchestra was a significant issue. Rightly so, let me add. Yet this afternoon we've added a takedown fee, and now you are willing to pay an additional sum for me to conduct. That's quite a turnaround."

"Yes, it is," Michael said.

"Care to elaborate?"

Michael smiled. *Where do I begin?* "Well, it's all a very long story. For now let me just say that I befriended a gentleman who recently passed away. He was aware of my hope to organize a concert, and he was aware of my financial limitations as well. I just recently learned that my friend, whose name was Henry Taylor by the way, made provision in his trust shortly before his death to ensure that the performance would happen."

Nicholas shook his head side to side. "This whole package grows more intriguing by the hour."

Michael nodded in agreement, and smiled. "It's been a roller coaster these last few months. Anyway, Henry's trust is bankrolling the performance. I met with his attorney and I've been given the green light to make arrangements. And now that we've gotten this far, I was hoping you'd join me in seeing this thing through."

Nicholas pondered the request. "It's pretty unusual for me to personally conduct a performance like this. I'm afraid there would have to be an additional fee."

"Carolyn made that clear to me in our first meeting," Michael said.

"And still you want me to conduct?" Nicholas asked.

"Absolutely," Michael replied.

"My standard fee for this type of appearance is $15,000. Will that fit within your budget?"

Michael smiled. If Henry only knew how he was spending this money. "That would be perfectly acceptable," he said. "I really appreciate that you'll be a part of this."

Nicholas smiled in return. "Very well then. Let's get Carolyn back in here to organize the next step."

As Nicholas turned away toward the door to retrieve Carolyn, Michael tapped his hand on the table as if he was giving the table a high five. He was grinning from ear to ear. Hearing the sound of the hand slapping the table, Nicholas looked back over his shoulder. "Everything all right over there?" he asked.

"Everything's fine. I was just thinking about my friend Henry. I wish he was here to be a part of this."

"He sounds like quite a generous man. Someday, I'm going to have to insist that you tell me the whole story behind this event. Agreed?"

"Agreed," Michael nodded.

Nicholas opened the door and requested that Carolyn return. Once she reentered, Nicholas told her that he would be conducting, and requested that she have the contracts for the orchestra and for his appearance prepared.

"We have agreed that the consideration for my conducting will consist of two items. One will be my standard appearance fee," Nicholas said, turning his eyes away from Carolyn and back toward Michael and pausing.

Carolyn then prompted, "And the second item, sir?"

Nicholas grinned. "A pledge to be told the entire intriguing story of this matter."

Carolyn didn't understand. "Do you want that included in the contract, sir?"

"I don't think that will be necessary," Nicholas said. "A gentlemen's agreement on that point should suffice. Would you agree, Michael?"

Michael smiled. "That's fine by me. The truth, the whole truth, and nothing but the truth, at a time to be determined."

"Excellent, now I'll leave the two of you to attend to these matters," Nicholas said as he waved to them both and departed the room.

Suddenly the room seemed larger because Nicholas was no longer within it.

Michael spoke. "He is a dominating figure, isn't he?"

Carolyn nodded. "That he is. You've already spent more private time with our music director than most non-musicians. And I take it we're to continue with the planning."

"So where do we go from here?" Michael asked.

"The first matter generally would be to agree on a date. That's problematic now with the takedown. I'm going to guess that the best we'll be able to do for you is to schedule the event at the end of the season, right around September 15th."

Michael was disappointed. September was a long way off, and there was no way he could be certain that his mother would be around at that time.

"Is there any way we could do it sooner?" he asked.

"Yes, there is," Carolyn said matter-of-factly. "Eliminate the selection that requires nine months for orchestration and we could schedule this in May or June."

Michael sat back and tried to balance the two notions in his mind. Scheduling it earlier as opposed to including one song that he was certain would touch his mother's heart. He had to err on the side of sentiment.

"Can it be done by September?" Michael asked.

Carolyn put her pen down, folded her hands. and looked up at Michael.

"It could happen. That's the best I can promise you. It's going to take a major effort to have the piece ready for per-formance by mid-September. For one thing, the deadline for the orchestration would be September 1st, so that the orchestra would have two weeks for rehearsal. But if the music director wants this done, I suspect it will be done. Yet even with his influence, it will take all summer to get the piece ready."

"I understand," Michael replied.

"Let's plan now for Friday, September 16th," Carolyn said, as she picked up her pen and resumed making her notes. "Next, I would like to schedule a site visit in one month. Would you be available to meet us on February 14th? Say at 9:30?"

"I guess I could," Michael replied. "What's the visit for?"

"These are special events, and sometimes tricky ones, too," Carolyn responded. "We're going to be communicating quite a bit over the next several months, so I'd like to begin with a site visit, just to get a feel for the entire event. The visit will take about an hour. I'll be accompanied by three other behind-the-scenes orchestra members: a technical director, a lighting technician, and a sound engineer. All of them need to get a feel early on about the event."

"I'll be there if you want me, but it seems pretty early for that," Michael said.

"We're not familiar with the site, Michael, and we need to ensure that the area will be large enough to accommodate a stage covered by our tent. If your courtyard isn't large enough we'll need to work out something else, like a smaller orchestra or a different location."

"I understand," Michael said. "I'll see you on the 14th."

With the schedule agreed upon, Michael stood, shook hands again with Carolyn and told her he could find his way out.

✱

The following afternoon Michael was scheduled to give Amy another piano lesson. His classes at the university were over by three o'clock. Amy had arranged to schedule part of her dinner break at four o'clock. They met at that hour in the empty auditorium.

Michael arrived first and began to loosen up on the piano. He was playing an old arrangement of "Beautiful Dreamer" when Amy entered. She heard Michael playing and hung back to hear the rest of the piece before walking all the way in. She loved it when he would play a short piece for her. She always asked, but he generally didn't want to play anything at their lessons for fear of showing off.

Once he finished the song, Amy walked forward and clapped.

"That was wonderful. I love to hear you play," she said

Michael looked up from the keyboard. "I didn't know you were back there."

"I didn't want to disturb you," Amy said.

Michael smiled. "That was one of my father's favorite songs. I love to play it."

"I wish you'd play more. You're wonderful."

"That's very kind of you, but I don't think I'm wonderful. Adequate maybe. And dangerous, too."

"Dangerous? How so?" Amy asked.

"Dangerous as an instructor. I'm probably committing piano malpractice just by agreeing to give lessons to you."

"I love a man with confidence," Amy joked.

"Instead you got me. Oh well ... let's pick up where we were last week. Come on up here and take a seat."

Amy joined him on the piano bench and began to practice the measures Michael insisted were the proper warm-up before each lesson could begin.

A half hour passed quickly. At its conclusion Michael launched into a few bars of the overture from "West Side Story." Once he stopped he asked Amy if she liked that song.

"Sure I do."

"Do you think the older clientele around here would like it, too?" Michael asked.

"I think so, but why do you ask?"

"Because they're going to be hearing it at a symphony concert live and outdoors this coming summer."

"What are you talking about?"

"I'm talking about how today was just a terrific day. I met with Nicholas Shefsky at the symphony today and we agreed on a concert to be held out in the courtyard in September."

Amy was flabbergasted. She could barely find the words to express her astonishment. "Michael, please, what is going on here? Why would you be scheduling a concert here?"

"It's a long story, one which I promise I'll tell you in detail some day. For now, though, through the generosity of the late Henry Taylor, I am coordinating a concert to be held by the symphony here."

"Who knows about this?"

"Actually, you're the first at Village Green."

"What? Have you gone mad?"

Michael laughed. "Actually I've met a few times with Carl Fowler. He's aware of it and has approved the idea. But today I agreed on a date for the concert, and you are officially the first person here to know."

"Well, I'm honored," Amy smiled. "When will this be announced?"

"Soon, I hope. There are still a few details to work out, like Carl informing Joanne Holly. I'd sure love to see her reaction when he breaks the news."

"So I should keep this quiet for now, right?"

"Please do. The news should break soon. Meanwhile we need to practice harder so that you'll be ready for your first recital with the symphony in September."

"Funny guy. Just let me catch up with my daughter eventually. That would be success enough for me."

"Sounds doable to me. I'll check back with you in a few days to see what day works best for you next week. And now I believe I'll pick up my mother and enjoy some of the gruel they pass off as the chef's special in the main dining room."

"You do that, Michael. And make sure you order dessert for her before they run out."

Michael began packing up the music books he had brought as Amy began to head back to the nurse's station.

As she neared the door, Michael called out to her.

"Amy."

She paused and turned back to Michael who was still seated at the piano. "I enjoyed our lesson. I'm glad we're doing this."

Amy was pleased to hear his sentiments. "Thanks for saying that, Michael. I enjoy it too."

CHAPTER 16

I t was an unusually warm February day when Michael met with Carolyn at Village Green for the site inspection. With her were the technical director, a lighting technician, and a sound engineer. Carl Fowler joined them as well, explaining that Joanne Holly was otherwise occupied.

Michael led them to the middle of the courtyard where the concrete patio held several benches, and was the central meeting point of several branches of walkway. His mother's room was thirty feet in front of and three floors above what would be stage left.

"Here it is," Michael declared proudly.

The technical director took a hard look in each direction of the courtyard. The others stood back to let him gauge the area. After pacing the width of the patio, he finally spoke.

"This is going to be tight," he said. "I'm going to need to measure this closely. Let me check it out."

Together, he and the lighting technician drew out their tape measures and began to mark out the area for the stage. After tallying their measurements, the technical director returned to Carolyn and reported that the patio was four feet shy on the width and three feet shy on the depth.

"Can we work with that?" Carolyn asked. She hadn't told the staff before now that her marching orders from Nicholas Shefsky were to do everything in her power to make this concert work.

"If we bring the full orchestra we'll have to squeeze at the rear. We can handle the width. That shouldn't present a problem. I can put a rail up on either end so the musicians don't fall off the side. It's the depth that's the real problem. We've never set up for the full symphony in this small of an area," said the technical director.

"I understand," responded Carolyn. "I know it won't be easy. But the maestro wants me to do everything possible to make this happen. So I need to know whether you can modify our setup some way to fit it all in."

The technical director was surprised at how persistent Carolyn was being. *This must be a big job,* he thought. "Well if you want it done here, we'll get it done here. It will be tight. Some of the controls will have to be off stage to the rear. We may have to put the trailer with the instruments on the other side of the portico, and we'll have to use some of this rear walkway to set up the whisper generator. But, yes, if you say we need to work with this space, then we can make it work."

Michael beamed when he heard those words. Carl clapped Michael on the back and said, "This is really going to happen, Michael, and right outside my window."

Carolyn joined the two of them in their smiles, then got down to business.

"Carl, can you have your plant maintenance personnel link up with our people to go over electrical locations and our needs? Then I'd like our technical director to walk the route our equipment vans will use to gain access to the courtyard. Finally, I'll want to see where you propose we have our musicians park their vehicles. We'll need to establish a reserved parking area."

Carl summoned the plant manager on his pager. "I'll have all the brainpower from here that you'll need in just a few minutes." Carl said.

"Thank you, Carl," said Carolyn, who then turned to Michael and added, "Looks like we're a go now. I'll tell Mr. Shefsky this afternoon that the site will work. He'll begin working on the takedown piece soon. I think that's all we'll need from you today,

Michael. Thanks for meeting us. I'll just do some more coordinating now with Mr. Fowler and his staff."

"Fair enough," Michael said. "Thanks for all you're doing." He offered a big smile to both Carolyn and Carl then went indoors to visit his mother.

*

Helen remained relatively stable for the next month. Michael, Mary, and Tom saw to it that one or the other of them visited her every day. Amy, too, took a special interest in Helen's care, making sure that she personally looked in on Helen during each of her shifts.

Michael and Amy still felt a connection between each other, but since Henry's death and the resulting postponement of their first date, they never got around to rescheduling. Michael realized he had strong feelings for Amy, and he loved to see her whenever he was at Village Green. But pursuing a relationship right now seemed to be too much. Dealing with his mother and the confusion which swirled around her was consuming all his free time.

Near the end of March the fall that Michael feared finally occurred. Carl Fowler informed him.

"Your mother fell this afternoon in her apartment," he told Michael in a phone call. "She's all right. No broken hip or anything. But she's showing signs of additional confusion now. It's possible she had a stroke, although I really don't think so. In any event, I want her checked out more thoroughly than we can do here. So I've called for an ambulance to transport her."

No matter how much he anticipated this type of call, it still rattled Michael. "Thanks for the call, Carl. Please send her to Christ Hospital. That's where her heart physician practices. I'll leave here shortly and meet the ambulance at the emergency room."

Michael met the ambulance when it arrived at the hospital. Tom and Mary joined him there. After a number of x-rays and blood work-ups, the emergency room physician concluded that Helen had not suffered a stroke, but that her blood pressure was irregular, and that she was experiencing atrial fibrillation, and what appeared to be a buildup of fluid around her heart.

She was admitted shortly after that diagnosis, and for the next ten days she was subjected to a host of treatments by both the cardiac and the pulmonary teams, including the removal of fluid around her heart by means of a syringe inserted through her back. The physicians informed the family that the fluid collecting around the heart now was chronic, and that Helen would need to be monitored regularly.

After seventeen days in the hospital, the doctors released Helen with orders to recover for a spell in Well Care before returning to assisted-living. The family agreed this was needed as, once again, the long hospital stay improved Helen's heart and lung condition, but at the cost of depleting her energy and spirit. She was exhausted most of the time now. Fortunately, a private room in the Medicare section of Well Care was available for Helen to begin her recovery from the hospital stay.

Although the skilled-care room resembled a hospital room, Helen's spirits began to improve as some of the residents of Village Green stopped in to visit her each day. Amy was a regular visitor for brief stays, and she could see that Helen's demeanor was markedly better with each visit. Somehow Helen associated Amy with being close to home again, and she began to talk about returning to her apartment.

Two weeks into the skilled-care stay, Michael began to lobby for a return to assisted living, and a week later the staff held a care conference to review Helen's status. The meeting was held in a small room with pink walls, pink striped upholstered chairs, a pink, flowered couch, pink lamps, and lampshades with pink fabric. It was all a little too much for Michael. He wondered if this was designed to foster more peace in these meetings or to encourage quicker meetings so that everyone could escape the room.

The staff was surprised that all of Helen's children were present for the conference. The three of them had agreed that they should all be on hand to show a united front insisting on Helen's return to assisted living.

The director of nursing began with an expression of concern over Helen's failing memory, and a compliment to the family on their efforts in visiting daily, and creating memory books and doing whatever they could do to help foster her recovery. The family nodded gratefully, but they each sensed from the tone at the outset that the position of the staff would be that Helen must remain in the skilled-care center, rather than be allowed to return to her apartment.

Mary spoke first. "I think my mother has made some real strides in her recovery. We know that she still has some instances of confusion. But she is much better than she was when she first left the hospital."

The director of nursing nodded. "I agree that she has made great strides and we are all pleased to see that. However, we are still concerned about her being alone in an apartment, particularly with her heart issues."

Michael spoke up. "We understand your concern. It's a fair one. But please consider that we are merely asking for a return to assisted living, not independent living. We will be there each day to look in on her and the staff will be there as they typically are. We don't see why there should be a reluctance to let her return to some measure of privacy and independence, surrounded by her own belongings."

The nurse in charge of rehabilitation commented that Helen was walking better and had been cooperative in her exercises. "She still needs to try to walk regularly. She has mainly been sitting or lying down these past three weeks, and she has begun to rely more on a wheelchair to travel around the ward if she is not encouraged to walk. If she would continue to try to walk, her recovery could improve dramatically."

It was a glimmer of hope, and Michael seized it. "We always try to walk with her and keep her moving. Sometimes she complains about it," he said with a smile, and the room laughed. "But look, the bottom line for us is that we don't think our mother has a whole lot of time left. We want to give her the opportunity to have more of a life in the assisted-living structure than she could find here. That's not an attack on the quality of care here. It's merely a reflection of reality. We understand that if she can't make it there, if she has another fall, or other issues, she may have to return here. But she wants to be home among her things and we want to afford her that opportunity, and we really feel strongly that she should be given that chance in light of where she is in life now."

Michael continued, "The director of nursing for assisted living examined Mother yesterday. I think your notes will indicate that she concluded that Mother does presently meet the minimum standards for return to assisted living. I know the decision is yours, rather than the assisted-living director's, but surely that should carry some weight."

The skilled-care head nurse nodded. "I agree with you that she does have the potential to continue to have some quality of life. We think it can be filled with quality here in skilled care, and I suspect that she will need skilled care again."

She paused for what seemed like an eternity then added, "For now, though, I'll give the okay for her to return to assisted living."

It felt like a great victory. They were springing her from skilled care once again. The paperwork exercise to go from skilled care to assisted living was just as bad as being discharged from the hospital. It was another three hours after the meeting broke up before Helen was permitted to leave. This time she left the skilled care ward in a wheelchair rather than on her own two feet. That wasn't lost on anyone.

As they headed back to her apartment one more time, Michael wondered whether she would make it until the concert. All the planning that had been conducted so far would result in a concert, he knew. Yet he couldn't help but wonder if it might be a posthumous event for both his mother and Henry.

CHAPTER 17

One week after Helen had returned to assisted living, Michael received a phone call from Carolyn Webster.

"Michael, we've just had a date open up in June. I wanted to let you know right away in case you wanted to move the concert up," Carolyn said.

"How is the takedown proceeding? Will the music be ready?"

"Our staff has been working very hard on it, but they're still at least three months away from completion. We thought we were going to catch a break last week when one of our staff members was told by an acquaintance in Seattle that the piece was scored for an orchestra several years ago, but never played in concert."

Michael sat up. This could be a dream come true. "Can you get the music?" he quickly asked.

"I'm sorry to disappoint you. We already have it in hand," Carolyn replied. "It turns out it was an adaptation for a single violin. It's not going to offer us much help at all. Mr. Shefsky himself took a look at it with the concertmaster and told the staff they needed to keep working on their own."

"That is disappointing," Michael said.

"I'm sorry, Michael. We can still plan for September and include the piece, but I thought I would give you a call to let you know about the break in our schedule, just in case you might want to reconsider. Tell me, how is your mother faring?" Carolyn asked.

"She just got back to her apartment from skilled care a week ago. That's been a great relief to all of us. But I'm afraid she's failing now."

"Perhaps a concert might help her," Carolyn said. "Is it absolutely imperative that we include this music in the program?"

"No, I suppose it's not. It would be wonderful to have something personal for her, but maybe your call is an omen that I should be more flexible. I was just beginning to worry that Mother might not be around in September. I think this call has come at just the right time."

"So do you want to grab the date?"

"What do you have open?" Michael asked.

"We can do it in June if we commit to it right now. We have one date available when the orchestra and Mr. Shefsky can appear."

"Whatever the date is, we'll take it," Michael said.

"How does June 6th sound?"

Michael sat in stunned silence.

After several seconds, Carolyn prompted him. "Michael, are you there?"

Of all the dates in the month of June. June 6th. The anniversary date of his father's birth and death.

"Michael?" he heard again in his ear.

"Oh, Carolyn, I'm sorry. I was just surprised about the date. June 6th would be terrific. Let's plan on it. But that will be here soon. Can we make it happen?"

"It's going to take some work," Carolyn said. "You need to make sure right away that the date is acceptable to Village Green. It's only four weeks and three days away. But we can make it work."

My God, this is really going to happen, Michael thought, before saying, "I'll get with Carl Fowler today and lock it up."

"Good. Let me know if that's a problem. Otherwise, we've got four weeks to pull it together," Carolyn said.

"Thank you so much, Carolyn, and please pass my thanks along to Nicholas as well."

"I will," she said as she hung up the phone.

The next several days found Michael on the phone or in meetings with Carl Fowler, Daniel Baylor, and, finally, with Jackie Taylor.

Michael drove to Jackie's home to seek her permission to declare the event a memorial concert in honor of Henry.

This was the first time Michael had ever been to Henry's home. As he drove down the tree-lined street he couldn't help but imagine Henry's last evening. The driveway at his home was steep and shaded by a canopy of trees and overhanging bushes. Michael marveled at the effort it must have taken for the old man to have walked up the drive on that cold evening three months ago.

Halfway up, the drive curved to the right, bringing the magnificent home into view. To the left was another grove of trees, at the top of which was a huge pine. Michael stopped the car and shut off the engine. *That must be the tree Henry chose.* He exited the car and walked over to the base of the tree. On the far side, previously hidden from his view, was a wreath of fresh flowers. Michael imagined that the wreath could be seen from the upper floor of the house.

So this was where Henry chose to lay himself down and die. He took a knee on the bed of pine needles that was part of the grove. Placing his left hand at the base of the tree, Michael offered a silent prayer in memory of a man who, in a very short period of time, had become such a good friend and confidant.

When he had finished his prayer, Michael looked up to see Jackie walking down from the house. He was distressed at seeing her, worried that his presence at this sacred spot would cause her more anguish.

Once she neared the grove, Michael spoke.

"Jackie, I hope it's alright with you that I stopped to pay my respects. Once I saw this tree on my way up the driveway I just felt like I needed to walk over here."

To Michael's relief, Jackie greeted him warmly, offering him a hug. "Hello, Michael," she said. "It's fine with me that you're here. Most people seem afraid to go near this area now. I guess they're worried that it will make me cry."

"I was worried about that as well."

Jackie bent over to remove a wilting flower from the wreath. As she straightened up, she softly touched the base of the tree.

Looking again at Michael, she offered a quick smile and said, "I don't cry as much these days as I did right after it happened. But I don't mind it at all if the tears come. I miss him. The last thing I do each night as I turn out the lights inside is to look out here."

"That must be awfully hard for you," Michael said.

"I try to imagine seeing Dad leaning up against this tree with a book on his lap, and his eyes closed as if he's taking a little nap. It doesn't always work, but that's what I try to do, and sometimes it helps."

When Michael had no words to reply, she added, "Leave your car there and walk up to the house with me. Let's talk inside."

Jackie showed him into the living room of the large, beautifully furnished home.

"This place is magnificent," Michael said, as he admired the marble fireplace. Above the mantle was an oil painting of what looked to be the grove of pines they had just left.

Jackie saw him stare at the painting. When Michael turned to her with an inquiring look she smiled and nodded.

"Yes, that's the grove. Call me gloomy if you want."

"It's beautiful. Was it always here?"

"No, I had a friend paint it for me recently." Jackie smiled as she walked over to the mantel to join Michael in examining the painting.

"When I asked my friend to paint the grove," Jackie continued, "he was very hesitant. He thought that commissioning a painting like this was a sign of some serious depression. But I assured him I wasn't going crazy. I just wanted a scene from our property, so why not Dad's favorite pine?"

"Does it ever bother you to look at it now?" Michael asked.

"No, strangely enough, it brings me some comfort."

"I'm glad about that," Michael said.

"Now let's have a seat, so you can tell me why you're here."

Once seated, Michael began to tell her about the plans for the concert.

"You know, Michael, that Daniel Baylor let me know about the plans for the concert."

"I knew he was going to call you, Jackie. Your father's generosity is just overwhelming to me. When I was told that the expenses of the concert were going to be paid by Henry's trust I just couldn't believe it. I still have trouble believing it even now."

Jackie smiled. "That was Dad. He liked to surprise people with his generosity. And he never liked anyone making a fuss over what he had done."

"I understand. But I was hoping you would consent to the concert being held in his memory."

Jackie's eyes began to fill with tears.

"That is so sweet of you, Michael," she said. "You know that's not why Dad made provision for the event. You don't have any obligation to do that."

"That's what makes it even more special, Jackie," Michael said. "I'd really like to honor Henry with the evening, but only if it's okay with you."

Jackie smiled through her tears, and nodded her head. "Okay, Michael. That would be wonderful. Thank you."

After clearing the idea with Daniel Baylor, who was also moved by the idea, Michael arranged with Carolyn Webster for the program to state that the concert was in memory of Henry Taylor.

News of the concert spread throughout Village Green, and the excitement of the symphony orchestra coming just for the residents was palpable. Even Joanne Holly, once she knew the event was really going to happen, grew enthusiastic and began to assist in the coordination, to a point, naturally, where she casually let others believe this had been her plan all along.

Although Helen was back in her apartment surrounded by the mementos of her life, over the next three weeks she was steadily slipping away. Her vital signs all appeared normal, but her appetite was decreasing at a striking speed and her general confusion over day-to-day matters grew at the same rate. Michael began to feel that putting on the concert was becoming a race against time.

Amy could see the change as well. One week before the concert she sat down with Michael outside the dining room to voice her concern.

"Michael, if Helen hasn't already reached the point where she needs to return to skilled care, she's right at the edge. You do realize that, don't you?"

Michael wasn't ready to concede just yet. "Amy, I know that if Mother goes back into skilled care she'll never get out again. I can see her slipping away, but she's getting the best of care now where she is. Why disrupt her again?"

Amy reluctantly agreed that she would not press the issue for the time being.

*

When the sun rose on the morning of June 6th, the sky was blue with only a few light wisps of clouds. It was the prettiest day of the year thus far. Temperatures were predicted to reach eighty-four degrees in late afternoon, and remain in the upper seventies throughout the evening, comfortably above the minimum level the orchestra could perform in.

Michael arranged to spend the entire day at Village Green. In her room that morning, Helen told Michael she was bored.

"What are you bored about?" he asked, "there's so much to do here."

"It's all so old to me, Michael," she replied. "Really, it seems like every day I find that I've got nothing to do and all day to do it in."

"Well, today there's going to be a lot of excitement. Do you remember that the symphony is coming for a concert tonight?" he asked.

Although signs were everywhere and Michael had spoken of the concert regularly over the last several weeks, Helen responded, "No, I hadn't heard. But that sounds nice."

"The concert is being held in memory of Henry Taylor," Michael said. "Do you remember Henry?"

"Henry?" she asked.

"Yes, Mother, Henry Taylor, the man who lived here at Village Green. He had supper with us last Thanksgiving at Mary's house. Do you remember?"

"Oh, yes. I went to school with Henry Taylor."

Michael decided to let that one go. "Well, there's going to be a big concert tonight outdoors. It's going to be a beautiful evening. I think we'll have a wonderful time."

"Oh, I don't know," Helen said. "Sounds like a lot of work to me."

"How about we get some exercise and take a walk around the grounds? We'll try to see some of the activity."

"I'm pretty tired today, Michael."

"Let's go, lazybones. Amy told me I needed to keep you moving."

"Okay, we'll take a walk. Now where's my key ring?"

After securing her key bracelet, the two of them walked to the elevator, then past the nurse's station, heading for the courtyard. On the way, they came across Carl Fowler, who was issuing instructions to Joanne Holly and some of the maintenance personnel on his staff. He had just sent them off with their orders when Helen and Michael approached.

"Good morning, Carl," Michael said. "Big day today."

Carl looked up from his clipboard at Michael's greeting. A big smile spread across his face. "Good morning to you, Michael. And you, Helen. It's good to see you taking a stroll this morning."

"Hello, Mr. Fowler," Helen said. She knew he was the boss of the place and she just couldn't bring herself to call him by his first name.

"You won't call me Carl, but you'll still let me address you as Helen, is that right?" Carl inquired with a smile.

Helen indulged him with another smile. "I'm just old-fashioned I guess," she said.

"Fine, Helen," Carl responded, gently patting her hand. "The early shift from the symphony is here already, beginning to put the stage together. I've asked the staff to try to keep the residents out of the courtyard for most of the morning because there is so much activity going on. But Michael, if you'd like to take a stroll through with your mother that would be fine."

"Thank you. Looks like a lot going on out there. What do you think, Mother? Do you want to check all this out, or would you like to sit in on the news of the day session back near the nurse's station."

Helen liked the morning activity when one of the nurse's aides would read parts of the newspaper to the group and let people comment.

"Maybe I'll go hear the news while you walk," she said.

"You know, I'm headed that way now," Carl said. "How about if I escort you there, Helen?"

Helen took Carl's arm, while looking at Michael, and asked, "Will you be coming back, Michael?"

"Sure I will," he said, giving her a kiss on the cheek. "I'll find you in a little while."

"Good," Helen replied, as she and Carl walked down the hall.

Outside, the courtyard was bustling with activity. The tent and stage crews had arrived at nine o'clock and were already busy trying to squeeze things in.

The stage was designed to be forty feet deep and sixty feet long. The crew was working on a modification because the courtyard pinched in too closely from the sides, and a garden interfered with the depth at the back of the stage.

Carolyn Webster had told Michael that this process would typically take four hours, but that it would likely be longer today because of the stage modifications they would have to make. Besides the stage size issue, another space demand existed for the parking of the climate-controlled truck which housed the precious instruments. The trailer alone was forty-eight feet long. The orchestra always insisted that the trailer be placed adjacent to the stage or at least within fifty feet. The best that could be done in this venue was locating the trailer in a parking lot that was to the right of the stage and was accessed through a portico that passed between two of the buildings. The distance to the stage was just over fifty feet, but the path was at least direct and flat, so the location was approved.

At noon, Carolyn arrived, and with her were the stage manager, lighting director, and technical director who had assessed the site a few months back. They also brought three extra stagehands to begin the process of unloading the instruments, chairs, music stands, sound, and lighting equipment. That project would take three hours. With the musicians expected to arrive at 6:30, starting at noon would provide a cushion of time in case any unforeseen problems arose.

The sound and lighting director marched off with the maintenance personnel from Village Green as soon as they arrived to ensure that the electrical lines were all safely in order. They also agreed on the location of a whisper generator in the event there was a power failure during the concert. It would be a long day for these three and their teams. After the concert was completed the load-out would keep them busy for at least another four hours.

Six stage hands had been present since nine o'clock. The setup team from the private company retained by the symphony for the tent included another six workers. In addition to the orchestra members, eventually the site team would include the operations manager, the librarian for the musical scores, the personnel manager, and a cover conductor who would take over if Nicholas Shefsky became ill.

With all the equipment and personnel running around, Michael began to wonder if there was going to be room for the residents to sit in the courtyard and enjoy the show. Carl Fowler, with the able assistance of Joanne Holly once she finally accepted the inevitable, had anticipated that problem, and had devised a plan for an increased level of staff members to escort the residents into the sitting area. A temporary boardwalk was laid out through the gardens so that the residents could safely pass with wheelchairs, walkers and canes. The seating area directly in front of the orchestra would hold 100 residents.

Michael had alternated all day between hanging out in the courtyard watching the work, chatting with Carolyn when she had time, and checking in on his mother. Just before five o'clock he returned to his mother's room and walked with her down to the main dining room. The dining room was generally busy at that hour with early diners, but tonight was especially so as many of the residents were anticipating the orchestra's performance and wanted to get outside early for a good seat.

Mary and Tom and their spouses wanted to hear the concert, so they drove out early and joined Michael and Helen for dinner. Helen ordered the chef's special, which looked delicious, but once again she ate very little.

"You're a bird eater, Mother," Tom said.

"I just don't have much of an appetite anymore," Helen replied.

Mary rested her hand on Helen's arm, and asked, "Are you feeling well, Mother? Your breathing seems a little short."

"When is she scheduled to see the doctor again about the fluid?" Tom asked.

"Tomorrow," Michael replied.

"I'm fine," Helen insisted. "If the old perfessor here wouldn't keep walking me all over the building every day I'd be even better."

"So it's the perfessor who's getting you down, is that it?" Mary asked, glad to hear her mother joke a little.

"Actually, it's Professor," Michael added.

"Not while I'm still living," Helen countered.

"Well, aren't you a feisty one tonight, madame," Michael said. "Do you think you want to battle the crowds and listen to the symphony after dinner?"

"That would be fun," Mary said. "What do you say, Mother?"

"That's not for me. I'm tuckered out."

Michael was not surprised that his mother didn't want to attend the concert. He knew she was wearing down. They hadn't been to an evening event at Village Green for several weeks because of her general fatigue. He knew that others would be shocked at the thought that he and his mother would not be in the front row for the show, but that was all right with him. In fact, being with her in the apartment during the concert was fitting. It might be just like Christmas Eve again. So it was without regret when he told her that going back to the apartment was fine by him.

"Okay, Mother. You and I will go back to your apartment when we're done here," Michael said.

"Aren't you going to be at the concert?" Mary asked Michael. "After all this work?"

It was Michael's turn to rest his hand on his sister's arm. "It's okay. I don't mind."

"But Michael, you should be outside tonight. I'm sure we could find an aide to sit with Mother during the show. Or at least let me stay with her and you go outside to hear it."

Michael offered Mary his most reassuring smile. "I prefer to be with her tonight. It's going to be fine," he smiled.

"Then we'll all join you upstairs," Mary said.

"It's okay if you attend the show. Why don't you sit with Jackie Taylor? She's going to be here. Mother and I will listen to the music upstairs and I'll join you in the courtyard later."

"I wish you'd let us stay with her," Mary pleaded.

"I'd really like to be upstairs with Mother tonight. But you could do me one favor before the show."

"What's that?" Mary asked.

"Would you walk Mother back to her apartment? I just want to take one more look around. Then I'll join her, and you can sit with Jackie for the show."

"I'll take care of it," Mary said.

Michael smiled then patted Mary on her hand.

"Thanks for understanding," he said.

Mary flashed a big smile at Michael. "Can you feel the excitement in here?"

"I sure can," Michael said, as they all rose from the table. "I'm anxious to walk around for a while and feel some more of it."

Once in the corridor outside of the dining room, Michael kissed his mother on the cheek and promised her he would be up soon to sit with her.

"Promise?" she asked.

"Promise," Michael said.

"Come on Mother, let's take another walk," Mary said as she began to usher Helen back toward her apartment.

"You're getting to be just as bad as him," Helen huffed.

"Well, thank you. I'll take that as a compliment," Mary said, laughing as they began to slowly walk back toward the assisted-living building.

Michael walked the other way with the rest of the family, and stepped out into the courtyard right next to Carl Fowler's office. He saw Carl eating a sandwich in his office with Carolyn Webster. They each waved to Michael, and Carl motioned for Michael to join them. Tom, Janice, and Bill walked on through the courtyard to watch the crowd build up.

Michael stepped back inside and walked over to Carl's door and into his office. Sandwich wrappers and soft drinks covered his desk. Boxes of programs were stacked in the corner. The smell of french fries was in the air. The office was a far cry from the tidy one Michael had encountered at his first meeting with Carl.

"Michael," Carl said as he put his sandwich down and stood. "Carolyn and I are catching a little bite before things get busy again. How are you doing tonight?"

"I feel great, Carl. It's wonderful to see this many people so excited."

"Isn't it though?" Carl said with enthusiasm. "We were just talking about that."

"I have a very good feeling about tonight," Carolyn said.

Michael beamed. "Me, too."

"Is your mother excited?" Carolyn asked.

Michael offered a smile and quietly said. "Well, Mother seems to have taken a step back this evening. I think she's probably the exception to the rule you've seen today with the residents hanging around watching everything come together."

"But she's coming to the concert, right?" Carolyn asked, with a touch of concern in her voice. "You know I've reserved seats for you and your family next to Mr. Taylor's daughter in the front row."

Michael was touched by Carolyn's concern. "Thank you, Carolyn. That is really sweet. I'm honored that you would do that. I hope to see Jackie tonight, but I'll be with my mother in her apartment during the show."

Carolyn looked crestfallen. She stared at Michael, her expression changing from sadness to disbelief. Carl, too, was surprised at the news. Silently, each tried to process what Michael had just said.

Finally, Carolyn said, "Michael, we don't know each other very well. I don't mean to be intrusive, but this whole dream has been your idea. You've pushed and negotiated and cajoled people into believing this could happen, and now that it's just about to begin, are you saying you won't be here to enjoy it? I can't believe it."

Michael smiled at Carolyn, then at Carl, and said, "It's okay, Carolyn. I know this has been a big part of my life these last several months. But please don't feel sorry for me tonight. This started as a gift for my mother. My place tonight is with her, no matter where she is. Honestly, I feel fortunate that she's even in her room above the courtyard, rather than somewhere else this evening. I promise I'll be listening to every note. It's going to be great for me wherever I hear it from."

Carolyn shook her head, still disappointed that Michael would not be sitting up front.

Michael glanced down and saw a program for the evening's performance. "May I see one of those?" he asked.

"Of course," Carolyn said. "Take a couple."

The cover announced:

Symphony Orchestra
Concert at Village Green
In Memory of Henry Taylor

Michael looked up, fighting to hold back a tear. Shaking his head slowly from side to side with a rueful grin he looked over at Carl.

Carl could sense the emotion, and he spoke first. "It does touch you, just seeing the cover and those words, doesn't it?"

Michael nodded in agreement, still unable to speak. He looked inside and saw that the introduction of the orchestra would be made by Joanne Holly.

"Joanne Holly is introducing the show?" Michael asked. "You're not doing that yourself, Carl?" Michael was stunned.

Now it was Carl's turn to smile. "Michael, you're taking a seat in the background now that the show is ready to begin. I know Carolyn here is also about to be out of the spotlight, even though she's been running this enterprise today. Now it's my turn to step back."

"But Joanne Holly?" Michael asked.

A bit of laughter came from Carl. "You know, Michael, once I made it clear to Mrs. Holly that this performance was going to happen, I encouraged her to embrace the idea as if it were her own."

Michael looked up from the program again. "So has that happened, Carl? Has this somehow become her idea?"

Carl smiled again. "Of course it has, which is why she's been so effective these last few weeks."

Michael smiled.

Carl laughed. "I'll take your smile as being complimentary. And thank you. Once I suggested to Mrs. Holly that she should handle the introduction she was in our camp."

That surprised Michael, but he had to give the Administrator credit. He looked up at Carl, joining him in laughter. "You old dog," he said.

"Another compliment. You're full of them tonight, Michael. I prefer to think of myself as an effective manager, but I suppose old dog will do for now."

Carolyn shook her head and joined them in laughter, before saying, "Well, gentlemen, I wish us all good seats tonight, wherever they may be located. Now I need to return to the staging area to make sure we're ready for the musicians and Mr. Shefsky."

"I'll walk out with you," Michael said.

As Michael was stepping out into the courtyard behind Carolyn, Carl placed his hand on Michael's shoulder and said, "I really hope the show tonight is meaningful for you."

Michael nodded and smiled. "Thanks, Carl," was all he could say as he stepped outdoors.

Now that the stage was covered with a sparkling, white tent it looked massive. Flanking each side and literally touching the edges of the stage were crabapple and magnolia trees. To the rear, the length of the stage was bordered by shrubbery. Some equipment, including the whisper generator, was on the ground behind the stage and shrubs, easily seen by Michael now as he approached from the rear.

Once he walked around to the front of the stage he saw that it was bordered almost its entire length by rose bushes. The scene was picturesque. The bushes, trees, and flowers were in meticulous order. The grounds crew for Village Green had been out all day planting fresh flowers, and addressing anything that had been stepped on or snapped by the stage and tent crews.

Just beyond the stage and its border of roses was the middle of the courtyard, featuring several more small patios where chairs had been set up. The mid-section ran the width of the stage and twenty yards deep. Beyond that, the courtyard stretched on for another forty yards. That area featured another concrete walkway seven feet in width. All across the middle of the courtyard and the walkway to the rear were folding chairs or spaces for wheelchairs, with a narrow aisle for people to walk through or wheelchairs to pass. At the very rear, the courtyard opened again and flared out around the fountain, which had been turned off for the evening.

To each side of the walkway and running to the rear of the courtyard were a variety of ornamental trees and bushes. The trees had been trimmed somewhat, but they would still interfere with the view of the left and right sides of the stage for those sitting near the fountain at the rear.

It wasn't surprising that most of the seats were already taken. The nursing staff was busy ushering residents to seats. He counted over two dozen aides assisting residents. He chuckled to himself. *I see Carl figured out the checkbook from Henry's trust was wide open, so he spared no overtime expense tonight.* There was room in the middle of the courtyard and to the rear for 150 people to sit, but many more than that would be on hand for the evening.

Flanking the middle of the courtyard and running to the rear on each side were assisted-living apartments. All of the units on the first floor—six on either side of the courtyard—had patios outside the units. Michael could see that those patios were filling up with guests. Carl had arranged with the residents to allow some of the more alert skilled-care residents to be transported to the patios. Each of those patios was squeezing in ten to twelve people.

On the second floor of the buildings were balconies. Again there were six on either side. The balconies were smaller than the patios, but each could hold up to eight people, and those were quickly filling up as well, even though the show was still a half hour from beginning.

Helen's apartment was on the third floor. There were no balconies for those apartments, but each unit had a large window overlooking the courtyard. It looked like all the windows were open tonight.

Also on the third floor of each building was a hallway wing that contained a twenty-foot wide bay window, which sat right above and about twenty feet from the stage. Those sites offered a terrific view above the orchestra, and each wing held up to thirty of the residents who preferred not to sit outside.

At that moment, just about every square inch of available space was filled with residents, all gathered close in their wheelchairs and walkers.

Michael had not seen Jackie Taylor or Nicholas Shefsky, the two people he had hoped to greet before the concert. Both were apparently running late. He had seen Daniel Baylor. Daniel had laughed when Michael told him that the overtime faucet was in full flow tonight. It was getting close to start time when Mary joined Michael and the rest of the family in the courtyard after having taken her mother up to the apartment. Michael introduced his family to Daniel Baylor, who offered to show them to their seats. Michael knew it was time to turn his attention to his mother, and headed off to her apartment.

He found her there watching television, just minutes before the concert was scheduled to begin. Her apartment was located at the rear of the building to the left of the stage, near the fountain at the rear of the courtyard.

"It's a beautiful night, Mother," he said as he walked into the living room. "Why don't we turn off the television and open these windows and get some fresh air."

"Sounds good to me," Helen said. "Where ya been?"

"Oh, just walking around the place. Did you remember there's an orchestra playing a big concert tonight?"

"I didn't know that," Helen replied. "That sounds nice."

Michael was disappointed she had forgotten again about the symphony, but he thought he would try one more time. "Care to go down to hear it?"

Helen shook her head side to side. "I'm just too tired to go out again, Michael. Let's just stay up here."

"Okay," he said. *So there it is,* he thought. *Six months of planning and we're here in the apartment with an obstructed view. Oh well.*

He knew that it had been a real effort on Helen's part just to walk down to the dining room earlier in the evening. Now she was breathing heavily again.

"Does your chest hurt?" he asked.

"No, it's just a little tight. I'm fine," she replied. It would have been unusual for her to have complained of any pain, not because she wasn't experiencing it, but because she didn't want to seem a burden on anyone.

Michael heard major applause from outside the window. The show was beginning. He could barely hear the speaker's words, and he guessed that Joanne Holly was on stage now. After a few minutes he heard the applause again, and then the strains of music began to carry through the evening air.

Helen didn't seem to notice any of the sounds coming from outside. She spoke for a while about her grandchildren, and wondered when Tom and Mary would be by to visit, even though they just had dinner with her that evening.

Michael reassured her that Mary would be there tomorrow, and that Tom was going to join her for dinner as well. He knew that tomorrow she probably would ask Tom and Mary about when he was coming.

"Say, I was looking for Jackie Taylor tonight. She was supposed to be here for the concert. But I didn't see her," Michael said.

"Who is Jackie Taylor?" Helen asked.

Oh my goodness, Michael thought, as the music drifted through the air. *She's forgotten someone else.* "Do you remember

Henry Taylor, the nice man who used to live here at Village Green?" he asked.

"Maybe so," Helen said, but Michael could see she was wise to his game now. She probably didn't remember Henry, but she wasn't going to admit it to him.

So they sat in the living room on a lovely summer night, with a full symphony orchestra playing outside their window, and talked about the days of yesteryear, one of Helen's favorite topics. She liked for Michael to recall some family activity or special Christmas present from the past. When he would bring one of those stories up she would be totally engaged. Sometimes she remembered the events with vivid clarity. It seemed like a funny thing to Michael that the older the story, the easier it was for her to remember it.

Today was June 6th. The date had slipped her mind, so Michael reminded her that today was the anniversary of her husband's birth. He remembered it was the anniversary of his death as well, but thought it best to stay positive tonight. At first Helen was upset that she had not recalled, but Michael helped her get past that, and they began to share stories of his father. After thirty minutes he could see she was tired from the talking and the mental activity of recalling the old stories.

They sat in comfortable silence for a few minutes, while the sounds of *West Side Story* floated through the room. Helen didn't appear to Michael as if she registered any of the music. Anxious to look out at the scene below, he stood and walked over to the living room window.

"How about some ice cream?" he asked, while gazing at the crowded courtyard. His view of the stage was partially obstructed, but he could just see the arm and baton of Nicholas Shefsky through the branches of a magnolia tree.

"Get behind me, Satan, and push," was his mother's reply.

Michael turned back to face her. He smiled at the little old lady that was his mother. "You've got a million of those lines stored up, don't you?"

"I've been storing them for a long time, Perfessor," she laughed. "I better start using them up."

"Oh, you've got time," Michael said.

Helen looked up at him with her lips pursed. She raised her shoulders as if to say, who knows.

"Are you all right?" he asked.

She sat quietly, just looking at Michael.

He asked her again. "What are you thinking about, Mother? Is everything all right?"

"Did Henry die?" she asked.

The question stunned Michael. He thought Henry had been erased from her memory. *Only a half hour ago she had no idea who he was. Was she recalling him now?*

"Do you mean Henry Taylor?" he asked.

"Yes, you know who I mean. Henry who used to live here. I haven't seen him for some time."

Michael returned to the couch and sat down next to her.

"Yes, Mother. He died about four months ago. We went to his funeral together."

"How did he die?"

Do I tell her that he crawled up next to a tree and decided to die? He couldn't say that. "Henry was sick for a long while. He had cancer, and it finally overtook him," he said.

She nodded her head as if it was all coming back to her now. "I thought so," she said.

"I'm glad to see you're remembering him. Your memory was playing tricks on you for a while," he said.

Helen offered another rueful smile then looked away from Michael until her eyes fell upon a photograph from her wedding day. The photo held her gaze for a minute.

Finally she said, "I'm so tired, Michael."

Michael didn't understand her at first, and asked, "Do you want to get ready for bed?"

"No, I don't mean it that way. I mean I'm just weary of living." She turned away from the photograph and reached out her hand for his. "It's no fun getting old, watching people die, and just waiting for your turn to come," she said.

"Are you just waiting now, Mother?"

She pursed her lips again and nodded. "I'd like to go home, Michael. Can we go there?"

"Where is home, Mother? Is this your home here in this apartment? Or do you think it's somewhere else?"

She shook her head as if she didn't know herself, and said, "I think I'll know it when I find it. I keep thinking of places other than this, and then I get confused over which one is home."

"You've lived in a lot of places, a lot of homes, Mother," Michael said. "Do you remember that Dad died six years ago, and that you lived a long time by yourself here in Cincinnati in another home?"

"Six years?" she asked in disbelief.

Michael nodded his head to say yes. "And today's the anniversary of his death."

"I know he's gone, but not for that long. It seems like only yesterday now."

"A lot of things have happened in the last six years," Michael said. "I wish he was still here to talk to and catch up on all those happenings."

It was Helen's turn just to sit and nod her head in agreement.

Michael wasn't sure whether to broach the subject directly. He didn't want to scare her, but it seemed like now was an opportune time to talk more about life and death.

"Are you thinking about dying, Mother?" he asked.

She raised her head an inch upon hearing the question as if she was taken aback, but she wasn't. Her response was more of an indication that she was ready now to hear the question from someone other than herself.

"I'm afraid, Michael."

"We're all afraid of dying, Mother."

"I can feel it around me some days," she said. "And sometimes I'm just so tired that I feel like I can't push it away any longer."

"Is that what you've been doing?" Michael asked.

Helen nodded again. "I feel like I've been pushing for a long time. And now I feel like I can hardly do it anymore."

"Does that make you feel afraid?"

"It does. I just don't know what's going to happen when I stop pushing. Where will I go? Will I be all alone, or will your father be there? Sometimes I'm ready to stop, but then I get afraid of what will happen, so I start pushing again."

Michael didn't know what to say. He wanted to encourage her not to be afraid. Yet, selfishly, he did not want to encourage her to die. But seeing her labor with her breathing in an apartment which she just didn't seem capable of calling her home weighed heavily as he considered his words.

"Mother," he said, taking her hand, "it's easy for me to say, don't be afraid. It's not me pushing hard like you say you're doing. I've always believed that Dad is in a wonderful place, and he's just waiting to see all of his family some day. Especially you."

Helen looked up at him. Michael could see the hope in her eyes. "Do you really believe that?"

Michael wanted to reassure her like he had never done before. "I've never been more certain of anything, Mother. And your mother and dad will be greeting you, too."

Helen smiled and squeezed Michael's hand. "I'd like that."

"Now, let's have some ice cream. Still want some?"

"You know it," she said.

While Michael was in the kitchen the music continued to drift through the apartment. As he returned to the living room with two bowls of ice cream, he heard his mother say, "Isn't that beautiful? It must be wonderful out there."

Michael paused to consider what she had just said. Those were almost the same words she used on Christmas Eve, the last time they had listened to a symphony together.

"Well, why don't we just see if that's true or not," he suggested, as he carried the dessert over to the table next to the bay window. "Let's sit over here and watch."

He walked back over to the couch and helped his mother up. After she was seated at the table she glanced out the open window to the crowd below, and began to take it all in. When her eyes settled on the stage she smiled and turned back to Michael.

"I told you it was wonderful out there."

"That you did, Mother. You were right."

"Of course I was right. Why wouldn't I be?" she said, as she returned her gaze to the scene in the courtyard.

No reason, Michael said to himself. He looked out at the orchestra, then back at his mother. She continued to stare out the window, now tapping her finger to the beat of the music. At that moment Michael knew the concert was a complete success.

Helen sensed him staring at her and looked over.

"Why are you staring at me?" she asked. "And what's that grin all about?"

Michael's grin grew wider. "I'm just glad you're enjoying the music. Now eat your ice cream."

Helen returned his smile, took a spoonful of ice cream, and turned back to watch the proceedings below.

Michael stole a glance at the clock and saw it was 7:50. *There can't be much more to hear now,* he thought. He looked at the program he had been carrying around and saw that the next song was the last on the program.

As the orchestra concluded a medley of songs from Porgy and Bess, the audience gave a tremendous hand. Nicholas Shefsky took a bow to acknowledge the applause then stepped to the microphone to address the crowd.

"You will note in your program that our next scheduled piece is our traditional finale, 'Stars and Stripes Forever.' But before we play that final selection we'd like to perform one more song for you from the good old days. As you know, the concert this evening is being held in memory of a generous man, and former resident of Village Green, Mr. Henry Taylor. Mr. Taylor was aware of the planning for this concert during his lifetime. Shortly before he passed away, he wrote a note requesting one particular song be played just before the finale. We've reached that point this evening, and would like now to play a special request for Mr. Taylor, and for all the wonderful friends he had here at Village Green. We're honored to have Mr. Jack Rendell with us this evening to provide vocals for this song. We hope you'll like it."

Michael was surprised to hear that Henry had made a request. He wondered when all this happened. He looked over to see his mother looking at him with surprise.

"Did he just say that Henry requested this next song?" Helen asked.

"He sure did. I wonder what it will be."

They both looked toward the stage and saw Nicholas raise his baton to begin the music. The next sounds they heard were familiar ones, as the vocalist sang the words, 'I'll be loving you, always.' They were playing the Frank Sinatra hit that Helen heard on the night of her engagement. It was the song she told Henry about at the autumn dance when the two of them reminisced about the good old days at Valley Dale.

Of all the songs they could have chosen, this was surely the one with the most meaning to Helen. When it began, she immediately recognized the strains of the melody and turned to Michael with a look of wonder in her eyes.

"They're playing 'Always,'" she said.

She didn't need a response from Michael, as she turned back to the orchestra and began to softly hum along with the music.

Near the end of the piece, Helen raised her hand slightly at the pause before the soloist sang the word *Always* for the last time. She smiled in that brief moment and nodded her head, recalling the night she was engaged. For Michael, the pause signaled another break, one from the guilt that he had been carrying for the last six months. Although the caesura was but a moment, to Michael time seemed to stand still as he thought back to the Christmas Eve past and everything that had happened since that evening. He wished that this moment when she was responding to the music could be frozen in time. Then his thoughts were interrupted by the sound of applause. The piece had ended and the response from the audience was tremendous. The old song, so seldom heard, had touched the residents.

While the applause went on, he continued to gaze at his mother and heard her say, "That is so beautiful out there."

He couldn't speak at first, choked with emotion, so he simply smiled and nodded. She clasped her hands as was her custom. As he tried to resume a grip on his emotions, he looked out at the sea of guests, then turned back to her. "You're right, Mother. It is a beautiful scene out there."

Helen looked at him funny, and repeated her words from just a few minutes earlier. "Of course I'm right. Why wouldn't I be?"

Michael sat back in his chair and grinned again. *Six months to try to make it right,* he thought. And he had. As the applause faded, the orchestra launched into its finale, "The Stars and Stripes Forever."

"I'm feeling tired, Michael. I think I'd like to lay down now."

"Don't you want to hear the last song?" he asked.

"What song is that Michael?" she said, suddenly having tuned out of the night's magic.

Michael was surprised she had stopped listening so quickly, but it was alright with him. The evening had already more than fulfilled his hopes.

"Oh, nothing. Why don't I help you get ready?"

Michael helped Helen to her bedroom just as a nurse knocked on her door with her evening medicine. Since so many of her patients were still outdoors, the nurse volunteered to help Helen get dressed for bed. Michael kissed his mother goodnight and walked out into the evening air just as the concert had broken up.

He saw Amy across the courtyard helping a resident with a walker negotiate the walkway safely. It was good to see Amy again. Their lessons had been pretty haphazard over the last few months with his mother's decline. Amy must have sensed Michael's presence in the courtyard, as she looked back over her shoulder toward the fountain and saw him standing there. She waved with a big smile. Michael smiled, hesitated for a moment, then blew a kiss her way. That surprised Amy and her smile grew even brighter as she reached with her hand to catch his kiss. Then she waved again and continued to help her charge back into the building.

Michael moved a little further into the courtyard and chose a magnolia tree to lean against to be out of the way of the pedestrian traffic. The stagehands had already begun their work, removing chairs and music stands from the stage. Nicholas Shefsky, resplendent in a white dinner jacket, was standing near the entrance to one of the assisted-living buildings. Michael was surprised but touched to see Nicholas greeting the residents as they passed by to enter the building. He was shaking hands, accepting hugs from some of the old ladies, and smiling at everyone. It looked to Michael as if Nicholas was just as moved by the evening's events as Michael was.

Michael continued to watch the parade and the greetings extended by Nicholas. After a few minutes he heard his name called from off to his left. He turned to see Jackie, Daniel, and his family waving to him. There was still a line of walkers and wheelchairs blocking their path to him. One of the nurses saw they were trying to cut through to see Michael so she stopped her residents and let them pass.

"Hello, Jackie," Michael said as they approached, extending his arms to give her a hug.

She returned the embrace and whispered, "Thank you so much, Michael. This was just wonderful."

Michael stood back and smiled. "Jackie, all credit goes to your father for this evening. All credit."

"Nonsense," Daniel said with good humor. "It took dreaming an idea, then money, and finally serious determination. I'd say you provided two out of three of those elements, Michael. Congratulations on a great success."

Michael beamed at each of them, feeling a great surge of pride. "Well, thank you both. I'll share the credit with Henry then. But I have to ask, when did Henry put in the request for 'Always' to be played?"

Daniel put his arm on Michael's shoulder, and said, "At our last meeting Henry told me about your mother and about the night of her engagement. Henry was a sentimental man, and wanted to insure that the program would include something very special for your mother. I spoke to Mr. Shefsky just after you selected the first date, and explained the meaning behind the request. He agreed to it immediately. It was his suggestion that the number not be included in the program so that it would be a surprise to you. I hope you and your mother liked it."

Michael gave Daniel a hug. "I can't begin to tell you how moving that was for her. Thank you so much."

Mary stepped over to her brother and embraced him. "It was wonderful, Michael. Did you enjoy it, too?"

Michael hugged her back and whispered, "It was everything I had hoped it would be."

"Was it really?" Mary asked with hope.

"I'll tell you all about it soon, Mary, but I promise you it couldn't have been better."

Mary beamed and hugged her brother again.

Michael then pointed to the doorway. "Look at Nicholas Shefsky. As if the evening wasn't a big enough thrill for these people already, there he is greeting them all as they leave the grounds. I bet having a word or a smile from the maestro might be even a bigger thrill for some of them than hearing the music."

Jackie agreed. "What a lovely scene. I wish I had a camera to capture that."

Daniel stepped forward. "I've got one. Let me try to catch that scene." Daniel walked a few feet further to the right for an unobstructed view and took his photo. "Got it," he said as he returned to the group. "I'll send you each a copy."

"Thanks, Daniel. In return I guess I'll have the administrator here at Village Green send you the bill for the overtime," Michael laughed.

Daniel and Jackie joined him in laughter. "Yes, I do believe that the administrator here, fine man that he is, took us up on our no expense to be spared proposition," he said.

They laughed again seeing the host of staff members that must have been on overtime that night. Jackie then said, "Money well spent. Dad would be proud."

She hugged Michael again and turned to Daniel. "Shall we go?"

"Absolutely," Daniel said. "Congratulations again to you, Michael. I hope your mother enjoyed the concert in her own way."

"Thank you. I know she did."

Michael then turned to his brother and sister and said, "Mother's in bed now. She's fine. Go on. I'll be right behind you."

The six headed off toward the portico connecting the courtyard to the buildings. At the doorway they paused to greet Nicholas Shefsky. Michael watched as Jackie gave Nicholas a hug. Nicholas spoke to them for a moment, at the conclusion of which Daniel turned back toward Michael near the tree and pointed him out.

Nicholas looked over and gave a hearty wave. Michael smiled and waved back. Nicholas quickly resumed greeting the balance of the residents returning to the building. When the final resident had passed by, Michael walked over toward the door. As Michael approached him, Nicholas let out a smile and exclaimed, "Well, at last, there you are. Where have you been all evening? I thought for sure I would see you and your mother in the audience. Where were you?"

Michael smiled. "I confess that I wasn't out in the courtyard to see you perform, Nicholas, but still I must say I had the best seat in the house."

Again Nicholas Shefsky was intrigued by this strange man. "How about joining me for a drink?" he asked. "Our work is done here."

"Sounds good to me," Michael said, as they left the courtyard and headed for their cars.

Nicholas suggested a quiet lounge near his home, and each of them drove away.

✳

Shefsky's condominium overlooked the city and the river on which the town was built 150 years ago. Two blocks from his high rise was the lounge overlooking the river. Michael parked nearby and met Nicholas in the lobby. They entered the lounge together. Nicholas had exchanged his white dinner jacket for a light blazer he kept in his car. He was clearly a regular at the lounge, greeted by the hostess and the bartender as they were led to a booth near the back.

The waitress served their drinks, and after she returned to the bar, each of them raised their glass in a silent toast. After taking a minute to enjoy the view of the river and the lights beyond, Nicholas asked, "So tell me, did you enjoy our version of 'Always'?"

Michael smiled. "What can I say? It was a magnificent surprise. The entire concert was all that I dreamed it would be. But to hear that special song was overwhelming. My mother recognized it immediately and loved it as well."

"Is that right?" Nicholas said, obviously pleased with Michael's response. "I was surprised myself how well it sounded. I'm glad Mr. Taylor requested it. Now tell me, where were you during the performance?" Shefsky pressed.

It's over now, Michael thought to himself. He felt relieved that the event was so successful. *Why not share the real reason behind the concert?*

"Well, it's a long story, which began with a promise I made to my late father almost ten years ago."

Nicholas leaned in. "Now this is what I wanted to hear — the real story behind this evening. Time to live up to our contract."

Each of them had almost finished their drinks, so Michael caught the eye of the waitress and signaled for another round. He took another sip of his whiskey, and began to tell his story, beginning with the promise he made his father one afternoon a long time ago that he would take care of his mother. He spoke of the long and inevitable decline of his mother as he and his siblings were unable to prevent the darkness from overtaking her mind. He continued with the story of Christmas Eve in the hospital, and his mother's certainty that a symphony was playing right outside her window, and the anguish he observed in her, and later felt himself when he corrected her that evening. He spoke of Henry Taylor, and the friendship he established with the man, and the incredible generosity Henry showed to Michael and his mother. Finally, he spoke of his conversation with his mother that very evening, and her thoughts on death, and then the special moment when she realized that an orchestra was playing right outside her window.

Throughout Michael's recounting, Nicholas intently watched and listened. After thirty minutes of storytelling, Michael sat back, held out his hands as if to say, 'That's it,' and smiled.

Nicholas was clearly moved by the story. "And you tell me she spoke the very words tonight that she used on Christmas Eve?" he asked in disbelief.

"Yes, she did," Michael replied, "and that's all I was hoping to achieve."

Nicholas leaned back in the booth, contemplating the incredible story he had just heard. "Amazing," he said, and sat silent again.

Michael then said, "Tonight's concert was the greatest I've ever heard, even if I didn't see too much of it. Tell me, Nicholas, how did you feel about the evening?"

Nicholas savored another sip of his cognac. "Let me put it this way. As you saw, some of the folks here knew me as we entered. This lounge is convenient to me, but it's not one that I visit frequently. It's more of a retreat for me on special occasions."

Michael was intrigued. "How so?" he asked.

"I've performed with the orchestra all over the world for many years. Through all the years and venues, I'm glad to say it's rare that I have ever felt disappointed with a concert. I feel a great passion about our music and all our performances. Some evenings, however, offer something that moves me greatly. When I feel something truly magical has happened, I like to take the time afterwards to visit this nice lounge or a similar establishment to unwind. On those occasions, I choose to sit back with a fine cognac and savor the evening past."

Nicholas looked intently at Michael, smiled and continued. "Now, I have to say that when I walked out to the stage and saw how tight everything was, I had some doubts. As I looked out across the courtyard at all the elderly people, I thought that we might be in for a long night. But then I saw the gleam and appreciation in their eyes as they anticipated the beginning of the performance and I was both inspired and touched. And each time during the evening that I faced the crowd I was touched again."

"Isn't that something you regularly see from your audience?"

"It's something I often observe, but not always. Don't get me wrong. Our audiences are unfailingly supportive and gracious. But this audience tonight… " Nicholas paused to consider his words. "Well, this may sound selfish or vain, but they made me feel so proud to be there entertaining them. You could see they were savoring every moment."

Michael nodded. "I understand. I don't think it's vain of you at all. Those folks gave as well as received tonight, didn't they?" Michael said.

"Precisely," Nicholas said.

"I was particularly moved by the sight of you at the door greeting the old-timers passing by."

Nicholas smiled. "Well, that was unusual for me. But it felt so natural tonight. As you say, those old-timers gave me as great a gift as the orchestra gave them. I couldn't help but think of my mother tonight as well. Sharing a few handshakes and hugs was the least I could do in return.

"So," Nicholas continued, "you ask how this evening went for me. To sum up, I would say simply that I'm having a cognac this evening, and I hope that answers your question, Michael."

Michael nodded his head and smiled, once again at a loss for words.

Nicholas then raised his glass. "To your mother, to my mother, to Henry Taylor, and to all those wonderful patrons this evening who are visited by the darkness. May those who are still with us be granted some light from our music."

Michael raised his glass again. "Hear, hear," he replied, and joined Nicholas in tribute.

CHAPTER 18

Helen continued to deteriorate over the next three weeks. More and more she was withdrawing from everyone. She still perked up when her children and grandchildren visited, but her energy level was bottoming out.

At another care conference, the staff pleaded with Michael, Mary, and Tom to consent to moving Helen back to the skilled-care ward.

"She needs more help now," the nursing director said. "I know you want her to remain in her apartment. We do, too, when it's at all possible. But for now she needs more than our staff in assisted-living can give her. Let's try the Well Care Center for ten days and see if we can't improve her energy level and her spirits."

Reluctantly, the family agreed. The second floor at Well Care had a private room. That was one small consolation. The siblings told each other this would only be temporary, but privately each was coming to realize that the darkness was settling upon their mother now, much like it settles in December, when the shortest days are at hand and the sun sets earlier each evening. They could see that the sun was setting earlier and earlier for her, so that most of her days now were lived in darkness.

The hope had been that the stay would improve things, but they knew better. It wasn't long before her stay wound down there as well.

It was now just over a month since the concert. Michael's Aunt Louise had her daughter drive her the hundred miles from Columbus to visit Helen at Well Care. Michael drove out the afternoon of the visit to see his aunt.

Helen was in a chair in her room, wrapped with a blanket, when Michael arrived. Louise and her daughter, Karen, were attempting to make conversation, but there was not much being said. Michael sat with them and tried to get his mother to talk a little. She seemed to rally for the next fifteen minutes, smiling at stories that Louise would tell of their childhood from seventy and eighty years past. Michael kept asking both of them questions about their pets and their early dating days. Louise loved to talk about those days. Helen mostly listened, smiling occasionally at some pleasant memory.

"A few months ago Mother told me for the first time about the night of her engagement," Michael said.

Louise smiled while reaching over to pat her sister on the leg.

"Valley Dale with Frank Sinatra, wasn't it, Helen?" Louise said.

That brought a smile to Helen's face as she nodded weakly.

"Were you in on the secret that night, Louise?"

"I was hoping he'd ask her soon, but I didn't know it would be that night. What a time to ask. I was standing near them. Frank Sinatra had just finished his song when your father dropped to one knee. As soon as I saw him down on a knee I pushed myself closer."

Louise smiled fondly at her sister again. "I've never forgotten that moment, Helen. It was the most romantic thing I've ever seen."

Helen perked up a little. "He charmed me, didn't he?" she said.

Louise was happy to have Helen participate in the conversation.

"Oh, that he did," she said. "He charmed and danced his way into your heart."

"Where did you all go after the big show that night?"

"Don't laugh. We went back to our home. The four of us. That was our usual routine. After a big dance we would go back to Mother's and have eggs and toast."

Michael laughed. "That was a big night out, huh?"

Helen waved her finger at him. "I told you not to laugh, young man."

"Those were still lean times," Louise said. "We would have spent all we could afford just to get tickets to the show."

"Do you remember Mother's rule about bringing the fellows back to the house?" Helen asked of Louise.

Louise scooted closer to her sister and held her hand.

"You can cook as many eggs as you want, but you have to clean the skillet before you go to bed," Louise said, trying her best to mimic her own mother.

"Sounds like a pretty loose household to me," Michael joked.

The two old ones smiled, with Louise speaking first.

"That's enough out of you now, Michael."

"You heard her, Perfessor."

"Okay, you two. I'm just glad that your mother had some kind of rules for you when you brought men back to the house in the middle of the night."

"Let's change the subject," Louise said. "His head's in the gutter, isn't it, Helen?"

They all laughed together, and for the next hour Louise and Helen continued to share their stories.

"Tell us another story about Valley Dale," Michael urged his mother. "What do you remember about Louise at the big dance hall?"

Helen looked over at her sister and gave her a wry smile. "Do you remember your wine and rose colored dress?"

Louise sat back and laughed. "You would remember that onc, wouldn't you, Helen?"

"This sounds like a good one," Michael said. "Come on you two, out with it."

"I'll tell you on one condition," Louise said.

"What's that?"

"That you don't call me a floozie when I've finished."

Michael laughed. "I have a feeling that might be a difficult promise to keep, but I'll try."

"Well, I had the most beautiful two-toned dress that I just loved. In fact, I loved it so much that I wore it three nights in a row to Valley Dale."

"The same dress three nights in a row, but not the same date," Helen said with a small wink at Michael.

Louise blushed while at the same time laughing at herself. "I was shopping around in those days, and I thought that since I had a different guy each night who would notice?"

"I want to say you're a floozie, but I guess I can't," Michael said.

"That's all right, Michael, the conductor of the band just about said it for you."

Michael laughed again. "What happened?"

"Well, on the third night, as I was walking past the bandstand the conductor looked down at me and gave me a big wink and a smile that to me said, 'I see why you wear the same dress every night. You always have a different man.' Boy did I turn crimson."

"You two must have been quite a pair," Michael said.

The hour passed quickly, but eventually Louise could see that Helen was hardly speaking now, and that she looked very tired.

At that point, Louise said that she and Karen should probably begin the drive back to Columbus. Karen gave Helen a hug, and she and Michael stepped out into the hall to give Louise a private farewell with her sister. After a minute, Louise emerged, clutching her handkerchief, tears in her eyes. Michael leaned back into the room and asked his mother to promise to stay in her chair until he returned from walking Louise and Karen to the elevator.

As the three of them walked down the hall, Louise had to choke back her tears. "Oh, Michael," she cried, as they reached the elevator, "she looks so sad and tired. I'm so worried about her."

"I know you are, Aunt Louise. You've been a wonderful sister. She's always said that. I'm so glad you could make the drive down here today. I'm afraid Mother will be leaving us soon. It was good that the two of you could share some tall tales once again."

In spite of her tears, Louise laughed at Michael. "Well, thank you for telling me that, Michael. I think Karen and I should get going now. You'll call me if there is any change?"

Michael hugged his aunt. *My God,* he thought to himself, *she looks so old today, too.* "You be safe now, Aunt Louise," he said. "I'll stay in touch."

When Michael returned to his mother's room he found her anxious to get out of the chair. She refused to take a walk down the hall with him, and insisted that she wanted to get back in bed.

"I'm so tired, Michael. Why do you suppose that is?" she asked.

"Too much excitement, I guess," Michael said. "Putting a couple of old ladies together in one room will wear anyone out," he joked.

"Oh, listen to you, perfessor." His mother smirked as he helped her move to the bed.

"It's professor, by the way," Michael offered.

"Not to me, young man. And don't you forget it."

It felt good to Michael to hear her old lines again. It was nice to know she could still remember some of her bantering ways.

"Okay, Mother, I don't know what I'd do if I ever heard you call me by my correct title."

He lowered the bed and helped her lay down to rest. *She weighs nothing*, he thought to himself.

"Why don't you get some rest now?" he urged. "Mary will be out to see you tonight."

"I don't know why I'm so tired, Michael. Why do you suppose that is?" she asked again.

The same question, maybe even the exact same words she used just one minute ago, Michael thought to himself. He decided to respond just as he had the first time.

"Too much excitement, Mother," he said. "I guess putting a couple of old ladies together in one room will wear anyone out."

He watched her face closely to see if she realized they had each said the same thing just a minute before, but there was no sign of that recognition.

"Funny man," was her reply. "I'm tired."

"You rest now, Mother," he said. "Mary will be here soon."

She closed her eyes and drifted into sleep. Michael sat in the chair by the bed and watched her in silence. He couldn't help but wonder how much longer this was going to last. After twenty minutes he quietly rose and returned to his office.

The next day Michael returned to Helen's room to find Mary bundling her up in a blanket. Helen was shivering uncontrollably.

"What's going on?" he asked as he joined in to help tuck the blankets around her.

"She told me she was so cold and begged me to wrap the blanket around her, but now she feels like she's burning up with fever," Mary said. "You better get the nurse in here."

Michael walked out to the nurse's station and found the RN who was supervising the shift. "I think you need to check on my mother," he said. "Something's happening."

The nurse returned with him to the room. After taking Helen's temperature, she called for an aide to bring some wet cloths for Helen's forehead.

"Her temperature is 101," the nurse said. "I know she hasn't eaten much for the last two days. I think I should call the doctor."

After giving instructions to the aide, the nurse left to make her call. She returned shortly to say that the doctor wanted Helen taken to the hospital right away. "I've called for an ambulance," she said. "She'll be taken to Christ Hospital."

"I'll call Tom," Mary said, and walked out of the room to call their brother. The nurse left as well to get Helen's chart ready for the hospital. Michael was alone with Helen.

"What's happening, Michael?" his mother asked.

"You've got a fever, Mother. The doctor wants us to go to the hospital for some tests," Michael said.

"Oh, not the hospital, let's not go there. Let's go home."

Michael took his mother's hand.

"Not right now. You need to see the doctor at the hospital first. Then we'll see about going home. How's that sound?"

"Sounds like you're trying to kid a kidder, Perfessor."

Michael laughed. *There she goes again, just when you don't expect it.*

"You know you're going to get this professor thing right one of these days. I just know it."

She smiled weakly. She'd used all her energy up with her quip.

"You rest easy now. We're going to follow you to the hospital and talk with the doctor."

"I don't want to go," was all she could reply.

It wasn't long before the ambulance arrived and Helen left Well Care Center for the last time.

The fluid buildup around her heart remained constant, which troubled the emergency room physician, and just as at her last hospital visit he concluded that she was experiencing atrial fibrillation. Her heart beat quickly and unevenly, which explained her constant weakness and occasional dizziness. X-rays taken two hours after she arrived also showed that Helen had pneumonia. She was placed on antibiotics and admitted.

The next day the staff physician advised the family that Helen was having difficulty swallowing and wasn't getting enough nutrition to fight off the pneumonia. With the additional fluid accumulating around her heart, the prognosis was poor.

Even though they had all anticipated that the end would come for their mother sooner rather than later, it was still a shock to realize that her time was literally now at hand. After the doctor left the room one of Helen's nurses suggested that the family meet with a hospice nurse for another perspective on what was happening to their mother.

The following afternoon, Ellen Wells, a registered nurse employed by hospice, joined the three siblings at Christ Hospital. The meeting was illuminating to each of them. Ellen, after reviewing Helen's chart, meeting with the head nurse, and personally examining Helen, sat down in a quiet room to talk about their mother's care.

She began by explaining how the difficulty Helen was experiencing in swallowing and her loss of appetite were indicators that her body was shutting down.

"We all need to eat on a regular basis because our meals provide the fuel that our bodies need to run correctly. When a person's systems are in the process of shutting down, the body doesn't want and doesn't need any food. Your mother is having difficulty swallowing because her body doesn't want any more fuel."

"How long has this been going on?" Tom asked.

"Judging from her chart and the notes that were sent over from the nursing home, I'd say this process has been going on for about two weeks."

"Two weeks?" Mary cried. "She's been dying for two weeks? Why didn't we know?"

Ellen maintained a calm and composed demeanor, something Michael found very comforting.

"Sometimes the process can take a while," Ellen said. "The signs of dying can be very subtle, and not all healthcare professionals are trained to see them. But it's very evident to me that your mother's body decided it had run its course a few weeks ago and began slowly to shut down. Now I believe her body has entered its final stages."

No matter how far she had deteriorated in memory and strength, it was still difficult for any of them to believe the end was near.

While each of Helen's children was speechless, Ellen continued. "I know this can be a difficult decision. But I would encourage you to consider moving your mother to the hospice center. She would be treated there with the utmost compassion and care. The nurses would make her as comfortable as possible so that she can live her final days in dignity."

The three of them looked at each other, not certain of what to say or do. Finally, Michael spoke. "Are you going to be in the hospital for much longer today?"

Ellen smiled, sensing that the family needed some private time. She'd been through this ordeal many times. "I can be here as long as you want me," she said.

"How about if we meet again in two hours and talk some more?" Michael suggested. Mary nodded her head in agreement.

"Okay with you, Tom?" Michael asked. "Maybe the three of us could talk about it some more over lunch."

"That's fine, Michael," Tom said.

Turning to Ellen, Michael said, "So let's meet back here around two o'clock."

Ellen agreed, and she excused herself from the room.

The conference room had a coffee and tea table. Michael prepared three cups of tea and brought them back to where Mary and Tom were still seated, staring vacantly at the walls.

After giving them each a cup, Michael said, "I believe what the hospice nurse is telling us about Mother. What do you think, Mary?"

Mary looked down at her hands, tears forming in her eyes. When she looked up at her brothers, she said, "It's so hard to accept. It's not hard for me to believe. I believe what Ellen said is true. Do you know what I mean? I believe her, but it's still so hard."

"I know," Michael said. "The idea that she's begun a final journey is hard to believe, but the medical facts are hard to argue with."

"I think we can argue with them," Tom said. "Can't we try a feeding tube, or something like that?"

"Oh, Tom," Mary cried. "You've seen her in there. She's so old and afraid. What would the tube accomplish?"

Tom turned to the window and stared. "I don't know," he admitted, "but I just don't think I can give up right now."

"Tom, we're not going to take a vote here," Michael said. "Mary and I think hospice is the right course for Mother. If you don't think so, we'll stay the present course. We're all going to agree before we act. Is that all right with you, Mary?"

Mary looked at both of her brothers and nodded. "Of course," she said.

"Let's take a break and go check on her," Michael suggested. "We'll come back here at two when Ellen returns."

As they left the meeting room Michael lingered back with Tom and encouraged Mary to go ahead of them back to Helen's room. Outside the room he asked his brother, "Tom, do you believe Mother is dying?"

Tom leaned up against the wall, staring off into space before answering.

"Yes, I do."

"Okay," Michael nodded. "It's hard isn't it?"

Tom could only nod his head.

"I need some time, Michael. I'm going to take a walk."

"Good idea. I'll see you in a little while."

Tom headed down the hall. Michael lingered at the door watching his big brother walk away. *The first-born child,* he thought. *For a long time it was just Tom and Mother and Dad. I wonder how different it is for each of us now.* When Tom reached the elevator, Michael turned to enter his mother's room.

Mary was sitting by the bedside holding her mother's hand. The floor nurse was checking vitals again. Michael waited till the nurse left, and walked to the other side of Helen's bed. She was lying quietly, eyes closed. Michael leaned down to kiss her on the forehead. As Michael lifted his head, she opened her eyes.

"Oh, Michael, thank God you're here," she said in a low, fearful voice. "Let's go home."

Michael quickly stole a glance at Mary, weeping on the other side of the bed. He took his mother's hand. "Do you want to go home, Mother?"

"I do, Michael. Let's go home."

"Who are we going to see when we get there?" he asked.

"All of us will be there. Dad and Mother. All of us."

"Your mother and dad will be there, too?"

Helen no longer looked afraid. Instead she looked puzzled by Michael's silly question.

"Of course they'll be there," she said, clearly mystified.

"How about our dad? Will he be there, too?"

"Oh, Michael. Why are you asking all these questions? You know your father's there waiting, too."

"I know, Mother," Michael said, a tear running down his cheek.

"But why are you crying?" Helen asked, and turning to Mary, asked again, "And you, too, Mary?"

"We just don't want to see you go home yet," Mary said, through her tears.

But Helen was already well down the final path to home.

"You'll be home soon, Mother," Michael said, patting her hand. "Very soon."

"Thanks, Michael. I'm tired now. I think I'll close my eyes for a while."

Almost as soon as she closed her eyes she returned to sleep. Michael and Mary looked across at each other and shook their heads, then each of them sat back, lost in their own thoughts of living with and now losing their mother.

Almost two hours had passed when Tom entered the room.

"Is she resting?" he asked.

Mary nodded yes.

"Let's go down the hall," Tom said. "It's almost time to meet with hospice again."

Outside Helen's room they saw the hospice nurse talking with the floor nurse. The three siblings headed toward the meeting room. Just before entering, Tom stopped and turned to his brother and sister.

"Are you each certain about this?" he asked.

"Even more so now than before," Michael said.

"I agree with Michael," Mary said.

Tom put one arm around each of them. "I needed some time," he said, tears forming in his eyes.

"It's okay, Tom," Michael said, as the three of them hugged.

"I know," Tom replied. "Thanks for that. I'm ready now."

Ellen Wells joined them in the hallway outside the meeting room.

"Let's go in and talk," Mary said, and the four of them sat down to resume their planning.

Tom was the first to speak. "Tell us what happens once we leave here for hospice."

Ellen smiled at Tom. That's all it took for her to know that the family was in sync again.

"Hospice offers dignity and care to those who are in the process of dying. Your mother will be given the finest care to help her be as peaceful and free of pain as is possible while she is dying. She will no longer be treated for her heart condition or any other health issue. The only medicines she will receive will be those designed to keep her as comfortable as possible. If she chooses to eat or drink she will be provided meals or snacks, as much as she might want, but she will receive no forced feeding. As I say, once she enters hospice care we are all recognizing that your mother is going to die. Our goal is to permit her to die with dignity and with as little pain as possible."

Tom looked at Michael and Mary, before asking, "When do we take her?"

That evening an ambulance transported Helen to the Hospice Care Center. The three of them followed the ambulance as it slowly made its way to the center. No flashing lights or sirens were needed.

Once in the care center Michael was immediately struck by the sense of peace that pervaded throughout the building.

Visitors talked quietly in the rooms, and generally not at all in the hallways. Helen's room was a comfortable size, with a couch and easy chair for the family.

The move had taken even more out of Helen. By the time she had been settled in to her room she looked exhausted. The nursing staff gave her some medicine to help her rest. Once she drifted off into a deep sleep, the family went home for the night.

Michael spent the next afternoon and early evening sitting quietly in Helen's room. She was growing weaker by the hour and communicated very little with anyone. Her eyes were often open, but they seemed to generally stare vacantly into the distance. Michael would occasionally try to speak with her, but for the most part she would lie still, almost in a trance.

At 7:30 that evening Amy surprised Michael with a visit to Helen's room. As soon as he saw her, Michael jumped to his feet and walked over to hug her. Amy was pleased by Michael's display of affection.

"What a wonderful surprise. Thank you for coming," Michael said as he led Amy to Helen's bedside.

"I couldn't wait for my shift to end so that I could drive out here. How is she doing?"

"She seems peaceful, but she's hardly communicating now," Michael whispered.

Amy was greatly moved when she laid eyes on Helen. She went to her side and took Helen's hand, squeezing softly. Leaning over the bed, she brushed a lock of hair away from Helen's forehead then whispered softly into Helen's ear. When she looked up at Michael she had tears in her eyes.

Together they sat in silence with Helen for the next twenty minutes.

At eight o'clock Tom arrived to spend the evening. After catching Tom up on the afternoon and evening events, Michael and Amy left. Once outside Michael asked Amy to join him for dinner. They found a restaurant nearby and they each ordered a glass of wine.

"I can't tell you how much it means to me that you came to visit tonight," Michael said.

"I really wanted to see Helen again," Amy replied. "Truth be told, I was really hoping that you would be there when I arrived."

Michael smiled. "I'm glad I was. Look at us. It's almost five months since we first agreed to go to dinner, and at last we've made it."

"I was thinking that, too," Amy said. "I'm sorry it's under these circumstances, but I hope you don't mind if I say I'm glad we're here."

"Me, too, Amy."

Through dinner they spoke mainly of Helen and the last two weeks of her care. When they were nearly finished, Amy shared a concern she had about the two of them.

"I wonder if the only common thing we share is your mother and if her death will signal the end of our friendship," she said.

"I hope it doesn't," Michael said as he reached across the table to take Amy's hand.

"I hope so, too," Amy said, thrilled that Michael had taken her hand.

"It's been a very long time since I felt like I wanted to spend more time with a woman," Michael said.

"What have you been waiting for?"

"Twenty years of mourning to expire, I think."

"You told me that once before. When are you are going to take a step forward with someone else?"

"When I'm alone with you, I feel like I can take that step."

"Tell me about her one more time."

Michael stared at Amy and smiled. "I don't think I need to talk about Lainie any more. I think I'd rather talk about you."

Amy smiled. "I'm glad to hear that," she said. "Why don't we continue this another night?" she suggested. "It's getting late, and I have a feeling you'd like to stop back to see how your mother is doing."

"Sounds good to me," Michael replied.

Michael walked Amy to her car, and once there they gave each other a lingering hug. Amy drove home, and Michael headed back to hospice just to look in before heading home himself.

The next day Helen seemed to rally. When Michael arrived at noon Mary told him how the two of them had talked briefly a few times in the morning. Mary was grateful that she had been able to tell her mother once more that she loved her, and to hear her acknowledge the words. Mary and Michael stayed together in the room for the next three hours. At that point Mary needed a break, and she went home for a rest. Michael remained in the room alone.

For the next two hours all was quiet. Michael would occasionally speak, but Helen had returned to her trance. The nurses told Michael the end could come anytime today or tomorrow. At five o'clock, just after the nurse administered some more pain medicine, Helen looked around the room and saw Michael sitting nearby.

"Let's go home," she said in a weak voice.

At first he was startled to hear her speak. Then he sprang from his chair to be closer.

"Why don't we call this home right here, Mother?" Michael said, as he sat on her bedside.

"Have you been here long?" Helen asked.

"Not long enough."

Then she lapsed back into her staring. Michael sat silently again with her for another hour. At six o'clock she rallied again.

"You don't have to stay so long, Michael," she said.

Michael was glad she had returned. "I'm happy to be here. It's nice to hear you talking. You've been pretty quiet today."

She gave him a small smile. "I'm tired, Michael, so tired."

He took her hand again. "I know. I think it's almost time for you to see Dad again, and your mother and father, too."

"Do you think so?" she asked with some hope in her voice.

"I sure do," he replied.

"Why don't you go get yourself something to eat now," she urged.

"Oh, no," he said. "I don't want to go anywhere."

She squeezed his hand slightly. "Go ahead, please. I'll be all right."

"Do you want me to leave?" he asked.

"Just for a while, Michael. Just long enough for you to get a sandwich. How about that?"

Michael felt like she really wanted to be alone. He leaned over and kissed his sweet mother on the cheek and whispered softly, "I love you, Mother. I hope you know that."

"I always have, son."

Michael sat on the bedside and smiled at her, holding her hands.

"Now do me a favor, Professor, and take a break."

"All right," he smiled. "But just a short one, I'm warning you."

Michael gave her another hug and walked out of the building towards his car. It didn't register with him that she had called him "Professor" until he got into his car. Then it struck him like a ton of bricks, and he was certain that was her way of saying farewell. He immediately jumped out of the car and rushed back to her room, but when he arrived, she had already finished her journey home.

Alone with her, he cradled her in his arms and wept, just as he had done for his father. In some ways it seemed like only yesterday when he was holding his father. But six years of looking after this dear sweet lady had finally passed.

CHAPTER 19

The day before the funeral, Nicholas Shefsky's assistant brought in the day's mail to the maestro's office, and a copy of the morning paper's obituaries. A note appended to the paper read: '*Mr. Shefsky: I thought you would want to know.*' He picked up the obituaries and read of the death of Helen Telford, survived by three children, Thomas, Mary, and Michael.

It had only been a month since the concert, and now Michael's mother is gone. What a touching story, to have planned a symphony concert for his mother. He put the paper down and continued with his morning mail.

Throughout the day, however, his thoughts kept returning to the death of Helen Telford, and his dealings with Michael. Late that afternoon he returned to his desk and read the obituary again. A funeral service was planned for the next morning at St. Joseph Church at ten o'clock. *I bet I can guess one song that will be played at the funeral,* he thought. He buzzed his assistant on the intercom.

"Ask Patrick Kelly to come to my office, please."

"Certainly, sir."

Patrick Kelly was the principal cellist with the orchestra. He was fifty-seven years old, and had served the orchestra for almost thirty years. He was a masterful musician, quick to commit any score to memory.

Patrick reported shortly after he was summoned.

"You asked for me?"

"Yes, I did, Patrick. Do you recall us recently working on a takedown of the old religious song, 'In the Garden'?"

"Yes. The one we had planned on using at the nursing home concert."

"That's right. Do you still have the score for violin that we received from Seattle?"

"I do."

"Good. Would you do me two favors then?"

"What can I do for you?"

"Would you take a look at the music for an adaptation to be played by violin and cello? And would you be so kind as to join me tomorrow to play it in memory of a lady I've never met?"

Patrick laughed. "I'll be happy to work on the music this afternoon and join you tomorrow. Will there be anything else?"

Nicholas clapped him on the back. "Let's meet at 8:30 tomorrow and go over it. We'll need to leave here by 9:30."

The funeral plan for the family had been easy to put together. A selection of traditional music was recommended by the church liturgy committee. There were only two items that Michael requested. He wanted to give a brief eulogy during the service, and he wanted the music director to play "In the Garden" as the family was walking the casket down the long aisle of the church to the waiting hearse. The liturgist had heard of the music, but suggested strongly that it be played just before the eulogy rather than as the family recessed out of the church, and the family agreed.

The funeral service began with the family marching into church to the sound of the mighty church organ and a deep baritone. That was the voice of the parish music director. As Michael took his seat in the pew at the front of the church he looked up at the choir loft which was raised at the back of the church. He expected to see only the music director, who was going to sing and play the organ for the service, but it looked like there were a few other men in the loft. He couldn't recognize them though, and he thought no more of it.

The music played by the organist throughout the service was very pleasing to Michael and the family. The priest's words were a comfort, too. After the bible readings and the homily, it was time for the family to sit and reflect while the organist played "In the Garden." Michael sat back in the pew and closed his eyes, anticipating the sound of the church organ beginning the opening passage. Instead, he heard the strains of a violin and cello begin the opening melody of the song that meant so much to his family. *Who is that playing?* he wondered. He looked over to Mary and raised his eyebrows as if to question her. She just shrugged that she didn't know who was playing.

Michael couldn't resist turning around and staring up at the choir loft. It was only then that he recognized that the organist was playing no music, and instead Nicholas Shefsky was playing the violin, and another musician was playing a cello. He couldn't believe it. The maestro played the opening stanza and then repeated it with the music director adding his voice to the mix. Hearing the song was already enough to move Michael to tears, but to see that the great conductor had taken it upon himself to honor the family was too much. Michael turned around in the pew and wept. He wept for his mother, and for his father, and for his lost love Lainie, and for his brother and sister, and, finally, for himself.

When the music ended he was still lost in his own thoughts. Mary nudged him and whispered that it was time for him to speak. Michael was unnerved at the thought of getting up now to speak of his mother. Mary took his hand and whispered softly, "Go on up now, Michael. Do this for Mother." He grabbed his notes and walked up to the dais at the altar.

After exchanging a nod of respect with the priest seated on the other side of the altar, Michael placed his notes near the microphone and looked out to the pews beyond. There was his family in the front row. His sister and brother, whom he loved so much, their spouses whom he loved as well, and his nephews and nieces were all gathered together looking at him. Behind them he could make out Aunt Louise and several of Helen's old friends from years past. Near them was Amy, and to his surprise, Jackie Taylor. And at the back of the church, seated at the railing in the choir loft, was Nicholas Shefsky.

On seeing Nicholas, Michael nodded. The conductor nodded his head to acknowledge in return. Then Michael began to speak.

"*I am home*," read the note, written in Mother's hand. We found it in her apartment a few months ago. Mother had written a note to herself, trying to come to grips with the loss of her memory.

"She waited each day in her last few years for someone in the family to come sit with her or take her to dinner. But we could not be with her every hour, and as her memory dimmed she wrote a note to herself that said, *I am home*.

"It can be difficult to deal with a parent who forgets what she asked you five minutes ago. But it also can be a gift. Here rests our mother, who fed us, raised us, spanked us, educated us, set an example for us, and who asked for nothing in return, except perhaps that we offer her our care as her years stretched on.

"One of Mother's regular refrains in the last few years was 'Let's go home.' She said it in the hospital, in the skilled-care facility, and for the final time just a few days ago at the Hospice Center.

"We used to think she meant her old home where she had raised her family. But we learned in this last year that she was thinking of a far greater place than a house in Cincinnati. She dreamed of a home where her husband, her mother, and her father would be there to welcome her.

"She visited her dream home often in her imagination after Dad passed away. Sometimes her imagination became more real to her than what we mortals consider to be reality. And so one lonely afternoon, when she became unsure, she wrote a note to herself that said, "I am home."

"Today we know what she meant when she would say 'Let's go home.' Today Mother has found the home that she was looking for. We can be thankful that she'll never need a note to remind herself again, because the home she was dreaming about is where she is headed now."

His remarks concluded, Michael returned to his seat next to Mary. The priest said a final prayer and stepped down from the altar to lead the procession out of church. The organist began to play a recessional hymn. Michael looked back up at the choir loft to find that Nicholas was gone without fanfare.

As Michael and his family proceeded down the aisle behind the casket, he came upon Amy in a pew near the back. She had tears in her eyes as the casket passed her by. Michael paused at the pew and asked her to join him and the family as they completed their procession out of church. Amy, moved by his tear-filled smile and invitation, smiled back, took his hand, and joined him.

After the cemetery service, Mary hosted the family at her home. Amy gratefully accepted Michael's invitation to attend. At the home, Michael found a quiet area where he and Amy sat. There he began to relate to Amy his sadness over not being in his mother's room when she died.

"I think she wanted to be alone at the end, Michael," Amy said. "It's not uncommon for someone to want to spare their loved ones from witnessing their last breath."

"You know, Mother and I talked about it the night of the concert. She told me then that she thought that when the time came she'd prefer to slip away quietly. So I know you're right, but still…" Michael stopped speaking and gazed off into space.

Amy attempted to draw him back. "You know, we haven't seen each other much since the big concert. I was hoping you'd tell me a little more about how the concert came about."

Michael turned back to Amy and smiled. "I'm afraid that's a long story."

"Then tell me a long story," Amy urged.

"You're sure you want to hear?" Michael asked.

"Start talking," Amy responded with a smile, just as she had at the restaurant a few nights before.

And just as he had with Nicholas Shefsky, Michael began to tell her of the evening in the hospital which prompted his desire to make things right. He spoke of his anguish over that Christmas Eve night, and about discussing the matter with Henry, and the ordeal of trying to arrange the concert and the great cost involved. Finally, he spoke of the generosity of Henry, and how the evening played out for his mother.

As he concluded, Amy smiled, touched his hand, and said, "That was wonderful. I'm honored you shared it with me. This may sound silly, but I'm proud of you, Michael. You made things right after all."

Amy stood and reached for her purse. "I'm afraid I have a shift starting in an hour, so I have to go," she said.

Michael walked her out the door and down the driveway to her car. As she opened her car door, he said, "Amy, you know I won't be back at Village Green any more. We may not be seeing each other as regularly in the future."

"I'm going to miss that, Michael," Amy said, another tear coming to her eye. "Who's going to give me piano lessons now?"

"You know there's a piano in my home. You're not going to get off that easy."

"Really?" she said.

"I'm going away for a week to decompress a little," Michael said. "I'll be back next Friday. Would you have dinner with me again when I return? We'll talk about it then."

Amy smiled and brushed away the tear. "I'd love to."

Amy started her car and began to back out the driveway. As she reached the street, she rolled down her window, and motioned for Michael to walk over.

"You know, Michael, I'm a firm believer that there is a wonderful reward for your mother and for Henry, too. They're at peace now. I know you're hurting today, but I just want you to know that I believe Helen is all right, and I think she'll find a way to let you know. So keep your eyes open. I think you'll see."

CHAPTER 20

Michael's week away had passed quickly, and he was returning now from his get-a-way. He had found himself walking the beach at all hours during the last six days, thinking of his mother, of course, but also thinking about where he was at this point in his life.

The pilot announced that the plane would be starting its descent soon. Michael refastened his seat belt and straightened his seat.

Casting one more glance at his bookmark before laying his novel down on the tray table, he thought, *that's a lot of memories circulating through my feeble brain.* And he wondered once again what it might be like to have one more chance to speak with his mother, and maybe even hear her voice, see her smile in return. *Was that asking too much, just to have her visit for a minute so that he could see that she was okay?*

The memory of leaving her to get a sandwich, and returning to find that she had slipped away was still haunting him each day. It didn't matter that he really knew that was the way she wanted it to be. The reflection on that moment, and the wish for another one with her, were now daily visitors, appearing in his mind unbidden.

The thought of her leaving without him having held her hand or, even more importantly to him, telling her one more time that he loved her, led him back to his final walk with his father six years earlier. Through all those years, at some point each day he would think of his father. Sometimes he would simply daydream of having another conversation with him, a moment to catch up with each other. Sometimes it was a thought of how his father told a story with such great relish. But invariably, most of those moments of recollection, having visited him now for almost a decade, would turn to that final walk together. He would remember his father's fear, their holding each other in what Michael did not know would be their last living embrace, their sliding dance across the floor. And finally, those silent thoughts of love he held at that moment. He sometimes felt haunted by that memory—that lost opportunity as he walked and danced the final leg of his father's journey home.

And now, his mother, too. He took some solace in Amy's belief that his mother must have wanted to be alone when she breathed her last. He recognized that the old man, Henry Taylor, had been of that mind. His intellect told him that Amy was right. Mother wanted to be alone at the end, and that it was good he had in effect granted her last wish. His intellect could also tell him that it was best not to tell his father that he loved him as they danced their way to the hospital, as his father was too afraid at that moment to hear what might have sounded like his son's farewell. Yet Michael's heart argued differently. Just one short visit with her, that's all he hoped for. But then rational thought stepped in again, cautioning him that the visit was not going to happen. *She's gone.*

Michael closed his eyes and drifted into sleep as the plane glided on. He was awakened by the touch of the flight attendant who asked him to put his tray table up as the plane would be landing shortly. Michael rubbed his eyes and stretched, and then realized he had been dreaming during his short nap. He immediately recalled seeing his father in the dream, and he concentrated to try to recall the details. Details of his dreams always seemed to slip away from him easily, and he especially wanted to capture this one.

He recalled that in his dream he was riding in an open-top vehicle, large and round, on a track through a park. There were others on the vehicle with him, but they were strangers. At some point, Michael saw that his father was walking behind. Once Michael noticed his father, the vehicle veered off the track and stopped in a field. Michael jumped off the back and ran to his father.

In all the years since his father was gone, he had never dreamed of him so clearly. His father held out his arms and embraced Michael warmly. It was a wonderful feeling. Michael recalled how surprised and happy he was to see his dad once more.

"Oh, Dad. I've missed you so much. It's so good to see you," he said.

"It's good to see you, too, son," his father said in the dream.

His dad looked happy and peaceful. Michael recalled his father looking off to his right with a great smile and Michael looked in the same direction, anticipating that he would see his mother next.

At that point Michael's recollection of the dream began to fade away. He was certain there was more. He could visualize the first part with his father very clearly, but the rest eluded him. He was frustrated that he could not recall any more details.

As the plane touched down he kept trying to recall the rest of the dream. Did he see his mother in the dream? He had a feeling that he did, but still he could not recall.

Once the plane coasted to a stop at the terminal there was the inevitable commotion of passengers anxious to get off the plane first, no matter where their seats were located, and Michael's thoughts dissipated into the air. He was midway back in the plane. Once the passengers seated ahead of him had begun to exit, he stood in the aisle and began to walk out. Three rows in front of him was an elderly lady. He guessed she must be in her early nineties, struggling to retrieve a small bag from the overhead bin. Her seatmates had abandoned her, and she was clearly perplexed at her dilemma. She was too short to reach up to get her bag. *Is she by herself?*. He offered to retrieve the bag for her and she blessed him with a sweet old-lady smile.

"Well, thank you so much, sir. This has been quite an ordeal for me."

"Here, let me help you out, ma'am," he responded, guiding her toward the plane's door, while anxious passengers behind him were breathing down his neck.

Once off the plane and walking through the gateway, he asked if she could use any more assistance.

"Oh, I'd love to find a ride to where my bags are. I'm so tired. Do you think that would be possible?" she asked.

"Sure it is," he said. As they reached the terminal he asked her to have a seat near their gate while he approached an attendant to arrange a ride for her.

He waited with her for a few minutes until the tram arrived. As he assisted her on to the tram he began to bid her farewell.

"Aren't you going to ride with me?" she asked.

He smiled, "Oh, I don't think so. It's all right if I walk."

"Oh please, won't you join me? You've been so nice."

She is a sweetie, he thought. "Okay, I'll climb on. Let's go for a ride."

She smiled in return and the driver beeped his horn at approaching walkers as the tram headed off for baggage claim.

"Is this home for you?" he asked, as they breezed down the long terminal.

"Well, it is now. My children are meeting me here to take me to my new home. I'm getting a little older now and they think I need more help. I think they're full of baloney if you ask me, but I do forget a few things from time to time, so I agreed to come here and move into a nice apartment where there are some other old ladies and some nurses to help with my medicines."

"Did you fly here all alone?" he asked, puzzled that she had no apparent traveling companion.

"Yes, that was at my own choosing. My kids always make a fuss over me, but for what I'm afraid will be my last trip I insisted on being alone. My house was sold a few weeks ago. The moving truck will be there tomorrow to pick up my belongings. One of my grandsons lives nearby, so he'll oversee the loading. Once everything was scheduled I decided I would stay in my home for one more day and told my children and grandchildren to go on home. I just wanted one more day in my home alone and one more trip alone as well. I lived in my home so long, and it meant so much to me. It was hard to leave."

"I can understand that," he replied. "My mother chose to leave her home a year ago, with a lot of urging from her children," he grinned sheepishly.

"There you go," she smiled in return. "Children always think they know what's best for their parents. How is your mother doing?"

That caught him by surprise, and he had to pause. This was the first time since the funeral that he had spoken of his mother with someone who did not know she was gone. He had no reason not to tell this woman that his mother had died. But for some reason he thought he'd answer in a different way.

"Oh, well," he stumbled, "funny you should ask. I was just thinking about her after a dream I had on the plane."

The old lady smiled and reached over and patted him on his hand.

"I bet you're a good son to your mother. A mother can tell," she said.

Michael smiled back at her and nodded. "Thank you. That's a very kind thing for you to say. My brother and sister and I have tried."

They were approaching the end of their ride. He could see a large group of middle-agers and young ones holding up signs that said, "Welcome, Grandma."

"It looks like you have a welcoming party waiting for you just ahead," he nodded to her.

"Oh, my," she exclaimed, as she looked up and noticed her family for the first time. "Aren't they wonderful? But they're just making too much fuss."

"Fussing is good for you," he smiled. "I think you're about to be swept up by a lot of folks who are happy to see you."

"I'm very lucky to have them," she confided with a wink, "even though they're putting me in an old ladies home."

He laughed and helped her off the tram. She took his arm as they walked toward her awaiting family.

Once across the secured area line, her family surrounded her. There were at least a dozen people waiting for her, and everyone wanted a hug. He stood there enjoying the spectacle. What he would give for the chance to enjoy that again. The greetings completed, she then announced to her family, "Let's go home."

Hearing those words, he felt a chill sweep over him. "Let's go home," he repeated to himself, as he stood there staring at the family scene. Suddenly he began to recall the details of his dream. He saw his father once again, and felt the warmth of the embrace, then followed his father's lead as he turned to gaze upon someone or something. It was the someone he hoped for. There was his mother, dressed in comfortable clothes, lying on a couch. Michael's father remained where he was standing, as Michael walked over to the side of the couch. He looked down at his mother who was smiling peacefully, just like his father was.

"Are you all right, Mother?" he asked, as he dropped to one knee next to her. Her hands were under her head like a pillow, a posture she often took when she was resting.

She looked at Michael with a smile again, but this time her grin looked almost sheepish, like she was embarrassed or reluctant to tell him something. That struck him as odd and he asked her again, "Are you all right?"

She remained calm and smiling, but still a little timid as she said, "Michael, I'm fine. I'm just resting right now, but I am very happy here."

She's not coming back, he thought to himself, *and she looks embarrassed because she doesn't want me to feel bad that she has chosen to move on to another place.*

He shook his head and smiled back, patting her on her shoulder.

"Don't be embarrassed about your happiness, Mother. I'm glad you're here."

She said nothing more as he stood and took one step back. And with that the dream was complete and he was back once again at the airport. He was slightly disoriented as to where he was until he turned and saw the little old lady again, surrounded by her family.

Her children started to usher her off, but she stopped them all first and, turning back toward Michael, she called out over the commotion, "Thanks loads, young man. I hope you talk to your mother soon."

He waved at her, and nodded with a smile. He could find no words. The chill was even stronger now. He felt he was standing alone in the crowded airport, watching her family whisk her away.

She was beyond hearing distance when he finally spoke.

"Thank you," he called out, but he could see she had gone away, and he was not going to see her again. And then softly he added, "I believe I just did."

He remained standing in the crowded terminal, watching the old lady walk away, hand in hand with a man that he guessed must be her son. Beside her was a young woman in her early twenties. From the back she reminded Michael of Lainie, his love from so many years ago, the woman whom he had found to be irreplaceable for the last twenty years. He pictured Lainie again, and then thought to himself that he hadn't dreamt of her for a long time.

After Lainie had died he had immersed himself in his studies. Then for the past ten years he had helped to look after his father and especially his mother. His life was encompassed by the desire on his part, and the need on his mother's part, for care.

Now the three people he had most cared for in the world were gone. He looked up to see a man his age escorting another elderly lady across the terminal. It was a portrait to his eyes of his mother and himself. Behind them another fifty-year-old man strolled by alone. Another portrait, he thought, of where he stands right now.

The transition of the two men passing by struck him as an indicator of the passage of time, depicting for him clearly where he had been and where he might be now. For he was in transition himself. He was alone. Lainie would never return to share his love. He remembered how much he had loved her, and in that moment he acknowledged to himself, finally, that he wanted to experience that feeling of love again. Just then another man that looked to be Michael's age passed by, walking arm in arm with a woman his age as well. *That could be me with Amy,* he thought.

A passenger brushed his shoulder trying to hurry by. The contact drew him back to time and place. He could feel a smile spread across his face, almost involuntarily, as he rejoined the throngs streaming away from the terminal. And with the smile came the thought, *maybe Amy will enjoy hearing this story. Why wait for our dinner date tomorrow? I'll call her now.*

listen|imagine|view|experience

AUDIO BOOK DOWNLOAD INCLUDED WITH THIS BOOK!

In your hands you hold a complete digital entertainment package. In addition to the paper version, you receive a free download of the audio version of this book. Simply use the code listed below when visiting our website. Once downloaded to your computer, you can listen to the book through your computer's speakers, burn it to an audio CD or save the file to your portable music device (such as Apple's popular iPod) and listen on the go!

How to get your free audio book digital download:

1. Visit www.tatepublishing.com and click on the e|LIVE logo on the home page.
2. Enter the following coupon code:
   b2fd-60eb-0d36-1f31-59b0-d1e0-757c-38c7
3. Download the audio book from your e|LIVE digital locker and begin enjoying your new digital entertainment package today!